Rola Press

THE ONES WHO DON'T STAY

Paola Mendoza was born in Bogotá, Colombia. She now resides in Brooklyn, New York with her partner and son. She received her Bachelors of Arts from the University of California, Los Angles and her Master in Fine Arts from Sarah Lawrence College. As a film director her movies include: *Entre Nos, Half of Her, Autumn's Eyes* and *Still Standing. The Ones Who Don't Stay* is her first novel.

THE ONES WHO DON'T STAY

A NOVEL

PAOLA MENDOZA

Rola
press

To my mother and Tita,
I am because you are.

To remember: To walk through one's heart again.

~ EDUARDO GALEANO

THE ONES,
WHO DON'T
STAY

PROLOGUE

Mariana Cabal Azcárate watched with a broken heart as her daughter limped away from her. She realized Andrea must have hurt her leg in her last fight and shuddered at the thought, pushing it from her mind, focusing instead on the simple fact that Andrea was there. She smiled as Andrea's dark chocolate-brown hair swayed from side to side, her fingers grazing the wall as she slowly walked down the Jetway. Her daughter was there, safe and alive. Mariana took in every detail: the stale smell of the airport, the flight attendant's voice as she announced the boarding doors were closing, the stranger who stood uncomfortably close to her at this unbearable moment. She prayed her daughter would turn around—she wanted to gaze into those beautiful brown eyes one more time—but Andrea turned the corner without looking back, leaving her mother's prayer unanswered.

Mariana let out a long, conflicted sigh. As the breath escaped her, the tears, which she had bottled up for the last few days, erupted. She buckled over, her shoulders heaving as her sorrow flowed out of her like the Magdalena River. She was relieved, horrified, heartbroken, and now completely alone. She cried harder. Andrea was gone. Mariana had barely known her while they lived under the same roof, and now that she was to live thousands of miles away, they would inevitably become complete strangers. Mariana knew what distance did to mothers and daughters. She knew that letters written with so much love and longing were heartbreaking to those who received them. Within the spaces, commas, and periods lived all the moments spent without one another. In the folds of the letters were the wrinkles of unseen faces; in the tattered corners of the envelopes were the frayed dreams of longed-for reunions. Mariana had accepted this reality for her and her mother, but she never imagined she would relive the story with her own daughter.

Mariana gasped for air as she wiped the tears and snot from her face. She dug into her purse for tissues but realized she had left them on the kitchen counter and chastised herself for being so careless. She'd known she would cry. She'd known she would need those tissues, but so often in her life, she seemed to leave behind the things she knew she should have.

Mariana closed her eyes; now was not the time to chide herself. There would be more than enough opportunities for that. She would spend plenty of sleepless nights staring at the orange-yellow glow splashed on her wall from the distant street lamp. Though with her wakefulness she tried to delay the inevitable, Mariana knew her insomnia would not stop time. She was painfully aware that the next time she saw her daughter, time would have done its job and transformed Andrea into a woman. Her heart broke at the thought of it. The image of Andrea as a woman had always delighted her. She had dreamed about it, imagined its every detail since the day her baby girl was born. She had always looked forward to the day when Andrea would stand before her no longer the girl she had cherished for years, but a magnificent woman. The woman she was destined to be. But Mariana never imagined she would not be there to witness the transformation. She never thought she would be forced to let Andrea go as a girl of sixteen and simply accept her as a woman when she returned. This painful reality had never even entered into her wildest nightmares. She stopped her thoughts abruptly. Now was not the time.

She imagined Andrea sitting in the airplane and smiled at the thought. She knew exactly how Andrea was sitting— the way she always sat when she was upset, her shoulders curled forward, right leg crossed over her left, both hands placed between her thighs.

Andrea was naturally small, and when she sat this way she practically disappeared. She was so tiny people always treated her as if she might actually break. They had a tendency to speak quietly in her presence so as not to knock her over with their breath.

Over time, Andrea had grown to enjoy this misperception. She relished her ability to shock people with her outspoken opinions, which she expressed passionately and as colorfully as a truck driver. Mariana was mortified by her daughter's vocabulary. She tried everything to stop her from saying *fuck*, *shit*, and *bitch*, but the words streamed from Andrea's mouth as casually as someone else might say *love*, *animal*, or *sleep*.

Unbeknownst to Mariana, it was she who had first inspired her daughter's famously vulgar vocabulary. Andrea had been six years old. She had just come to the United States with her mother and her older brother, Gabriel. She did not know why they had left Colombia, but she knew she was supposed to be happy to see her father again. Andrea wanted to be happy when she saw Antonio, but he was a stranger to her. She had no memory of his stringy black hair, his greenish-brown almond-shaped eyes, or his funny-looking teeth, which were nearly perfect in their whiteness and straight angles but looked as if they had been shaved down by a nail file. She searched for the happiness that Mariana had promised would be there with her father, but she never found it. Gabriel, on the other hand, was ecstatic. He never wanted to leave his father's side, and Andrea never wanted to leave Gabriel's side. She quickly learned that if she pretended to be happy, Gabriel would play with her and even be nice to her. So Andrea was happy to pretend.

Andrea loved the name of her new home, Los Angeles: "the angels." She felt that she was among angels the moment she walked off the plane and inhaled the sweet, dry air. She was astounded by how big everything was and instantly wanted to tell her *abuela* how they now lived in a palace, but she would soon find out that hearing her *abuela*'s voice was a rare treat, reserved only for birthdays and Christmas.

Gabriel and Andrea shared a mattress on the floor of their small studio apartment. Andrea loved the setup. Gabriel hated it. Mariana and Antonio's bed was right next to theirs. Privacy was never Mariana's concern; it was a luxury she hadn't had in years. Mariana knew life in Los Angeles would be hard, but she had held out hope that she and her husband would have the simple luxury of their own room. She tried to conceal her disappointment when she saw the tiny apartment. She was touched by the effort Antonio had made to turn the small box into a home: The beds had matching sheets, and there was a tattered rug at the door. Throughout the apartment, family pictures were meticulously taped to the walls. There was only one window in the apartment, a sheet serving as its curtain. Mariana walked from the beds to the kitchen in five steps and sat down at the table, which was the only furniture that fit in their new home.

Their circumstances had not changed, only the city they now lived in. Years of loneliness had brought them back to the same place they had started from. Mariana was crestfallen. She knew she had to say something, but she could not find the words. She smiled at Antonio; it was the only thing she could do. He smiled back. It was the only thing he could do. Each was disillusioned with the other. It was only the first in the litany of disappointments to come.

Soon after his family's arrival, Antonio left temporarily to Miami for work. Mariana hated to sleep alone, so she let Gabriel or Andrea, or sometimes both of them, sleep with her. Summers in Los Angeles were hot and dry. The family's open window offered little respite during the unbearable heat waves. On what seemed like the hottest night of the summer, Andrea was lying in Mariana's bed. She was restless. Sweat dripped down her forehead, and no matter how hard she tried, sleep refused to come. She felt Mariana roll over and was comforted by the fact that she was not suffering alone in the stifling heat. Mariana got out of bed, and Andrea smiled. Her mother was going to wet a towel and place it over the two of them, their secret weapon against the heat.

Andrea listened to her mother's footsteps; they were different somehow. The pitter-patter on the floor was quieter and quicker than normal. Mariana moved about the apartment, searching for something. Andrea was wide-awake, but she pretended to be asleep. She tried to decipher exactly what was going on. Her mother did not walk to the bathroom, but instead walked quietly toward the front door. Andrea held her breath as she heard her mother put on her shoes. The front door creaked as Mariana opened it and slid out into the hallway.

Andrea bolted straight up as soon as the door closed. She looked at her brother; he was still asleep. She thought about waking him, but decided not to. Even though he was older, he did not like making decisions quickly. He took his time, weighed his options, and would decide only after carefully analyzing every angle. Andrea did not have time for that. She heard the gate to the apartment building open and then slowly close. Mariana had just left the building. Andrea still had time to catch up to her, but she needed to hurry.

Quietly but very quickly, Andrea got out of bed, put on her shoes, opened the door, and ran out of the apartment building. She opened the front gate, which only moments earlier she had heard her mother close. She looked down the street...nothing. It was dark and eerily quiet. Andrea marveled at the silence. Parked cars lined the streets, and every light in every house was off. Only then did Andrea realize just how late it was. She suddenly felt giddy; she had never been awake when the rest of the world was asleep. Her mind quickly snapped back to the task at hand: Why was her mother leaving?

Andrea looked down the other side of the street. At the very end she saw Mariana's silhouette, with its rigid walk, a walk she would recognize anywhere. She ran toward her mother. Mariana turned the corner. Andrea ran faster. As she approached the corner she slowed down, aware of her every step. She tried to calm her shallow breathing, but it only grew louder and harder. Just as she turned the corner, Andrea saw her mom talking on a pay phone. She ducked into a doorway and held her breath.

Mariana's voice rose above the hum of the streetlights, the distant cars, and the music blaring from the lonely bars. Her voice ripped through the night and found its way into Andrea's blood. Who was that woman, viciously screaming words into the phone? Who was she speaking to? What had they done to deserve her mother's wrath, this anger Andrea had never seen before? She peeked through the doorway. The words assaulted her.

"You fucking asshole! I hate you! How could you fucking do this to me, you bastard?"

Mariana hit the receiver against the phone booth over and over. Andrea stood transfixed, unable to move, unable to breathe; all she could do was stare in awe. The woman who stood before her amazed her. She wanted to be just like her. Her strength, her power, the force of her anger mesmerized Andrea. The sound of the receiver crashing down on the phone booth finally broke her trance. Mariana stopped abruptly, the phone broken in her hands. She dropped the shattered pieces of plastic onto the sidewalk and walked away, passing the doorway without even noticing Andrea.

In the shadows, Andrea repeated her mother's words to herself. She said them quietly, for her own personal pleasure. She pronounced every consonant precisely. She loved how the *F* flicked off her lips, how the *U* connected to the *C* and *K*, which felt like rapid gunfire escaping from the back of her throat. She said the word over and over. Quietly at first, but with each repetition it became louder and louder until she screamed "Fuck!" at the top of her lungs. She covered her mouth with both hands, her eyes darting from side to side. Her heart beat fast. It thundered inside her head. She dropped her hands to her sides and thanked God no one had heard her.

Suddenly, her moment of relief smashed into her realization that she had to get home before her mother did. She ran down the street and prayed that Mariana was not in bed or, even worse, had noticed that Andrea was gone. What would she tell her? How would she explain to Mariana what she had seen and heard? Her thoughts rushed a mile a minute in her head as she approached her building. The apartment was dark, a good sign. The front gate squeaked as she opened it. *Fuck* was all that ran through her mind. A smirk crossed her face. She continued toward the apartment building and approached her front door. Her heart was beating so fast she was certain Mariana would hear it. Her hand shook as she turned the doorknob; she held her breath and pushed the door open. Darkness. The bathroom light peeked from underneath the door, and the sound of the shower calmed Andrea's heart. She jumped into bed. She had made it.

Andrea tried to stay awake until her mother got out of the shower, but sleep overtook her. Just as she was dozing off she muttered to herself, "Fuck," and fell asleep with a smile on her face.

From that moment, Andrea loved how the bad words made her feel. But more than anything, she was overjoyed by the reactions she got from other people when she said them. She used them very strategically, carefully choosing when and with whom she let the words slip from her mouth. Her favorite targets were old ladies.

The first time Andrea wielded her newfound power in public Andrea, Mariana, and Gabriel had been waiting for a bus. An old lady sat down next to them at the bus stop. The heat was unbearable. Beads of sweat dripped down everyone's foreheads. In the distance, the long-awaited bus crawled toward them. After what seemed like hours in the hot sun, Mariana stood up. She grabbed Andrea and Gabriel by the hands and stepped toward the curb. The old lady struggled behind them. They waited in the blazing sun, but the bus did not stop. They watched with gaping mouths as the crowded bus passed them by. Andrea simply said what everyone was thinking: "You gotta be fucking kidding me."

The old lady gasped, stunned, while Mariana smiled uncomfortably and Gabriel burst into laughter. This scene played out time and time again. Andrea never reacted outwardly to any of it, but she loved the attention, the power to shock. She lived for those moments. She sought them out, and unfortunately for Mariana she found them quite often. Mariana tried everything in her power to stop her daughter, but no matter the threats, the punishments, or even the beatings, Andrea never stopped saying *fuck*.

Now, Andrea sat in the airplane just as her mother had imagined her, shoulders slightly hunched forward and hands tucked between her legs. She stared out the airplane window. Andrea was furious at Mariana for sending her to Colombia, a country she had left ten years ago, furious that her mother was sending her to live with a family she did not know. And while she would never admit it, she was deeply hurt that her mother was able to send her away so quickly and so easily.

Andrea was in shock. She could not accept that she was leaving Little Quartz, the only home she had ever known, for a city that she could barely find on a map. The word *Bogotá* was on constant repeat in her mind. The more she said it to herself, the angrier she became. Without her even realizing it, a single tear rolled down her cheek. Instinctively she wiped it away.

"Fresca mija, it gets better *en nuestra tierra querida,"*a man said as he plopped down next to her. He pulled out his

handkerchief and wiped his sweaty bald head. Andrea grimaced through clenched teeth. She was disgusted by his small pointy nose and the fat, flabby paunch that hung over his worn khaki pants. He revolted her. This was what awaited her in Bogotá. Her stomach tightened into knots. She seethed with anger. These were the people she was going to live with, these disgusting, wretched people.

"So where are you heading?" he asked in Spanish.

Andrea's worst nightmare, a chatterbox.

"*A ver, a ver, a ver, paisa?* You're *paisa?*" He smiled a huge, grotesque smile.

"*No hablo español.*"

A complete lie, but she did not care. All she wanted was silence. She needed silence to think. The year before her seemed to stretch infinitely toward nothingness. Andrea was staring directly into the unknown for the first time in her young life, and she was buckling at the knees with fear. The man looked at her in surprise, not sure whether he should believe her. Her luminous brown eyes, her *café con leche* skin, and her perfectly heart-shaped lips screamed Colombia. She turned her back to him before he could ask her another question.

Andrea looked out the window. It was a cold and dark night in Los Angeles. The sky was moonless and the stars were hidden behind clouds of smog. There was nothing spectacular about the city. It was not a place Andrea particularly loved, but it was home, and being forced to leave it made her feel heavy with rejection.

The plane backed away from the terminal. The people in the airport became smaller and smaller. Andrea's eyes filled with tears. *No*, she told herself, *no tears*. Tears had always been a bad omen for her, and more bad luck was last thing she needed.

Andrea inhaled deeply. She knew this would be the worst year of her life. She was sure of it. But she also knew she would survive it. Andrea doubted many things about herself—she was not as beautiful as she wished to be, at times she was not as brave as she needed to be, and while she would never admit it to her friends, most of the time she felt she was not as smart as she should be. However, there was one thing that Andrea was sure of, and that was her strength to survive anything. She was a survivor. At an early age, life had brought Andrea such unbelievable pain that it had created an unshakeable confidence in her ability to survive anything. Even what was certain to be a year of living hell.

The plane slowly crept onto the runway. Andrea heard the pilot's voice crackle over the loudspeaker, but it sounded faint and distant, her mind filled with thoughts of the twisted pleasures of revenge. Her mother had insisted she was sending Andrea away for her own good. She pleaded for Andrea to understand that this was the only way she would not end up dead or in jail. Mariana promised her daughter Colombia would save her. Andrea did not need to be saved. She liked her life. She vowed that once she returned to Little Quartz her life would be her own. The plane rumbled down the tarmac, faster and faster. The wheels lifted off the ground and the plane rose into the night sky. Andrea mumbled to herself: "Fuck you, mom."

chapter

ONE

Buga, Colombia, 1972

Mariana grabbed the light blue dress out of her closet. It was beautiful. Simple, but its beauty was in its simplicity. She laid it out on her bed, sighing in resignation. Outside her window, the streets of Buga bustled with preparations for the Saturday night parties. She tried to reassure herself that at least this Saturday night would be different. At least this Saturday night she would be in Cali.

Her sister Esperanza had convinced her to buy the dress the week before. Esperanza, Mariana, and their mother, Amparo, had driven into Cali for the sole purpose of buying Mariana a dress. Amparo and Esperanza insisted she needed one because now that Esperanza lived in Cali, the invitations to parties would be endless, and of course she could not go to them by herself; her little sister had to be by her side at all times. Mariana reluctantly agreed, since once her mother and sister set their minds on something, arguing with them was pointless. Mariana tried to make the experience as painless as possible by simply trying to disappear into the background while her mother and sister buzzed about in a flurry of dresses, shoes, and purses, explaining their mission to anyone within earshot.

"Mariana doesn't hate to wear dresses; she dislikes the process of choosing them. So we're helping her. That's what family is for, right?"

The truth was Mariana disliked shopping, but she hated dresses even more. She despised how they clung to her shapeless body. She was most comfortable in bell bottoms, sandals, and T-shirts. The looser the clothes, the better. Mariana was happy to disappear into the freedom of the ordinariness her jeans and T-shirts gave her. She knew she was plain, and sometimes even ugly. This truth seeped into her bones; it weighed heavily on her chest, making her shoulders curl slightly forward. Mariana was thin as a rail. There was not a curve on her body where there should be; instead, she was simply a series of connected flat lines. Her hair was untamable, her frizzy curls bursting out in all directions, making her look as if she had just rolled out of bed, no matter the time of day. The only thing that managed to distract from her unruly hair was her infamous hooknose. Amparo spent her days telling Mariana she was beautiful, sometimes even spectacular. She said it so much Mariana was convinced her mother was trying to will the words into being. But try as she might, her mother's words could not change the truth in the mirror.

Amparo was an imposing and unforgettable force. Her skin was as white as milk and as smooth as pearls. Her magnificent brown eyes hypnotized anyone brave enough to hold her gaze. Physically she towered over most everyone in town, but her height seemed only to accentuate her grace. Her voluptuous hips naturally swayed to the rhythms of the *cumbia*s that seeped into the streets from the kitchen windows as the maids prepared elaborate dinners. She belonged to a small and very tightly knit community of families that had protected their wealth, their names, and their Spanish ancestry because they believed their lives depended on it. The Azcárate family was known for its pearly-white skin. The women were sought after for their curvaceous bodies and their splendid cooking, the art of which was a gift passed from generation to generation. The recipes were family secrets, carefully transcribed onto parchment paper and kept in trunks with hidden compartments that only the women in the family knew existed. Amparo loved the time she spent at the stove. As a child in the kitchen with her mother she had felt a warmth that she did not feel anywhere else. In the heat of the kitchen, Amparo was able to forget the lonely nights spent in cold, strange beds as her mother traveled throughout Colombia with her stepfather. The large archways protected her from the isolation and solitude she felt whenever she was in the same room with her stepfather. She blocked out his bitterness with the warmth of the oven. The kitchen became her refuge.

As soon as she returned from school each day, Amparo ran into the kitchen. She stayed there with her mom, alone, or with the maids until her head bobbed from exhaustion. It was in the kitchen that she was able to hear her dead father, Juan Ignacio, whisper into her ear how he liked his *sancocho*, a broth brimming with flavors of the earth, thick with chicken, succulent pieces of *platanos*, potatoes, and *yucca*.

It was her father's ghost to whom she always gave credit for her delicious *sancocho*. By the age of sixteen Amparo was famous in Buga, Palmira, and even among certain families in Cali for her *sancocho,* her beauty, and her boisterous laugh.

When she was seventeen Amparo married her second cousin Hernando Andrés Cabal Martinez. Hernando Andrés came into the world with his eyes wide open and his hands ready to explore the secrets of life. Hernando Andrés was cursed with a burning desire to understand how things worked. As soon as he could hold a screwdriver he began taking apart phones, inspecting every detail, following every wire, until he fully understood how a person's voice could travel for miles through a wire and into someone else's ear. He took apart car engines and put them back together haphazardly. The maids had to hide the blenders and the toasters and keep their eyes on him in the kitchen so he would not take apart the oven and blow up the house in the process. The Cabal Martinez home was his laboratory of destruction until his fascination with things was replaced by his attraction to women.

When he saw Amparo at her *fiesta de quince* he knew that he wanted her to be his wife. The courtship was long and uneventful. Amparo behaved with impeccable social grace; it was not until the hot and humid day the Cabal Azcárate family was bound together by marriage that Amparo finally kissed Hernando Andrés Cabal.

The Cabals were celebrated for their delicate freckles, which were flawlessly placed all over their bodies. Their dark hair perfectly accentuated their fine lips and small circular eyes. Since their arrival to Buga more than three hundred years ago, both the women and men had always been the tallest in town. It was said God made their height to match their social standing, and with each generation they grew inch by inch, and the land they amassed grew acre by acre. The Cabals were famous for two things: The first was their *finca*, El Arado, which had been in the family since Juan Andrés Cabal-Igarreta from Navarra, Spain, came to conquer the unruly new world. Their second claim to fame was the unforgettable Cabal nose.

With each passing generation, the Cabals became taller, their wealth larger, and their noses bigger. From as far back as anyone in Buga could remember, before the birth of every Cabal descendent the town buzzed in anticipation as wagers were made about whether the infant would be born with the curse of the Cabal nose. Too many family members, both men and women, had had their otherwise lovely faces ruined by the infamous hooknose.

Amparo was petrified that her children would be cursed with the horrid Cabal nose. When she became pregnant, Amparo began the obsessive rituals and the frenzied prayers to break the curse of the hooknose. In one of her most desperate attempts to cheat fate, Amparo found herself on Doña Circua's decrepit porch.

Doña Circua was as short as she was round. She was a forgettable woman except for her hair, which she kept over her right shoulder in a perfect braid. Doña Circua spent her days sitting in her rocking chair, content to watch the drama of life unfold before her. She did not speak to anyone about the comings and goings of Buga, because the wind spoke to her at night in her dreams. It whispered to her the passions of new love, the heartbreak of death, and the tears of financial ruin. The wind brought to her the faces of the unknown visitors that knocked on her door all too often. The visitors came for spells to win back cheating husbands, concoctions to end surprise pregnancies, and special prayers in unknown languages to halt the promise of an early death.

Doña Circua woke up earlier than normal on the morning of Amparo's visit. She stepped onto her porch and took in the empty streets. A breeze gently caressed her ankles, crawled up the insides of her legs, slithered its way over her chest, and whispered in her ear that she should make her *aguapanela* extra sweet that morning—Amparo would need the extra sweetness in order to navigate the bitter road life was going to take her on. Doña Circua inhaled the breeze and knew Amparo's request would be a difficult one. She wanted change, a complicated and very expensive endeavor.

Amparo came to Doña Circua's house quietly. She did not ask Wilson, their chauffeur, to drive her. She told the maids she was going for a walk because she was tired of being locked inside the house on such a hot day. No one questioned her. In her state, everyone pitied her. She was fat, her legs were swollen like sausages, and her breasts were on the brink of exploding. She was miserable, and she let everyone know it. Her pregnancy was painful, difficult, and soon to be very dangerous. In her horrid state she had the audacity to believe that her next pregnancy would be easier. She convinced herself that this one was difficult because it was her first. Little did she know that each subsequent pregnancy would become more difficult and more dangerous. As she lay in her own blood after the birth of her sixth child she realized she had reached her limit. Six was her gift to the world. Six almost killed her.

Amparo saw Doña Circua's house from a distance, a small cinder-block box with a scrap-metal roof and a bright turquoise door, which allowed those who were lost to find their way to her house. Doña Circua sat in a rocking chair, her eyes closed and a slight smile on her face. Amparo approached her, not sure what to say or what to do. Doña Circua's eyes remained closed.

"Sit down. I made you some *aguapanela*."

Amparo sat down. She looked at the murky water in the tin cup. Her stomach turned.

"I came here—"

"Drink. I know why you came, but you need to drink first."

Hesitantly, Amparo picked up the cup and brought it to her lips. She smelled the sweetness of the *panela* and it instantly soothed her stomach. The cold water relieved her parched mouth and slid down her throat. She was refreshed at once. She wanted to ask for another glass but was ashamed to ask for more from a woman who clearly did not have very much to give.

Both women sat with their thoughts. In their silence they forged a trust with each other, an understanding of mutual need. The silence was piercing, but within it their bond was firm. Doña Circua pulled out a small green pouch tied with a thin purple string. Amparo reached out with both hands, unsure of what was in the pouch but convinced it held the cure to her curse. Doña Circua looked out to the street in front of her. She never bothered to make eye contact with Amparo; why should she? If the circumstances were different, Amparo would not look twice at Doña Circua, and she most certainly would not refer to her as *Doña*. As far as Circua was concerned, it was best to be honest in all aspects of one's life, particularly when it came to matters of business.

"Take these stones and go to the water. Let the water cover your ankles. Wait until you see yourself as you are now. Walk away from the water and throw the stones over your right shoulder one at a time until they are all gone. Don't look back. Ever. You will have many children; not all of them will be saved."

Silence. Amparo concentrated. She repeated everything Doña Circua had said, word for word. When she was certain she had memorized the instructions, she stood up, pulled a bundle of cash out of her purse, and placed it in Doña Circua's outstretched hand. Amparo walked home as fast as her pregnant body could move. She stormed into the kitchen where Wilson was having lunch.

"Wilson, I need you to take me to the Guadalajara River right away."

The moment Esperanza was born, Amparo checked her nose. She was astounded. Esperanza was a perfect angel with the most beautiful nose. Convinced her family was free of the Cabal curse, she soon became pregnant again, with Mariana. As with her first pregnancy, Amparo's nine months with child were not easy, and the second birth was even harder than the first. Once Mariana came into the world, the doctors could not stop Amparo from bleeding. Rivers of blood poured from between her legs. The hospital floor was an ocean of red. In all the chaos, Amparo was not able to check Mariana's nose. Three days later, when Amparo finally regained consciousness, the first thing she asked for was to see Mariana. The nurse brought Mariana to her bundled in pink blanket. *A girl*, she thought to herself. *Esperanza will have someone to play with*. She took Mariana into her arms and pulled back the blanket that covered her face. Her heart sank. She stared directly into her worst nightmare: the Cabal hooknose. Doña Circua's words roared back into her head: *You will have many children; not all will be saved*. Amparo stared at Mariana for hours. She knew her only hope to save Mariana lay in El Señor de Los Milagros. Without anyone seeing her, Amparo hobbled out of bed and walked the mile to the church that housed the famous Señor de Los Milagros. The ostentatious basilica had always seemed out of place to Amparo in the quaint town of Buga. Its soaring pink towers shot into the sky like sore thumbs refusing to be ignored. Its white trim was too modern for Buga's adobe homes, cobblestone streets, and historical roots.

Amparo stumbled up the stairs. She slowly kneeled on the cold tile floor. The silver cross, adorned with gold and intricate silver juxtaposed with the wooden Christ, made this crucifix like no other in the world. Time folded into itself as Amparo prayed for her tiny miracle. Little Mariana's hunger pangs shot through her breasts and forced Amparo off her knees and back to the hospital. When she arrived she looked into Mariana's sweet, angelic face. Amparo saw a nose that was not perfect, but in its imperfection she found glimmers of beauty. The ridge of Mariana's nose had a slight bump on it, which caused it to curve slightly to the right. Amparo thought the bump made her daughter look aristocratic. The thinness of her nose made her appear European. Soon Amparo saw Mariana as the most beautiful Cabal child to have been born in centuries. But the tongues on the streets of Buga moved with the speed of lightning. They said that Mariana was cursed with the worst nose since the family's arrival from Spain, that the curse had skipped right over Esperanza and had doubled down on poor Mariana. One year later her twin sisters, Catalina and Juliana, were born, and the Cabal curse was split in two, leaving each of them with a nose not as big as Mariana's but not as beautiful as Esperanza's. And by the time the boys, Diego and Mario Andrés, were born, the curse had miraculously disappeared, leaving Mariana to carry the burden of her ancestors alone.

Mariana was seventeen, and it was the first time she had worn a dress since she was a little girl. Amparo was thrilled, after so many years of jeans, to finally see her daughter in a dress, to see her as a woman. She opened Mariana's bedroom door and froze at the sight of her. Mariana's younger sisters, Catalina and Juliana, rushed past their mother and stopped short, mouths agape as they stared at Mariana. The light blue dress gently hugged her thin body as the fading sunlight cast a warm glow over her, making her wavy hair glimmer in a mass of beautifully organized chaos. She was radiant. Mariana did not yet understand that beauty enamors people, that it makes strangers kind, that it causes life's doors to open with greater ease, that lovers are lost and gained without worry because beautiful people know they will never be left alone. Most people walk into beauty for fleeting moments throughout their lives; unbeknownst to Mariana, she was in the midst of her own first encounter with beauty.

Mariana felt ridiculous in her short dress, makeup, and painful high heels. Amparo saw Mariana sinking into her shell of insecurity and rushed Esperanza and Mariana into the waiting vehicle. She told the chauffeur to drive as fast as he could to Cali, ordering him not to stop until they got there.

The truck parked in front of a towering house. The lights were dimly lit, and music and cigarette smoke billowed out of every crack and crevice of the sprawling home. Silhouettes danced close to one another. *Another overcrowded house party*, thought Mariana. The girls opened the door of their rugged red truck and carefully got out. The truck was an eyesore to everyone in the family, except for Mariana and her father. They both loved it, if for different reasons.

Hernando Andrés loved the truck for its practicality. He needed a truck in order to work in El Arado. He needed to haul, pull, and transport sugarcane, mechanical equipment, and people—anything and everything to make sure their five hundred acres of land were producing and functioning as they had for more than three hundred years. Mariana loved the truck because she felt most alive when she lay in the back and looked up at the sky, when she was able to let her thoughts wander to a different life. She was able to ignore the life she was living, a life where she was a passive participant in a story that was not her own, a story that did not incorporate her, a story that happened without her. Mariana could not put her desires into words. She did not know exactly what she wanted, but she knew that she did not want what she was living at the moment.

The sounds of Lucho Bermúdez blared from the radio that sat upon the large dining room table. Esperanza quickly disappeared into the haze of smoke and laughter. Mariana moved through the maze of strangers and made her way to the back of the house, where it was quieter and much less crowded. She knew how this night would play out: Mariana would not move from her corner, a few people would speak with her, and when they found out she was Esperanza's sister the conversation would inevitably turn to Esperanza. Mariana would smile, laugh, and pretend to be interested in whatever dull conversation was happening. She might go and dance a few songs here and there to break up the monotony, but at the end of the night it would be like all the other parties she had been to. On the long ride home Esperanza would fall asleep on her shoulder, and Mariana would stare out the window, unable to sleep because of a nagging heaviness in her bones.

Mariana stopped at a window near the back of the house. She turned toward the crowd, and her eyes caught those of a stranger. They were dark, like the moonless nights of El Arado, with specks of green, accentuated by eyelashes as thick as the smoke that billowed from the *chivas* as they made their way through the Pan de Azúcar Mountains. His black eyebrows were delicately painted onto his coffee-brown skin. Mariana's eyes left his and wandered to his hair, straight as straw, black as night, and tumbling into his eyes. He brushed his hair away from his face and walked toward Mariana. She held her breath and turned her gaze to the floor. She wanted to disappear into its cracks. With his every step her back tightened, pulled, contracted, and tied itself into a hundred knots. He was so close that she could breathe in his smell. It was sweet and bitter, full of history and complexity. His smell overtook her, invaded her very being, and made her knees buckle. She walked away before he could speak to her. She saw a chair, her saving grace. She sat down and fussed with her heels. And then she heard his voice.

"I understand."

She looked up. He pointed to her heels and smiled.

"Well, not really."

They both laughed.

"What's your name?"

"Mariana Cabal Azcárate."

"Nice to meet you, Mariana Cabal Azcárate. I'm Antonio Rodríguez García."

Antonio came from a family full of holes. His paternal grandmother had died giving birth to Antonio's father, Juan Carlos. Antonio's maternal grandmother and grandfather were drunks, and his mother, Beatriz, was their only child. Beatriz was determined to give her children the childhood she never had. She wanted to be the loving mother she had dreamed of having in her childhood, and she was. She wanted her children to have a father who was honest, kind, and loving, and they did. Juan Carlos was all of that and more. Beatriz wanted lots of children and so they had ten healthy, rambunctious kids. But such a big family came at a price. Juan Carlos had so many mouths to feed, the only way he could manage was to work in the bustling ports of Buenaventura. Colombia was sending away its coffee, bananas, and coal, and Juan Carlos' strength was needed to load the ships. He worked day and night and sent every peso back to Beatriz. Beatriz was both mother and father in the Rodríguez home. Antonio saw his father only once a year, but his father's presence was always felt. His pictures hung on the chipped walls. The presents he bought Beatriz were always proudly displayed. The clothes he brought home during Christmas were passed down from child to child for years and years.

Antonio had bought a new shirt for that evening's party. His mother thought it was an extravagance, but since he had recently started working, it was his money he was spending rather than his father's. Juan Carlos had been trying to convince his son to come work at the docks, but Antonio imagined a different life for himself. He wanted his back to never know the weight of his country's treasures, the weight his father's back was so accustomed to.

Mariana and Antonio's conversation ebbed and flowed as if they had known each other for years. They laughed shamelessly at their own private jokes, danced until sweat drenched their clothes, and, by the end of the night, finished each other's sentences. Mariana was caught up in the whirlwind of chemistry and did not hear the whispering around her or feel the scornful, disapproving eyes on her.

Esperanza looked through the haze of people for Mariana. When she finally found her she was shocked by what she saw. Her sister was someone else; she barely recognized her. Mariana seemed to have stolen her mother's laugh. Her long, sensual legs, crossed at the ankles, seemed to be the legs of another woman. Her blue dress no longer clung to her protruding bones but wrapped around the full figure of a woman. Esperanza knew at that moment that her sister was lost in a maze of love.

That night, on the ride home, it was Mariana who slept on Esperanza's shoulder. She dreamed of Antonio, of his smell, his touch, his eyes, and his lips. Esperanza looked toward the night sky. It was a moonless night. *Not a good night to fall in love,* she thought to herself.

The following morning the house thundered with the sound of a ringing telephone. The sound jumped from the sparkling tiles to the cool stone walls, bounced off the wooden beams, and clamored its way into every corner of the house. The call was out of the ordinary. It was much too early for a friendly call. Everyone's thoughts turned to Hernando Andrés. He had rushed out of the house early that morning because a pipe had burst at El Arado. The family now held their breath and imagined the worst. The phone rang incessantly; Amparo's hand shook as she picked up the receiver. Her mind raced with images of how her life would be without Hernando Andrés, and within the second it took her to pick up the receiver and place it to her ear she had made up her mind: She could not survive without him. How could she raise six children without Hernando Andrés? Things were far from perfect between them; his countless lovers had left Amparo empty and dry. Love was a distant memory to her, but at least she and her children had security. The children stood in their doorways, close enough for their mother to reach out to them but far enough away to give her privacy. Amparo mumbled, "Hello."

The children listened intently to the one-sided conversation.

"Good morning."

Silence, silence.

"With whom am I speaking?"

The heavy quiet was unbearable.

"Who? You want to speak to who?"

Amparo turned to Mariana, utterly confused.

"Mari, someone named Antonio wants to speak with you."

Mariana let out a childish laugh. She ran down the hallway, grabbing the phone from her mother's hand and cradling it to her ear. Her heart melted when she heard Antonio say, "I wanted to be the first to tell you good morning."

Everyone retreated back into their rooms, confused by what they had seen. Amparo went directly into Esperanza's room, where she interrogated her oldest daughter relentlessly. She wanted to know everything about Antonio: where he lived, who his parents were, what they did, what he did. She demanded to know it all. Esperanza could not answer her questions because she did not know anything about Antonio. She had never seen him before, had never heard his name until last night, and she knew nothing about him, good or bad. *A bad sign,* Amparo thought to herself. If Esperanza did not know anything about him, then he was not part of their world. He was an outsider trying to get in. Amparo's only hope was to stop the romance before Mariana fell too deep, which meant she would have to act fast. Amparo called out to Mariana.

Mariana floated into her sister's room and sat down on the bed. She let out a wistful sigh and stared out the window. It was a beautiful, sunny day; few clouds dotted the deep blue sky. Mariana lost herself in the beauty of the sky; it had never seemed so radiant. Then her mother's piercing voice brought her back to reality hard and fast.

"Mariana! I'm asking you a question!"

Amparo did not have one question, she had a thousand. Mariana did not have the answers to most of them and was baffled by her mother's agitation. Amparo was relentless. But by the end of the interrogation, Amparo's questions remained unanswered.

"I cannot have you seeing him when we know so little about him. It's not right. I want to meet him."

"That's great! When should I tell him to come over?"

"As soon as possible."

"Mami, I can't wait for you to meet him. He's so wonderful!"

Annoyed by Mariana's giddiness, Amparo stormed out of the room and slammed the door behind her.

Mariana looked at Esperanza, confused.

"Mari, I'm glad it's you and not me," Esperanza said.

Mariana playfully pushed her sister down on the bed. Esperanza grabbed Mariana and pulled her close.

"Tell me everything," she whispered.

Amid giggles, sighs, and silences, which were filled to the brim with love, she told her sister how Antonio's voice made her heart thunder, how the butterflies in her stomach had still not gone away. She told her how the night before she had dreamed of kissing him. They squirmed with laughter when Mariana told her how Antonio said she was beautiful. They kicked the air in excitement after she confessed that Antonio had said he missed her already.

Antonio was scheduled to arrive at the Cabal home the following weekend. Normally the weekends were reserved for the family to go to El Arado, but this particular Saturday Amparo asked Hernando Andrés if the whole family could stay in Buga. Hernando Andrés berated Amparo for being melodramatic. She pleaded with him. She knew this was not just a passing boyfriend. Mariana was already changing, and Amparo needed Hernando Andrés there to help her navigate the treacherous waters of young love. Hernando Andrés refused. Saturday morning came and Diego and Mario Andrés went with their father to El Arado.

Antonio knocked on the heavy wooden door. He took in the stained-glass windows along the sides of the door. The Virgin Mary held Christ in her arms but seemed to offer him to Antonio. His eyes locked on hers, and suddenly the nerves in his stomach eased a bit. He looked above him and counted four balconies; each faced the street and each overflowed with red, white, and pink roses. He inhaled their sweet smell and was instantly brought back to the moment when Mariana's hand was in his as he twirled her on the dance floor. He closed his eyes and relived the moment in excruciating detail.

"What do you want?" a raspy, harsh voice asked.

He opened his eyes and saw a short, stocky Indian girl standing in the doorway.

"I'm here to see Mariana."

Dandaney was taken aback. This was the man who had Mariana singing in the shower, unable to eat or sleep. This brown, scrappy boy was the one causing so much chaos in the house. *How sad,* thought Dandaney. *With Mariana's nose and his dark skin, they'll have the ugliest babies in all of Buga.*

Antonio could not ignore the obvious as he entered the house. He and Dandaney were cut from the same cloth. Walking down the street they could be mistaken for cousins, or even worse, siblings. He wondered how many people she had guided down this very hall. He knew she wanted a life without bruised knees and worn fingertips, a life free of nightly visits from unwanted hands and whiskey-infested tongues as much as he wanted a life free of grease-stained fingers and hunched-over backs forced to carry the riches of his country to boats that ventured north.

Dandaney left Antonio in the dining room to face his fate alone. Antonio slowly took in the room. Statues and paintings of Christ's crucifixion surrounded him. He heard Amparo's heels hit the tile floor as she approached the dining room. He quickly smoothed his shirt, took a deep breath, and reminded himself this was his destiny. Amparo entered the room. She was as regal as he had imagined her to be. She approached him with a faint smile; it was all she could muster. She was shocked that this was the man who held her daughter's heart. This was the man with whom she was going to go to war. At first glance he looked like a respectable young man, but Amparo zeroed in on the details that spoke his truth. His newly pressed shirt could not hide its worn collar, his freshly polished shoes were in tatters under the shine, and his cheap cologne made Amparo nauseous. She grimaced and asked him to take a seat.

Mariana entered the room. Antonio jumped to his feet. As soon as they laid eyes on each other, the world around them melted into nothingness. The anticipation had been building for a week, and with each passing day Mariana had been increasingly unable to contain her exhilaration. She skipped around the house like a child, forgot her train of thought in midsentence, and hummed while she read, played tennis, and did her homework. The maids teased her, but Mariana was oblivious to everything around her.

Her mind thought only of Antonio, her eyes saw only his beautiful face, and her ears heard only his deep, husky voice. Antonio was even more perfect than Mariana remembered him to be.

"You look beautiful," he said.

"Thank you," she whispered back.

Amparo cleared her throat. It was all she could do to keep herself from slapping Mariana's smile off her face. They did not hear her. They continued staring at each other. Amparo cleared her throat again, louder this time. Antonio snapped out of his trance and smiled at Amparo in embarrassment. Antonio knew there was business to attend to, so he stretched out his hand and offered a seat to both Mariana and Amparo.

Amparo did not have time for subtlety; she needed answers, and she needed them quickly.

"Where do you live?"

"In Cali. In Siloé."

Amparo had never been there; she had only heard of the neighborhood. A distant cousin had been forced to move there after her husband left her for another woman.

"I see. And what does your father do?"

"He works at the shipping docs in Buenaventura. He's in the import-export business."

Of course he's a fisherman's son, thought Amparo. Antonio's cheap cologne could not hide the slightly pungent fish smell that seeped from his skin.

"Interesting. What exactly does he import and export?"

"Electronics."

Liar!

"How did he get into the electronics business?"

"During his time in the army."

Amparo did not need to hear anything else. She needed to end this quickly. A fisherman's son was never going to be part of her family.

"And tell me, Antonio, what do you do?"

"I'm in between jobs at the moment. I specialized in repairing refrigerators. Any refrigerator out there, I can fix it. It took me a year to study every brand, but today I can fix them all."

God help us, thought Amparo.

"The problem is, there are only so many refrigerators in town, which limits the amount of work I can get. So right now I am in the process of expanding. I'm learning how to fix ovens."

"In other words, you're unemployed."

"No, not at all. I'm just expanding my business."

"Thank you so much for stopping by today. I just remembered we have a family dinner and must be on our way."

Amparo stood up. Mariana looked at her mother in utter confusion.

"It was nice meeting you, Antonio."

Antonio rose to his feet.

"The pleasure was all mine, Señora."

They turned toward the front door.

"Wait! You didn't tell me we had a dinner. Where are we going?"

"Tía Rosa's."

"I don't want to go. I'm not going. Are Cata and Juli going?"

Amparo's chest puffed up with anger, the blood rushed to her face, and her upper lip twitched with fury.

"It's not for you to decide, Mariana."

Antonio gently took Mariana's hand in his.

"I actually have to go home as well. My mom asked me to come home early today. We don't want to make our mothers angry."

They smiled at each other.

"I'll call you tomorrow."

He walked to the door, his head held high because he believed now more than ever that this was in fact his destiny. Mariana opened the door for him. He gently kissed her on the cheek and whispered into her ear, "I'll dream of you tonight."

Mariana blushed. She watched Antonio walk down the cobblestone street and closed the door only after he disappeared around the corner. Mariana turned to face her mother. She was startled by what she saw. The regal, dignified, and honest woman that she had always known had been replaced by a frigid, bitter, and spiteful hag. Mariana's eyes narrowed with anger. She slowly spit out: "Liar."

She walked past her mother. Amparo stood in the hallway completely alone. The lines were drawn, and the battle cry was spoken. The war had begun.

chapter

TWO

Mariana nervously tapped her foot on the cold concrete floor. She looked at the clock that hung above the chalk-board: 2:12. Three minutes until she could breathe in Antonio's presence, three more minutes until she could caress his hand by pretending to accidentally graze it as she fixed her hair, readjusted her bag, or pulled up the socks that constantly slipped down her skinny legs. She let out a sigh that overflowed with pent-up desire. Three minutes felt like an eternity.

Mariana's eyes wandered to her classmates. She had shared the last eleven years of her life with the same twenty-one girls. She had memorized their faces; she could recognize the inflections of their voices; she knew when Maria Andrea got her period, that Ana María would soon follow, then Natalia and she would be fourth in line, almost always starting and ending on the same day. Mariana learned to both hate herself and love herself in the arms of these twenty-one girls.

School had always been difficult for Mariana. From the moment she started tracing the alphabet, the letters had flipped and twisted and turned, and sometimes disappeared altogether. Unable to read what was on the page, she stuttered and stammered trying to buy time while she waited for the letters to reappear. The girls laughed and the teacher, out of frustration or embarrassment, moved on. These were the days Mariana learned to hate herself. She retreated into silence. She pushed herself away from the giggling groups of girls she knew so well. She found solace as she lay on the grass in the open fields of her school. There, in her solitude, she imagined epic battles between monstrous creatures and a girl who rode a colorful dragon. The girl's name was Evalina, and she was beautiful and brave. Her blonde hair, green eyes, and quick wit saved the universe time and time again. The world loved her, but more important, the world *needed* Evalina, just as Mariana needed her. Mariana was happiest when she was with Evalina. With her, she was able to forget the confusion that letters caused her. She did not have to worry whether a letter was upside down, twisted around, or standing up perfectly as it should be.

By the time Sister Nubia, the principal of La Merced School, sat down on the damp green grass next to Mariana, she was immersed in Evalina's most epic battle against her arch nemesis, El Jején. Sister Nubia knew all about Mariana and her difficulties in the classroom. She knew about how she preferred to be alone at lunch, her annual battles for barely passing grades, and her inability to read aloud in the third grade. None of this worried Sister Nubia because she saw what no one else saw in Mariana. She saw curiosity in her eyes, and she had learned many years ago that curiosity was the key to knowledge.

Sister Nubia ran La Merced School, as she liked to say, "with an iron fist holding a dozen roses." Sister Nubia was timeless. No matter the years a student spent at La Merced, Sister Nubia did not change. Her small steel-rimmed glasses always rested on the tip of her nose. Her blue-and-white headpiece framed her heart-shaped face exactly the same way, and her habit was always as flawless as her skin. She never raised her voice because she did not need to. Her students listened to her every word. They went out of their way to impress her, hoping she might give them an approving glance, a word of encouragement, or a smile filled with pride. She insisted that her students strive for excellence from the time they started kindergarten through their last year of high school. She was equally demanding of everyone. It did not matter if the girl was six or if she was sixteen; she insisted on honesty, hard work, and, above all, discipline. She believed the problem with their beloved homeland lay in the fact that everyone was constantly looking for a shortcut, a simpler road to success, a get-rich-quick scheme. She believed that this lifestyle was at the core of the corruption, violence, and injustice that had plagued everyday life for millions of Colombians for hundreds of years.

As a novice, Sister Nubia's ideas had kept her up at night. She tossed and turned on her paper-thin mattress. Knowing the problem but being unable to find the solution was torture to her. In her bed she prayed for enlightenment, asked God to give her answers to her burning questions. Then, after years of self-doubt, sleepless nights, and screaming matches with God, Sister Nubia's answer finally came, in the form of a little girl who sold coffee.

Against her wishes, Sister Nubia's work took her to the cold, mountainous city of Bogotá. To ward off the cold, Sister Nubia wore multiple pairs of socks and layer after layer of sweaters, shirts, anything she could get her meager hands on. But she could not keep the frigid air from creeping into her joints. She was miserable in Bogotá. She missed the warm breeze of El Valle, the kindness of strangers of her hometown, and the glorious sun that made people infinitely happier than the rain-soaked bitter souls who lived in the country's capital. Rolos, as people from Bogotá were called throughout the country, were true to their reputations; the cold air that rolled off the steep Andes mountainside seeped into their blood and made them an unfriendly and miserable lot.

On one particularly gray and dismal afternoon Sister Nubia found herself caught in the rain. The hem of her habit was soaking wet. Then the torrential rain stopped just as quickly as it had begun, the sun waging a battle against the thick black clouds. The empty streets sparked back to life as people came out from doorways, bus stops, and stores. Sister Nubia was agitated. Her need to leave Bogotá was consuming her, but even more problematic was the fact that she did not have a plan. She did not know what her purpose was. She felt lost and utterly alone, and the cold only intensified her feelings of failure and desperation. Suddenly Sister Nubia was brought back to reality by a small, high-pitched voice offering her a cup of coffee.

"It will warm you from your head to your toes, Sister."

Nubia smiled at the little girl in front of her. Her brown face was smeared with black dirt, the corners of her mouth were so chapped they were scabbed over with dried blood, and her sweater was two sizes too small, leaving her skinny arms half-exposed to the cold air. In the capital, street children were as ubiquitous as *arepas* and *huevos pericos*, but there was something different about this little girl.

"I'll give you a ten-percent discount if you pray for me," said the little girl through her toothless smile.

"I'll pray for you without the discount. How much for a cup?"

"Fifty pesos without the discount, forty-five with."

Sister Nubia placed the fifty pesos in the little girl's dirty palm.

"You want two *caramelos* for five pesos, or four for six?"

"What if I only want one?"

"That would be three pesos."

"What if I want a coffee with the discount and eight *caramelos*?"

Without missing a beat, the little girl answered, "Fifty-seven pesos."

Sister Nubia presented the little girl with a series of rapid-fire math problems, and the little girl responded correctly every time. Their game continued for more than thirty minutes, and with every answer Sister Nubia's heart fluttered in excitement. She heard a whistle in the distance and turned toward it, and when she turned back around the little girl was running down the street carrying her heavy hull of coffee and *caramelos*.

"*Niña*, where are you going?"

"My papi's calling. Sorry. Don't forget to pray for me, Sister!"

Sister Nubia watched the girl disappear down the wet and crowded street. At that moment the sun finally broke through the thick wall of clouds, and in an instant Bogotá radiated in its own light. The sun had come out for her. It was calling her back home. The following week, she moved back to El Valle and settled happily in Buga. Within six months, Sister Nubia started La Merced, a private Catholic school for girls.

Mariana and Sister Nubia's relationship was built in the grassy fields of La Merced's playground. They spent hours on the grass after school. It was there that their unbreakable bond was formed, but it was in Sister Nubia's fourth-grade math class that Mariana's respect for the principal cemented itself into a deep love. Sister Nubia made Mariana want to learn again; she awakened her desire to know. She taught Mariana the secrets of how to make the letters that eluded her reappear as they were supposed to be. She taught her songs to remember the direction of *B* versus *D*, she showed her how to draw in order to focus her concentration, and in the end she gave Mariana the gift to live in the world of the living.

Now Mariana looked at the clock: 2:15. She looked down at her notebook; the pages were blank. *Another wasted day,* she thought to herself. She closed her notebook and placed it inside her desk. Mariana used to take great pride in her meticulous notebooks; they were the reason for her success in school. Since the fourth grade she had blossomed into an ideal student. Her good grades did not come easy; she worked hard, studied long hours, and took excruciatingly detailed notes. Sister Nubia had unlocked her intelligence and her discipline, but ever since Antonio had come into her life she had been unable to concentrate on anything but him. The simplest things overwhelmed her with emotion. A butterfly resting on a flower made her eyes well with tears because the splendor of life was so astounding. A song about longing sent her into an uncontrollable fit of rage, stomping and screaming down the hallway, cursing God, because to need someone so intensely was just so unfair. During class she stared out the window, doodled in her notebooks, or sighed repeatedly. She thought only of Antonio.

Mariana exited the classroom and inhaled the hot, humid air. The smell of deep-fried empanadas drifted through the air, and the butterflies that had been asleep in her stomach all day woke with a vengeance. The thought of watching Antonio's lips envelop the corner of a steaming empanada as he bit down on it caused waves of excitement to pulsate through Mariana's body. She saw her sisters Catalina and Juliana waiting for her by the front gate. They whispered the words she had been anticipating all day: "He's here." Her breath grew shallow. Her hands trembled. They kissed her good-bye and promised to stay out of their mother's sight until sundown. They ran off giggling in the other direction. She took a deep breath and walked out through La Merced's front gates. Her eyes settled on Antonio. He stood in exactly the same spot as he had every Friday for the past month.

Antonio leaned against a flimsy metal gate. His eyes were closed, his head tilted toward the sun. Mariana stared at him. This was a rare moment; she could take her time and revel in his every detail. She did not need to worry about appearing too forward, too obvious, or too desperate. She did not have to play the games that were expected of her; instead, she was able to admire him without any inhibitions. His muscular arms bent just so as his hands rested inside his jean pockets. His yellow shirt was dotted with sweat from the unrelenting sun that beat down on him. His thick lips were relaxed in a subtle smile. *Perfection,* she thought. Suddenly her feet became as heavy as concrete blocks; she could not move, could not take a step. Her body reacted to what her heart and mind desired. Mariana wanted to live in this moment forever, to stop time, to be free of the necessity to breathe, because breathing meant time was passing, and in these moments of ecstasy time passed far too quickly. She wanted to reach out and grab time, wrestle it to the ground and stop it from pushing her out of her moment of bliss.

Antonio opened his eyes and saw Mariana staring at him. He waved her over. She glanced down both sides of the dirt road and crossed the street, her wild hair blowing in every direction as she expertly avoided puddles, motorcycles, and stray dogs. He could not take his eyes off of her as she crossed the dirt road. This was the moment he looked forward to all week. As Mariana crossed the street, he was able to let his mind linger on her beauty; he was able to imagine her as a woman. Antonio pictured Mariana's silky-smooth thighs rubbing together underneath her plaid skirt. He imagined her soft lips against his, his moist tongue entering her mouth and discovering her sweet taste for the first time. He took quick, shallow breaths. Mariana was just a few feet away from him, and the hollowness in his stomach grew deeper with her every step. She finally reached him. She stood perfectly still before him. He was in awe of her imperfections—it was in her chaotic hair, her freckled face, and her ungraceful nose that he saw her beauty.

Antonio noticed the small beads of sweat that rested on Mariana's forehead. He was overwhelmed with the desire to kiss every droplet, one by one, taking in her taste. He imagined a mixture of salt and roses, because, unbeknownst to Mariana, her clothes, her hair, and even her breath were invaded by the sweet smell of the white and red roses that bloomed on her balcony. Wherever she went, the slight smell of roses followed her. He took in her aroma. His heartbeat thundered like a Mack truck on La Calle Quinta, and he was certain she could hear it. She smiled at him, and yearned for his gentle kiss. He leaned in; she held her breath as his lips gently kissed her cheek. It was a slow, tender kiss filled with trepidation and anticipation.

Mariana and Antonio walked over the bridge of La Libertad. The Guadalajara River roared below them while they walked. Each second spent with the other felt like an eternity wrapped inside a bullet that was moving at the speed of light. A walk that normally took ten minutes stretched out to over an hour. Without realizing it, Mariana and Antonio zigzagged back and forth, repeatedly crossing the street. They meandered into El Parque Cabal and stopped to buy a *chocolatina jet* from a toothless woman, single cigarettes from the kid who always asked for a little extra money for his school books, and the dreaded cup of *tinto*, which forced them back into reality because old Don Julio's shop was a mere ten steps from Mariana's front door.

Mariana and Antonio knew prying eyes watched their every move, snooping ears listened to their every word, and gossiping tongues were at the ready to inform Amparo of any indiscretions. They wanted nothing more than privacy so they could laugh wildly, share their secrets, and confess their fears and dreams. They knew that truly private moments were too much to hope for, but they did manage to share short flashes of intimacy without the meddling and snooping souls of Buga ever realizing it.

Mariana and Antonio developed a clandestine language of love. Antonio scratched his knee, which was Mariana's cue to walk closer to him. His pinkie finger reached out across the abyss of desire, desperately searching for Mariana, for any part of her angelic body: her thigh, her calf—even her knee was magical. Once he found her, his finger caressed her in small, gentle circles. His burning desire was satisfied only for an instant, though, because inevitably someone would walk down the street, poke their head out the window, or drive by on their way to church, forcing Mariana to step away from him. Their separations never lasted very long.

As they crossed the street, Mariana told Antonio what she wanted with a simple flip of her hair. They stepped to the sidewalk and Mariana rested in the shade under a white balcony with dark wood accents. She complained about how hot she was. She turned toward the street, fanning her face. She then twisted her fingers in her hair on either side, creating a curtain of wild black curls. Antonio stepped behind the dark curtain and tenderly grazed his forehead against her back, in the space between her shoulder blades. Mariana's core trembled with yearning. Antonio sighed to stop himself from bursting with desire. His breath found its way through Mariana's white-collared shirt, wrapped itself around her back, and rested on her unexplored breasts. There they stood in complete, torturous silence, both loving and hating their torment and tormentor. Their anxious longing muffled the sounds of the honking horns, the barking stray dogs, and the horse-drawn carts around them. Each felt as if they were going to burst, but neither said a word because to utter a sound would break the spell of their desire. Unable to contain herself any longer, Mariana finally walked back across the street. Antonio followed behind her. He watched how her skirt swayed from side to side. He imagined his rugged hands wrapped around her soft, slender hips. His eyes worked their way up her back.

He wondered what color bra she had on. He imagined a crisp white bra with translucent lace letting her soft pink nipples peek through. The hollowness in his stomach became deeper and turned into a hard knot. His eyes stopped at the nape of Mariana's neck. Beads of sweat glistened in the radiant sun as one droplet slid down her neck. He watched it disappear into her shirt and imagined how it slowly slid down her shoulder blade, over the meaty part of her lower back, and then disappeared into her white lace panties. Antonio wanted nothing more than to be that drop of sweat.

From the corner of his eye he saw Don Julio's coffee stand, and his heart roared in his chest. He could not leave Mariana, not now, not like this. Without thinking, he grabbed Mariana's hand and pulled her into an alley. Mariana did not put up a fight. She was delighted by his audacity, his bravery, his manhood.

The alley twisted and turned between the backs of two houses. There among the garbage cans and peeling walls, Antonio and Mariana lost themselves in each other. He leaned her against the wall and placed her perfectly inside a nook, making them invisible to everyone. They looked into each other's eyes, each accepting, each knowing that this moment was a crossroads for both of them. This moment changed everything. Antonio's fingers caressed Mariana's soft cheeks, traced the outline of her heart-shaped lips. He let his fingertips discover every curve. He was enraptured by their flawlessness. His hands trembled as they made their way back to the nape of Mariana's neck. He brought her slowly toward him. She closed her eyes.

Mariana lost herself in the warmth of Antonio's lips. She felt as if she were in a vast ocean, bobbing and weaving in the waves, which were on the verge of consuming her.

Her world spun as Antonio's tongue entered her mouth. He tasted of sweet mangos, and she was overwhelmed with the urge to devour hundreds of them. She wanted to fill her body with their sweet, stringy meat, she wanted their juice to run down her hands, she wanted to tear and chew their rubbery skin. Mariana's knees buckled. Antonio held her in his arms. He brought her closer to him, his supple tongue searching, discovering, tasting Mariana for the first time. Antonio pressed his body against hers, and he felt her nipples harden through her shirt. He grabbed her hips and thrust her toward him. Mariana was like clay in his hands; however he twisted and turned her, she melted to fit perfectly into his body. Antonio's hands slid under her skirt and slowly crept up her thighs. Mariana leaned her head against the cracked wall behind her and looked to the sky. She was adrift in an ocean of desire, and she knew Antonio was the only one who could save her. Antonio's fingers found their way inside her. He played in her wetness, pushed against her insides, and went deep into her earthy smell. Mariana wanted more. She wanted to be full of him. As if Mariana's desires had been whispered into Antonio's ear, he grabbed her legs and wrapped them around his waist. She felt his hardness against her. She was frightened and excited by the animal inside him. She knew the thin piece of cotton that stopped Antonio from entering her would not protect her for much longer. His hands fumbled as he moved her underwear aside. Mariana was completely exposed, open, and wanting to be explored.

Antonio looked into Mariana luminous brown eyes. He felt her gaze penetrate the depths of his soul, and suddenly he lost his nerve. This was not how it was supposed to be. In a dirty alleyway, standing against a crumbling wall in broad daylight, unable to enjoy the sight of Mariana's naked body. In his moment of doubt Antonio looked to Mariana for guidance. She nodded.

The warmth between Mariana's legs invited him in. He entered slowly, cautiously, and filled her with love. His love ripped through Mariana. She felt as if she were tearing in half. With every thrust came a small burst of agony. She suffered quietly. The first of many painful moments in her life she would endure alone.

Antonio's heavy panting intertwined with Mariana's hushed moans created a symphony of pleasure and pain. Lost in the discovery of their bodies, they were unaware of the sweet smell of roses that surrounded them. The thick adobe walls that gave Antonio and Mariana their privacy could not contain the scent. The sweet smell flowed from the alleyway, burst into the streets, and invaded parks, kitchens, and bedrooms throughout Buga. The smell of roses awoke the passion of lethargic couples and angry ex-lovers and the curiosity of complete strangers. People flooded the streets, looking for that one person who could satisfy their crushing desire. The scent of roses grew stronger with every couple who slid into a closet, hid behind a tree, or devoured each other beneath the sheets. For a brief moment, Buga was transformed into a concerto of passion. Inspired, unbeknownst to the town, by two forbidden lovers as they made love for the first time in a decrepit alleyway.

Mariana unwrapped her legs from around Antonio's waist. Her feet touched the ground, but it did not feel solid under her shoes. She felt as if she were sinking into the riverbank of the River Cauca. She closed her eyes and tried to convince herself she was not disappearing into its muddy waters. With each breath, she tried to make herself feel the firm ground beneath her. Every sound was amplified around her. Her breath was as loud as her father's red pickup truck when it raced down the dirt roads of the sugar fields in El Arado. The distant clacking of the horse hooves over the cobblestone streets as they made their way back to their stables was as piercing as an exploding bomb. The clinking of Antonio's belt buckle mixed with his heavy breathing made Mariana's knees buckle in despair. What had she done? She had given herself to Antonio without a fight, in an alleyway, standing up. She would be remembered as the girl from the alleyway. Shame flooded her heart. She wanted to stay behind her closed eyes forever. She wanted to disappear into the dark and never face Antonio again.

The sounds grew louder around her. Antonio and Mariana's breath mixed with the running faucets in the homes that surrounded them, while the radios crackled with salsa, *cumbia*, and news of the countless murders in the countryside. The noise built into a crescendo. Mariana was on the verge of collapsing. Her breath was shallow and she was weak from the pain of having Antonio inside her. Antonio's deep, raspy voice broke through the madness around her, landing gently on her ears. His tender voice whispered, "I love you." Mariana opened her eyes and their gazes locked. She tried to say "I love you" in return, but nothing came out. She tried again, but again her voice failed her. Antonio smiled. He kissed her ever so sweetly, adjusted her skirt, and held her by the hand as they walked out of the alleyway.

The smell of roses followed them past Don Julio's coffee stand, and continued with them on the last ten steps to Mariana's front door. They kissed each other on the cheek and lingered in each other's necks, enjoying their deep, earthy smell. Antonio pulled away from Mariana. His fingers caressed her cheek as he said good-bye. Mariana leaned against her front door. She watched him saunter down the cobblestone road. As soon as he was out of sight, her sisters turned the corner, just as they had planned.

Mariana walked into the house, and the scent of roses followed, sinking in to every crevice around her. Amparo came out from the kitchen. Mariana walked past her mother, muttering an almost inaudible hello. This had become their customary greeting over the last four weeks. At first Amparo had been tortured by the coldness in her daughter's voice, but as the weeks passed she became accustomed to Mariana's aloofness. Not expecting a response, Amparo asked her about school. Mariana walked past without saying a word. Embarrassed for their mother, Catalina and Juliana kissed her hello and retreated into their rooms. Amparo stood in silent fury, unsure what to say or do. Mariana slammed the door behind her, sending the sweet scent of roses bursting past her mother.

Amparo had smelled that same distinct sweetness earlier in the day. This was the same smell that had awoken her from her siesta with a burning desire she had not felt in years. This was the smell that had her pacing in her bedroom like a rabid animal. This was the smell that inspired her to look at her naked body in the mirror, to venture to touch herself in ways that only Hernando had done. This was the same smell that had let her escape her dismal life to find a few seconds of ecstasy alone, under her sheets, as the cooling winds from the Guadalajara River soothed her sweaty body.

Amparo hunched over in despair at the realization of what the sweet smell of roses meant. For the past four weeks she had been delighted by how the roses on her balconies had bloomed. She had called over her neighbors, who had gushed over the roses' deep reds and pinks, astounded by their size. And above all, everyone was in awe of the glorious scent emanating from the marvelous flowers. She never doubted that the lustrous roses were as magnificent as they were because of her own tender love and care. Only as she took in the sweet smell of roses that lingered behind Mariana's bedroom door did she realize that it was not her fastidious care that made her roses glorious. It was Mariana's lovesick eyes and doting heart that gave the roses their purpose for blooming, for growing, for living. They no longer existed for the mere sake of beauty. Now the roses lived to bear witness to forbidden love.

Amparo was knocked down by the crushing truth of what Mariana had done. Speed and discretion were needed to untie the knot with which Mariana had bound herself so tightly.

chapter

THREE

Mariana grabbed the vase of flowers next to her bed and hurled it across the room, smashing it into hundreds of little pieces. She held her breath, shocked by her own audacity. Water mixed with shards of porcelain covered Amparo's body. She released the doorknob and slowly turned toward her daughter. Their eyes locked. Amparo's clenched jaw made the sides of her cheeks bulge. As a child, when Mariana saw her mother's cheeks bulge like that, she knew what was coming next: rapid footsteps down the hall, followed by the high-pitched squeak of her mother's closet door as she opened it, the loud snap from the leather belt in her mother's hands, the begging for forgiveness from the guilty child, Amparo dragging the child down the hall, chilling screams from both mother and child as she brought the heavy belt down on the child's naked behind.

Mariana was scared to death of her mother's ferocious eyes. Her bulging cheeks were bigger than she had ever seen them, but she refused to let Amparo know how afraid she was. Amparo took one step toward Mariana.

"Do not come near me. I'm warning you, if you come near me, I will tear your eyes out."

Amparo was blinded by her own fury and mistook Mariana's composed voice for a sign of weakness. She pounced on her daughter like a tigress attacking her prey. She grabbed Mariana by her hair and slapped her across the face. Flying into a rage, Mariana grabbed her mother with both hands and flipped her over on her back. Amparo's fury instantly turned into panic as Mariana towered over her. She went limp in her daughter's arms. Overcome with anger and heartbreak, Mariana lost all sense of control.

She pinned her mother on her bed, sitting on her chest and holding her arms down with her knees. Amparo tried to hit and scratch her way free, but it was pointless. Mariana easily overpowered her mother. She grabbed Amparo's hair and pulled her head back. Only inches away from her mother's face, she screamed at the top of her lungs: "Why did you make him go away? To Los Llanos, to Los fucking Llanos. I'm never going to see him again!"

Amparo tried to speak, but Mariana just screamed.

"Shut up! Why don't you want me to be happy? Just because you're miserable you want to make everyone around you miserable! Why do you think papi leaves every weekend? Why did Esperanza leave? Because you're horrible to be around! Everyone hates you! I hate you! I hate you! I hate you!"

Mariana collapsed in tears on top of her mother, sobbing uncontrollably. Amparo was unable to move. She was stunned by her daughter's words, and her heart was shattered by Mariana's cruelty. Amparo's mind raced, trying to find a way to make her daughter understand that Antonio going to Los Llanos was the best thing that could happen to Mariana. Yes, it was true that Amparo hoped the vast distance between them would end their ridiculous relationship, but she'd never intended to hurt her daughter. On the contrary; she was only trying to help her. She was only trying to save her.

Amparo had spent hours thinking of the perfect plan that would cause Mariana the least amount of pain but would also accomplish her goal of getting Antonio out of her life. During her restless nights she came up with various plans to separate them, some more extreme than others: She toyed with the idea of sending Mariana to a convent in Argentina where a distant aunt lived, but the mere thought of Mariana being a nun sent shivers of sorrow down her spine. She considered using her connections in the government to have Antonio arrested for a petty crime, but she could not live with the idea of sending an innocent man to jail. She seriously contemplated paying him off to leave El Valle, but that plan's success depended too much on Antonio, so she quickly discarded the idea.

Then, on an extraordinarily hot and humid night, inspiration struck. As had become her custom, Amparo restlessly tossed and turned for hours. Trying to quiet her racing mind, she stepped out onto the balcony and sat down on her favorite weathered chair. She leaned her sweaty back against the hard, cold chair and looked up at the moon. She was surprised by the moon's fullness, by how alive it was. As she was lost in its beautiful allure, Amparo's moment of inspiration arrived.

Antonio needed a job. It was the first thing he had told her when they met. Hernando Andrés was hiring men in Los Llanos to herd cattle for a new business he was starting. The opportunity could not be more perfect. Going to Los

Llanos to work for her husband would be as good as going to another country. Antonio and Mariana would never see each other again. If they were lucky, one out of twenty letters written would actually make it into the other's hands. Amparo's heart raced with excitement. She was thrilled.

The next night, as Hernando Andrés was getting into bed, Amparo broached the subject.

"*Mi amor*, did you enjoy Cata's tennis game?"

"She's playing very well. So much better than the last time I saw her."

"I knew you would enjoy seeing her before you left. How is everything going with Los Llanos?"

"Good. We've hired everyone. We're in good shape."

"I wanted to talk with you about hiring someone—"

"Amparo, I'm done with doing favors. The last time we hired someone because of a favor it was—"

"It's not for me, it's for Mariana."

"For Mariana?"

"I told you it was serious. I told you I needed you to help me, but all you could think about was El Arado and work. We could have taken care of everything then—"

"What is going on with Mariana?"

"There is a man who is very interested in her. She thinks she's in love with him, and if we don't do something about it, she will do something stupid. Stupid and very serious."

"What's his name?"

"You don't know him. He's a fisherman's son."

Hernando Andrés' world went silent. Amparo's lips moved, but he did not hear her. Love was a difficult thing for Hernando Andrés to grasp because it did not fit inside a box. Love was something he could not dissect in order to see how it worked, and then put back together again, like the telephones of his childhood or the airplanes he dreamed about constantly. He could not weigh it, box it up, and ship it away like the sugar he was obsessed with. Since he was unable to understand love, he shied away from it. He found it an unnecessary and silly distraction that created more problems than it was worth. Hernando Andrés wanted Mariana to be happy. He knew she was simpler than her sister Esperanza, less susceptible to complications and exaggerations than Juliana, not quite as beautiful as Catalina, and more disciplined than Diego and Mario Andrés combined, but regardless of her oddities he knew his daughter was meant to be more than a fisherman's wife. He raised his hand to quiet Amparo's nonstop babble.

"Send him to Los Llanos."

The irritatingly loud ring of the telephone bounced off the bare concrete walls in Antonio's home. His mother was in the kitchen, watching as her delicious *pandebono* turned a light golden brown in their small, overused oven. Antonio yelled to his mother from his bed.

"Ma, can you please answer it?"

"You know I don't waste my time answering the phone. Nobody ever calls me. It's always for you."

Antonio stumbled out of bed, eyes half-open, head pounding from his late night out.

"Hello?"

"Hello. May I speak with Antonio, please?"

"This is he. Who's this?"

"It's Amparo Azcárate de Cabal."

"Oh, good morning, Señora Amparo."

"Good morning, Antonio. I need you to come to my house today. It's very important."

"Is everything okay?"

"Well, that will depend on you. I'll see you here after lunch."

The phone went dead. Antonio's heart raced. What could Amparo possibly want from him? Was it possible that someone had seen him disappear into the shacks where women gave their bodies to the transient pleasures of men? Antonio was always discreet when seeking out his women. Unlike most of his friends, he went alone. He never boasted about the secrets the women shared with him, and he was kind and respectful to the naked bodies he found lying there on withered sheets. It was a lesson his father had taught him on the first night he was introduced to the pleasures of a woman. He pushed the thought out of his mind. It was impossible for Amparo to know anything about his nightly excursions.

Antonio sat patiently waiting for Amparo. The large house was empty of the Azcárate children, making it eerily quiet. He tapped his leg in anxious anticipation. He had arrived after lunch, just as Amparo had requested, but Dandaney had told him he would have to wait for Amparo to finish her lunch, as she had decided to eat later than usual today. He waited for over an hour before Amparo announced her arrival by the clicking of her heels on the marble floor. Antonio stood as she entered the room.

"I hope you were not waiting long."

"No, Señora. Not long at all."

"Good. So tell me, Antonio, have you found a job yet?'

"As I mentioned to you before, I am in the process of expanding—"

"Antonio, please. Those stories might work with my daughter, who knows very little about the world, but I can assure you they will not work with me. Do you have a job?"

"No, Señora. I do not."

"Are your intentions serious with Mariana?"

"Yes, of course. I love her."

"Love? Really? So tell me, how are you going to provide for her?"

"Well, once I am able to expand my business, I can begin to save, and with time I'll be able to give Mariana everything she needs."

"Everything? To give her everything with your little business will take quite a long time."

"Yes, maybe."

"You don't know Mariana very well, but she's not very patient. She hates waiting for things. Just waiting to see you every week is horribly painful for her. So waiting until you can give her everything…well, I don't think she'll be able to do it. But lucky for you, I have a solution."

"I bet you do."

"My husband has a new cattle business, and he is looking for help with herding. It's good pay because it will be hard work."

"Where's the job?"

"Los Llanos. You have to commit to six months. You won't be able to come home at all during that time. Hernando Andrés won't come home, either. You'll be working side by side with my husband, which could be a good thing or a bad thing. That all depends on you."

"How much is the pay?"

"You'll have to discuss that with my husband."

"No, I think it's best if we figure it out. This opportunity, I'm very well aware, is not out of the kindness of your heart.

And let's be honest—it's really not about helping Mariana, either. You're placing your bets. Hoping distance and time will do what you haven't been able to do. So let's really raise the stakes. I don't want to get paid a penny while I'm there. Instead, when I get back, if I marry Mariana I want a house. A house we can start a family in."

The silence in the room was deafening. Amparo glared at him with hatred. Antonio stared back with the promise of the future.

"Fine. But you have to leave today. I'll let Mariana know that you left."

"Be sure to send her my love."

Mariana's body trembled as she lay on top of Amparo and cried. Puddles of tears and snot formed on Amparo's chest. Amparo wanted to wrap her arms around her broken daughter, but she was afraid. She was afraid Mariana might hit her again, or even worse, that she might lose her mind and never find it again. She thought it best to leave her alone. Amparo slithered out from under her daughter's quivering body. Mariana did not fight her. Her body went limp, and she rolled over on her side. She brought her knees to her chest and wrapped her arms around them, weeping.

Amparo stood at the edge of Mariana's bed, and for a brief moment she regretted having caused her daughter so much pain. She looked down at Mariana, wracked with grief, and was reminded of her own broken heart and the unbearable sorrow that came with it.

When Amparo was merely fifteen, her own heartache had almost killed her. She had fallen madly in love with a boy named Camilo. He was smart, kind, and adventurous, and above all, he worshipped the ground Amparo walked on. Their love affair was as innocent as they were young. They never went beyond the few kisses he stole from her in the dark recesses of her house. But with each kiss, Amparo fell deeper and deeper in love with him.

Camilo's dream was to travel. He wanted to venture to the farthest corners of the world and lose himself there. By the age of sixteen he had traveled to the jungles of El Pacifico, the highest mountaintops of his homeland, and the most remote deserts of La Guajira. Amparo loved his free spirit and had grown accustomed to his good-byes.

Only seven days after his final good-bye, Camilo lost his life like so many countless Colombians, murdered at the hands of his own countrymen. The war between Liberals and Conservatives made rivers of blood flow through the countryside; Colombia's fertile land was soaked in the blood of more than two hundred fifty thousand of its people, butchered in the nightmare of La Violencia. La Violencia bound and twisted every state, every city, and every town in Colombia into savage knots that erupted without cause, logic, or an ounce of humanity. The blinding desire for revenge fueled the carnage. The thrones of power were drenched in blood. Greedy landowners and dirty politicians became savages as they stripped the murdered of all their earthly possessions, leaving only their skeletons behind in unmarked graves, to be found by future generations fighting their own endless wars.

Camilo's seven days alone on the back roads of Colombia had brought him to a quiet path surrounded by sugarcane fields. He stopped abruptly in mid-step and stared at the most beautiful sunset he had ever laid eyes on. The sky was splashed with pinks and purples, the scattered clouds washed with an iridescent orange glow. He marveled at the sun dipping behind the mountains. He was so entranced by God's perfection that he did not hear the group of men emerge from the sugarcane field behind him.

The men were rowdy after a long day of backbreaking work under the pounding and unforgiving Antioqueño sun. They knew Camilo was an outsider by the way he looked at the sunset. The locals were used to the vibrant colors splashed across the sky; outsiders were always spellbound by it. The men passed Camilo. He tipped his hat to his countrymen and kept walking north.

Seconds later the men descended on Camilo. He was an outsider, which could only mean that he belonged to the other side. The quiet evening was shattered by the piercing screams of the dying young man. They grabbed and pulled him by his arms, his legs, his head, whatever they could get their hands on. Camilo fought as hard as his sixteen-year-old body could fight, but he was no match for the ten men who pulled his body apart bit by bit.

By the time the men dragged Camilo down to the Cauca River, Camilo was barely conscious. Blood gushed from his nose. His mouth was covered in dirt and blood. His eyes were swollen shut, and deep purple black bruises cloaked his face.

"You piece-of-shit Conservative. You'll see what we do to people like you."

Camilo smiled. They were right, he thought; his father was a Conservative, but at the age of sixteen, he had never voted. Then a blow to his head stopped all the thoughts in his mind. Camilo's body went limp. Chaos broke out. The men screamed and yelled at one another. They did not want Camilo to die, at least not yet. The men wanted to mark his death in a special way; they wanted this day to be remembered.

A fat, toothless man pulled out his machete and scraped it on the ground. Sparks flew as he sharpened it for the beheading that was to come. A man with a cigarette in his mouth salivated at the thought of killing the boy with the *corte de mica*. He envisioned holding the boy's body as the fat man decapitated him in one fell swoop. Their favorite part was placing the decapitated head on the boy's chest while they made a special toast to all their compatriots killed mercilessly at the hands of Conservatives. The men had grown tired of the *corte de corbata*, which required cutting along the neckline and pulling the tongue out through the cut. It was too messy to enjoy. Inevitably, blood sprayed everywhere as the men grabbed the tongue and pulled it through the incision. The men craved something new.

An old man with white hair asked, "Is the boy still alive?"

They checked for his heartbeat. Miraculously, it was still there. The old man pulled a knife from his pocket.

"How many cuts do you think it would take for the bastard to bleed to death?"

The men roared. Their excitement only grew with each cut Camilo's body endured. Camilo withstood five hundred forty-four slits in every conceivable part of his body before his heart finally stopped beating. As they left Camilo's naked body at the river's edge the old man laughed and said, "All those cuts make him look like the *bocachico* fish I ate last night."

"Well, then I guess we just *bocachiquiar* him!" said the fat man, whose shoes were soaked in blood.

So it was there, on that quiet, beautiful night, at the river's edge, that one of the most violent deaths in Colombia took place. To be *bocachiquiar* became more terrible than death itself.

News of Camilo's death traveled through the coffee plantations, rode on the backs of horses, and bounced alongside a myriad of goats until it was finally whispered into his father's ear. His family was spared the most violent details of his death, but like so many before him, Camilo's father vowed to avenge his son's murder. After the memorial service he set out with a gun in one hand and a machete in the other to kill as many Liberals as he could find. He found twenty-four Liberals before he himself was killed with the *corte de mica*.

Amparo was in her kitchen when she heard the news. As soon as the words *Camilo has been killed* were spoken, her world went dark. Eighty years later, on her deathbed, Amparo could still vividly recall the pain of her heartbreak. She remembered how the heaviness filled her body, how breathing was an effort she could barely endure. She remembered what it felt like for her shattered heart to pump blood filled with shards of glass throughout her broken body.

Now, looking at her daughter, Amparo shook away the memory of Camilo. To remember such pain did nothing for her. She tenderly placed her hand on Mariana's leg, trembling upon the sheets. Amparo understood Mariana's tears, but she also knew that tears eventually dry and hearts mend—maybe not as perfectly as they once were, but well enough to love again. If she could survive, so could her daughter. Mariana pushed her mother's hand away. Through her sobs she managed to whisper, "Get out… please, just get out.…"

The bedroom door clicked shut behind Amparo.

After Antonio left, Mariana was lost in her grief. At school her classes were a blur of faces and voices that made no sense. The world kept moving forward, but her thoughts were only of Antonio. What was he doing while she stared at numbers on the chalkboard? Where was he while she sat in her bedroom looking out her window? Who was he with while she was forced to sit at the dinner table with her family? Did he think of her the way she thought of him? Did he miss her until it hurt? The same questions circled in her mind with no answers. Every day she waited for letters that never came. Days of pain turned into weeks of torture. Time and silence were driving Mariana mad. She stopped talking to her classmates. Their lives seemed so trivial to her. While they were concerned about test scores and what this boy or that boy thought about this or that girl, Mariana was fighting for her survival, for her future, for her reason to live. Her only respite was to retreat to the grassy hill where years before Evalina had offered her solace.

The morning dew seeped through Mariana's crisp white shirt as she lay on her back and stared up at the clear blue sky. The world around her disappeared, just as it had when she was a child. She found a quiet stillness in her thoughts, a brief reprieve from her broken heart. It was there among the green grass and splendid sun that she replayed every moment lived with Antonio, every conversation spoken, every kiss exchanged. Within each moment replayed, she searched for answers to the questions that kept her up at night. Why had he left so easily? How could he leave without even saying good-bye? Did he really love her?

As she pondered these questions, Mariana's faith in Antonio was slowly restored. She realized Antonio had left to prove himself to her father, to her mother, and in many ways even to Mariana herself. Antonio knew he was an outsider, unwelcome in her world. He knew he had to show Hernando Andrés that his daughter was safe in his arms. Antonio also knew that if he were able to win over her father, then her mother would have no other option but to accept him into the family. The only way to gain Hernando Andrés' approval was to work with him side by side, man-to-man, in the excruciating heat and unbearable conditions of Los Llanos. She was certain he was aware of the risks involved in leaving; distance has a way of twisting and turning relationships inside out until they are unrecognizable. Mariana found comfort in the fact that Antonio had so much faith in their relationship that going away to Los Llanos was a risk he was willing to take in order to win acceptance into the Cabal family.

In the safety and comfort of the grassy knoll, Mariana realized that Antonio's silence was in fact a battle cry. With his silence, he was telling Mariana to search for him. If she wanted him, she would have to find him. She would have to fight for him. She would have to find a way around Amparo.

Sister Nubia sat down beside her and took Mariana's hand in hers.

"My dear Mariana, my heart is heavy with your pain. How can I help? Tell me: How can I take away your hurt?"

Mariana looked into Sister Nubia's crystal-blue eyes and saw a kindred spirit. *A sign from God,* she thought.

Mariana told Sister Nubia about her mother's immense cruelty, her sleepless nights, and the tight knot in her chest that never loosened no matter what she did.

Sister Nubia had not lied to anyone in over thirty-seven years. She abhorred lying, but she had always allowed for one exception: She knew love sometimes required lies. To lie for love was admirable, at times necessary, and could even be revolutionary.

During the past thirty-seven years Sister Nubia had devoted every ounce of her soul to God. But the path of her devotion had been filled with pit stops, accidents, and gaping holes. The holes were left by a young man she had once loved. At the age of seventeen she had fallen in love with Gilberto. He was tall, with dark chocolate skin and beautiful honey-brown eyes. The details of her love story were stored in the deep recesses of her memory. Time had warped them into half-truths that still had the power to make the earth under her feet tremble with her desire.

Gilberto came into her life by accident, but once he was there, Nubia never let him go. She clung to him like ink on paper. She fell hopelessly in love with his eyes, because they reminded her of the irresistible sweetness of honey.

She told a thousand lies so she could spend time with Gilberto, but it took only one lie to send her to the convent. Nubia had blocked the details out of her mind. She only remembered looking at Gilberto's hand as it slowly moved up her stomach and gently clutched her breast. She remembered her hardened nipple sliding under his fingers, and the fire between her legs spreading into her stomach. She remembered a door crashing open, screams all around her, things smashing against walls, hands pulling and pushing her away, tears. She remembered lots and lots of tears, and then silence.

Nubia found God in the silence. In God she found the love she had been searching for in Gilberto, she found the love her mother never gave her, and she found the love she wanted to give to others. Now, Sister Nubia felt Mariana's love was pure, honest, and worth fighting for. So, nestled in the safety of her beloved school, Sister Nubia altered the course of Mariana's life. She came up with an elaborate plan to bring the two lovers together again. The first order of business was to find out where exactly in Los Llanos Antonio was working. To do this, Sister Nubia said, Mariana needed to transform herself into a madwoman.

That same night Mariana's howls echoed through the hallways of her house, her screams reverberating off the tile floors and crashing over Amparo's bed. Her brothers and sisters did not know what to make of the madness that was invading their home. Diego, Mario Andrés, Catalina, and Juliana each knocked on Amparo's door, and every time she sent them back to their rooms, saying, "Your sister's fine. She just needs to rest, and so do you." But Amparo was wracked with guilt. She buried her head in her pillow and desperately tried to ignore her daughter's screams. Each second felt like an eternity; each scream was a dagger piercing her heart. Despair forced Amparo down the cold, dark hallway, but nothing could have prepared her for what she saw in her daughter's room. Mariana was drenched in sweat, her sheets soaking wet, her body wound into a tight ball that shook uncontrollably. With each scream her head arched back like that of a wolf howling at the moon. Amparo did the only thing she could do: She held her daughter through the night, singing her lullabies, hoping her voice would bring her back to this earthly plane.

The next day Sister Nubia phoned Amparo.

"Señora Amparo, it's imperative that you come to my office and discuss Mariana. I'm very worried."

"Yes, of course. I'm so glad you called. I've been up all night, worried sick," Amparo said, holding back tears.

When they met, Sister Nubia was shocked by Amparo's appearance. Her hand shook uncontrollably as she brought the cup of *tinto* to her parched lips. Her normally perfect bouffant was a heap of stray hairs. Sister Nubia had never seen Amparo as anything but the dignified and astute matriarch of the Cabal family. *Mariana must have put on quite a show,* she thought to herself. She felt a twinge of guilt, and for a second regretted their elaborate scheme. But the image of Mariana alone on the grassy hill staring off into nothingness quickly pushed aside her guilt and forced her to focus on the task at hand: obtaining Antonio's address.

Sister Nubia told Amparo how Mariana was not participating in classes. She told her how Mariana spent her days staring off into nothingness. When people spoke to her, she did not respond. She spent her lunches alone on a hill, looking at the sky. Sister Nubia's concerns went on and on, and by the time Amparo took her last sip of *tinto,* she was so distraught she burst into tears.

"Señora, when does Hernando Andrés come back from Los Llanos?"

"Not for another six months."

"Well, if that's the case, I think it would be best to write him to let him know the terrible condition Mariana finds herself in."

Amparo shook her head in agreement. Calls were reserved for emergencies, though, and while Mariana was suffering tremendously, Amparo knew the situation was not what Hernando Andrés would consider an emergency. Hernando Andrés did not normally concern himself with the trivial matters of daily family life, so Amparo had to play her cards right. She believed a letter from Sister Nubia would give the situation enough gravitas that Hernando Andrés might be more inclined to come home.

Sister Nubia held the black fountain pen in her left hand. Her heart thundered as she wrote the address Amparo dictated to her. Written on a piece of crisp white paper, in black ink, was the key to Mariana's heart.

"Go home and get some rest, Señora Amparo. I'll take care of everything."

Amparo shuffled out of Sister Nubia's office. She walked in a daze all the way home, where she collapsed onto her bed.

That very same day Sister Nubia and Mariana composed their first letter to Antonio. At first glance, the letter was a casual hello from an old nun to a dear friend inquiring about his well-being, how his work was progressing, his co-workers, and when he might be coming home. But the passion in the spaces between words, the caresses in the question marks, and the devotion in the perfect penmanship breathed life into the love-starved, nearly broken Antonio.

Antonio missed Mariana desperately, but it was the lacerating life of Los Llanos that had him on the verge of giving up. Los Llanos was a cruel, hot, uncompromising land. The Llaneros told Antonio every day how lucky he was to have come during the rainy season, because the dry season was hell on earth: the dust storms from the waterless land slashing at the eyes, the inescapable stench from the never-ending piles of water-starved, dead cattle. The Llaneros swore it got so hot that people's shadows disappeared, only to return when the first rains came. Antonio thought he would prefer those horrors to the blood-sucking mosquitoes, flesh-eating sand flies, and devilish vampire bats that hovered above him all night. He would rather work under a hot sun than under the wet, gray sky.

Antonio lay in bed in excruciating pain. The pounding rains made his head throb even more. Breathing made his back ache. Two hours earlier, his horse, Payaso, had violently bucked him off. Antonio and a few other men had been moving cattle through a slightly flooded wetland when out of nowhere Payaso reared up on his hind legs, throwing

Antonio into the water, where he landed on a pile of rocks. The Llaneros knew only two things could spook Payaso that way: a poisonous snake or an electric eel. The men scooped Antonio out of the water and within seconds found and killed the eel before it could kill the horses, the cattle, or Antonio. Now he seethed as the smell of cooked eel wafted into his room. He knew he should be grateful that the men had saved him, but he was well aware their help came at a price. How could he prove himself to Hernando Andrés if he needed the Llaneros to save him? *Thank God Hernado Andrés wasn't there,* he thought to himself. A knock on the door interrupted his thoughts.

"Come in."

Hernando Andrés opened the door. Antonio tried to sit up.

"Don't bother. This came for you."

Hernando Andrés handed him a crumpled white envelope.

"Mail goes out in two hours if you want to write them back; otherwise you'll have to wait until next week."

"Thank you."

Hernando Andrés left. Antonio ripped open the letter. There in front of him was what he needed to keep him going: Mariana. Antonio read and reread the letter so many times that by the time he started writing his response he had only twenty minutes before the mail would leave on its long journey to Buga. He wanted to tell Mariana of his fear, his pain, his doubt, and his undying love, but he knew he needed to tell her everything in between the lines, to allow what went unspoken to speak the volumes he could not.

Antonio told her about the thousands of cattle he was poised to move across the rolling flatlands that stretched to the edge of the earth. He told her about the hot and muggy days and the boredom of the constant rain. He wanted to tell her about the bugs that burrowed inside one's skin and the deadly disease that ate away one's flesh. But instead he told her about the most beautiful river in the world, Caño Cristales. Caño Crystales was a river Antonio had heard the Llaneros whisper about, but he had never actually seen it; the Llaneros were weary of showing outsiders their secrets. But he described the river as if he had been there a thousand times. He told Mariana how he went swimming in the magical river and how every color of the rainbow shimmered and glistened in its waters. He described how the deep holes in the earth were filled with pink, purple, and green waters, and how those very same waters cured every sickness imaginable. This was only the first of Antonio's many lies.

Antonio ran out of his room just as the man with the satchel of letters was mounting his horse. He gave the man with the large mustache and deep brown skin his letter.

"The last letter is always the best."

The man tipped his hat, nudged his bare feet against his horse, and road off toward the horizon. *To be that letter,* thought Antonio. Just then Hernando Andrés grabbed Antonio by the shoulder and said, "Feeling better, I see."

"Yes, Sir."

"Good. I need you out in the field."

Antonio ran to find Payaso. His head still hurt and his back ached like never before, but Mariana had given him the strength he needed to endure the callousness of Los Llanos.

Mariana's recovery was miraculous. From one day to the next she turned from a raging madwoman to the old Mariana. She began raising her hand in class again; she stopped sitting on the grassy hill, staring off into nothingness; and the walks home with her sisters were once again filled with laughter and incessant chatter.

The morning after Mariana and Sister Nubia mailed Antonio's letter she ran into her mother on her way out of the house. She smiled at Amparo, kissed her on the cheek, and happily said good-bye as she closed the front door behind her. Amparo was flabbergasted. Her daughter had not shown her that much affection in months. She rushed down the hall and called Sister Nubia.

"Sister, I think the worst is behind us. Did you mail the letter already?"

"Not yet."

"Wonderful. I don't think it's necessary anymore. Thank you. Thank you, for all your help!"

Sister Nubia hung up the phone with a smile on her face. Her plan had worked perfectly. She knew she was not the one responsible for the plan's perfection. It was God's divine hand that had written that Antonio and Mariana were destined to be together.

chapter

FOUR

Mariana closed the door quietly behind her. She turned around and caught sight of her reflection in the beautiful gilded antique mirror that hung above the sink. She stopped and looked at herself. Growing up, Mariana had avoided mirrors. She did not like to be reminded of her unruly hair, her hideous nose, or her countless freckles. But that night she saw something she had never seen before. She stared at the beads of sweat as they rolled down the sides of her face. She was as pale as a ghost, her black hair more chaotic than ever, but for the first time in her life she found beauty in her rough edges. Mariana stared at her eyes; they were still the same plain brown eyes she'd always found so boring, but now she saw how lovely her eyelashes looked, curling toward the sky. She looked at her lips. They were so thin it seemed as if God had painted them on as an afterthought, but at least he had chosen a beautiful deep pink with which to paint.

Mariana's stomach rumbled and churned. She remembered why she was in the dark bathroom at the far end of the house in the middle of the night. She turned on the faucet, just barely letting out a trickle of water. As her hands cupped the cool water, her stomach slowly settled. She let out a long sigh of relief. Mariana had tossed and turned in her bed to the point of nausea. She sat down on the toilet, unable to remove her hands from the trickle of soothing water. Mariana rested her head against the cold countertop and was finally able to find the comfort that had escaped her in her bed. But her relief lasted only a few seconds. Mariana's stomach erupted like el Nevado del Ruiz. She lifted the toilet seat, leaned over, and threw up the *arepa* and cheese she had eaten for dinner the night before.

Mariana quietly moaned. She felt a mixture of pain and relief as she kneeled down before the porcelain toilet. She opened her eyes and focused on the half-digested cheese floating in the toilet water. Suddenly a flash of terror ran through her body. *When was my last period?* she wondered. Mariana never paid attention to when her period was supposed to come; it just showed up like an unannounced dinner guest. She never paid attention because she never had a reason to. Now the video in her mind rewound itself to the quiet evening when her body had twisted and turned and fit perfectly into Antonio's body. She replayed every major event in her life since that fateful evening two months ago. A quiet panic rose from her toes to her chest. Her unannounced diner guest had not arrived. She doubled over the toilet again and threw up what was left of her *arepa* and cheese.

Mariana eased herself onto the floor and stared into the darkness. *Pregnant. Seventeen. Unmarried.* She felt as if she were living someone else's life. As if she were a spectator in someone else's tragedy. Her mind raced with a thousand thoughts, but nothing made any sense. Her body trembled with fear on the tile floor.

Mariana watched as sunlight began to seep under the bathroom door. The outside world slowly crept into the cocoon of her distress. Time was no longer suspended. Time and reality crashed into each other, and Mariana knew she had to do something…anything. *I have to take a shower* was the only rational thought she was able to form.

Mariana turned on the shower and stepped into the stream of ice-cold water. Every part of her body was yelling for her to step out from under the freezing water, but she forced herself to suffer through the pain. In her discomfort she found a moment of clarity: Falling apart emotionally was a luxury she could not afford. She knew tears were pointless. Self-pity was destructive. Clarity of vision was what she needed. She stepped out of the shower, her teeth chattering. Her fear zipped back into her chest. *I have to go to a doctor,* she thought.

Mariana kissed her mother good-bye, telling Amparo she had to get to school early to study for an exam, and that Catalina and Juliana should walk to school without her. She grabbed her book bag and closed the big heavy wooden doors behind her. She walked down the cobblestone street as usual, but instead of turning left to go to La Merced she continued straight, toward the office of the doctor who had attended her own birth.

As she held the cold metal doorknob in her hand, Mariana prayed the doctor's office would be empty. She took a deep breath, begged for strength, and opened the door. Pilar, a plump woman with over processed curly hair, looked up from behind the reception desk. She was surprised to see Mariana.

"Mari, what are you doing here?"

"I just need to see the doctor really quickly."

"You don't have an appointment. Do you?"

"No, I just need to ask him something."

Pilar looked at her with concern.

"Everything's fine. I just need to ask him something."

"Give me one second."

Pilar disappeared behind the heavy oak doors. Mariana tried to calm the fluttering butterflies in her stomach. Mariana's father always told her, *If you ever need anything and I'm not here, go to El Doctor.* The thought sent the fluttering butterflies in Mariana's stomach into a frenzy. This was not where she should be. Doctor Martínez was one of her father's best friends, which meant he would never understand how she could be pregnant without being married. In the worst-case scenario, the doctor would tell Hernando Andrés she was pregnant. In the best-case scenario, he would tell Amparo she was pregnant. She grabbed a piece of paper from Pilar's desk and scribbled: *I'm having trouble sleeping. I was hoping you could help. I'm late for class, so I'll stop by after school.* She ran out of the office and into the street like a wild horse. A car slammed on its brakes and swerved around her, missing her by inches. Mariana did not even stop to acknowledge the driver as he screamed every obscenity imaginable. She needed to find a place where no one knew her. She needed to hide in the shadows of unrecognized faces. There was only one place in Buga where no one cared about her infamous nose or her famous last name: Palo Blanco.

Mariana focused on a bus in the distance. The red bus with the cracked window that spewed a constant stream of black clouds from its exhaust pipe was her only escape. The rickety red bus in the sea of chaos before her was her savior.

She flailed her arms like the wings of the butterflies raging in her stomach. The red bus slowed down just enough for Mariana to run alongside, grab the rail on the door, and pull herself into the overflowing crowd of people. She pushed and squeezed herself into the bus and settled between two women who were half her height and triple her weight.

The decaying bus with its frayed seats and its shattered windows was Mariana's sanctuary, except it was as hot as an oven. It could not fend off the dreadful heat that engulfed it. Sweat poured down the passengers' faces, men's shirts stuck to their sweaty backs, and women's makeup melted. The smell of sweaty armpits made Mariana nauseous. A sour taste pierced the back of her throat. She knew she did not have much time. She looked around the crowded bus, bracing herself. Bodies were pushed against bodies. In order to get to the nearest window she would have to crawl over mounds of people. Her stomach rumbled. She closed her eyes.

The bus made its way up the road at a snail's pace. It tried to avoid the gaping potholes, but with every swerve it slammed into another hole. Each crashing thump brought Mariana's stomach one step closer to exploding. She opened her eyes, hoping for a distraction to bring her stomach some sort of peace. As she looked around, Mariana took in the poverty of Palo Blanco. She had never actually been there; she had only seen its hills, dotted with square cinder-block homes, from a distance. Until that moment she did not know that the roofs of the humble homes were made of tin and held in place by large rocks their inhabitants had found at the edge of the road. The windy, poorly maintained roads were meant for buses she never rode and for the feet of people she only interacted with to say a cordial "hello" or "thank you" to as they served her food or made her bed.

Mariana's eyes focused on a young woman as she slowly wobbled up the dirt road. The woman's stomach bulged out of her shirt. She looked as if she might burst at any moment. The woman winced in discomfort as she waddled up the hill. Suddenly the rattling from the loose screws on the bus went silent, and Mariana realized she had a choice to make. Would she have the baby, or would she find a doctor to make her problem disappear? She had to take a chance on a stranger with a coat hanger, or she had to take a chance on Antonio. Both scared her. Both were uncertain.

Taking a chance on a stranger with a coat hanger meant taking a dangerous risk. Mariana had heard of girls who ended up bleeding to death on the edge of the Guadalajara River or in the dark alleyways of Palo Blanco. She also heard of women who spent years behind metal bars because a coat hanger had penetrated too deeply and sent them rushing on a river of blood to the hospital and then to jail.

She placed her hand on her stomach. Mariana knew whatever decision she made would dictate the rest of her life. The bus stopped momentarily at a red light. Mariana looked across the street and saw a sign that read DOCTOR'S OFFICE.

"Stop! Stop! Stop!"

The bus door slammed open. Mariana pushed her way through the crowd and got off. She walked into the small, dilapidated office. She took in the room around her. The walls were fighting a losing battle against the yellow stains of time. The small windows were covered with pieces of old bed sheets. An oversize wooden desk, which the ravages of time had left alone, stood proudly in the center of the room. A woman in a dark blue fitted blazer and matching skirt with bright red lipstick and pitch-black hair greeted Mariana kindly. Mariana's shoulders relaxed a bit.

The woman knew why Mariana was there. For years, countless young women just like Mariana had walked through those doors. They were all scared. They were all out of place. They all needed guidance. Luckily for each of them, destiny guided them into the caring hands of El Doctor.

The woman asked Mariana to take a seat while she let the doctor know she was there.

"I don't have an appointment."

"I know."

She disappeared behind the scraggly hanging curtains that served as the door to what Mariana assumed was the doctor's office. Mariana sat down. It was all she could do. She heard mumbling from behind the curtain, and her heart sank as she realized she was wearing her school uniform. Everyone in Buga knew the white-collared shirts, the blue-and-green checkered skirts, and the sparkling black shoes belonged to La Merced. In her haste to leave her house she had not thought about the implications of wearing her school uniform. It made her an easy target for wagging tongues: A girl from La Merced in a doctor's office in Palo Blanco meant only one thing. She had to leave, now. She bolted up just as the doctor stepped out from behind the curtain. Mariana froze. The doctor's kindhearted smile, salt-and-pepper mustache, and small, slender frame did nothing to calm her anxious heart.

"Come in, Señorita…?"

"Thank you, doctor, for your time, but I have to go."

"But I haven't even seen you."

"I know, but I have to go."

El Doctor cut right to heart of the matter.

"If you're worried about your uniform, I don't even know what school it's from."

"Neither do I," said the woman in blue.

Mariana looked into the doctor's deep brown eyes. They reminded her of Antonio's eyes. They were kind, honest, and judicious. This stranger was her only option. Mariana stood before El Doctor in his rundown office and trusted the first of many strangers who would help her along life's difficult road. Mariana swallowed the knot in her throat and walked through the curtains into the doctor's office.

His office was not much different from the reception area. The walls were fighting the same battle with time, and losing. They were bare except for the crucifix that hung above the curtains. The doctor sat down in a plastic chair and offered Mariana a seat on the cot, which was covered with a white blanket. She sat.

"How can I help you?"

Mariana stuttered, she stammered, she could not form a single sentence. He looked at her with pity. How many girls had he seen in this ugly child's predicament? How many young women's hands had he held as they cried tears of fear, anger, and repentance? El Doctor offered the young women a shoulder to cry on, but more important, he offered them options. He never gave them advice. El Doctor was simply the conduit that fulfilled their wishes. He had heard the words *What should I do?* thousands of times, and his response was always the same: "That's for you to decide, and once you do, I am here to help you." He never pushed one option over another. Often it took weeks for a woman to decide what she wanted. Once she decided, he worked as hard as a mule to make it happen, and just like a mule the only thing he got in return was a pat on the back.

El Doctor offered the women who came to his office three options. If they decided they did not want to keep the baby, El Doctor could discreetly arrange a stay at a convent for nine months. Once the baby was born, the nuns would care it for and the mother could return to the life she had left behind nine months earlier. Or he had a friend in Cali who would have the young lady back in three days, miraculously without child. He also knew of a priest who for the right price would happily marry a couple within days, no questions asked. None of the options was a perfect solution, but as El Doctor had accepted long ago, life is not about perfection, it is about concessions.

The hardest part of his job was not the ocean of tears he saw, but the mysteries the women left behind. He rarely if ever saw any of the women again. He assumed most of them disappeared into the unforgiving landscape of single motherhood. On very rare occasions he would see a picture of one of the women in the local paper. The pictures were always the same: The woman was a glorious vision in white, so different from the broken soul who had visited his office a few weeks before. At first glance the pictures seemed to be a dream come true—a beautiful wife, a handsome husband, smiling at the life that lay before them. But El Doctor took his time with these pictures. He studied the details. He looked into the woman's eyes, and there behind the veil and the mascara, he always saw her hidden truth. He saw her doubt, her fear, and her anger. He empathized with her; the first lash of life's lacerating whip always hurt the most.

El Doctor asked Mariana again, "How can I help you?"

Mariana struggled to get the words out. They tripped over one another as they wrestled their way out. He smiled, a gentle, kind smile.

"When was your last menstruation?"

Mariana's eyes darted to the ground. She bit her lip in shame. El Doctor took her hand in his.

"Do you not remember?"

Mariana did not have to fight the words any longer. He knew why she was there.

"Two months."

Mariana barely believed the words as they came out of her mouth. How was it possible that her life had changed so drastically in such a small amount of time? How could the pendulum of life swing so seamlessly from carefree innocence to extreme uncertainty within the blink of an eye?

El Doctor handed Mariana a small, clear plastic up.

"The bathroom is over there."

Mariana walked slowly across the room. Her heart pounded in her chest. Life as she knew it was about to change. She opened the door and turned on the light, locking the door behind her. A cracked mirror hung on the wall in front of her. Mariana looked at her reflection. The beauty she had discovered earlier that morning was gone. The abyss of fear had swallowed it. Her eyes welled with tears as she wondered, *What will Antonio say? What will he do?* She fell further into the hole of the unknown. Her hands trembled. She pushed the thoughts away and wiped the tears from her cheeks. *Pointless...tears are pointless.* Mariana lifted up her skirt, straddled the toilet, and peed her truth into the plastic cup.

As she awaited the results, Mariana's leg bounced uncontrollably. A solitary fan at the edge of the room failed miserably against the suffocating heat. A hand pushed aside the curtain. Mariana's heart dropped. Her eyes were fixed on El Doctor as he walked toward her. She searched for clues about her future in his almond-brown eyes, in his slightly hunched shoulders, in his crossed legs as he sat in front of her. He was as guarded as a penitentiary until he smiled. His smile betrayed the truth. He confirmed what Mariana already knew. She was pregnant.

"Thank you for your help, doctor. I need to go and speak with my mother."

"Yes, of course." He stood up and pushed aside the curtains to the reception area. "If there is anything you need, please come back. There is a lot we can do."

She nodded and walked toward the woman in the blue skirt. The doctor and the woman in blue looked at each other. Words did not need to be exchanged. Mariana was exactly like the thousands of others who came before her. She walked in a daze past the woman in blue.

"Excuse me, Señorita. There is a small fee for seeing the doctor."

Mariana's face flushed in embarrassment.

"Yes, of course. I'm sorry."

Mariana dug into her book bag, but she soon realized that in her rush to leave her house she had not brought extra money. She looked up at the woman with dread in her eyes. The woman in blue wondered why rich girls never had money in their purses.

"Don't worry. You can come by tomorrow or the next day, but please do come back."

"Yes, of course."

"I don't want to have to find out where that uniform is from. Okay?"

Mariana nodded. She understood exactly what the woman was saying without her having to say it.

Mariana stepped out onto the unpaved road. The reality of having to tell her mother she was pregnant hit her so hard it knocked the wind out of her. She gasped for air. She needed time, but time was a luxury she did not have. So

Mariana walked. She walked the long, solitary route home through the town of her childhood. She walked down the streets that held all of her memories. She walked on the same cobblestone streets where her mother had fallen in love, her grandfather had died, and her unborn child had been conceived.

Mariana found her mother sitting in her favorite chair on her balcony, fanning herself and reading one of her favorite romance novels. Amparo looked up at her daughter and thought she looked absolutely beautiful. She had noticed that for the last few weeks Mariana had been enveloped in an entrancing glow—the radiance of becoming a woman. Amparo felt a twinge of sadness knowing that her daughter was leaving behind her childhood and entering the thorny complexities of womanhood. But she was comforted by the fact that because of this transition, a new bond between mother and daughter was forming. They were bound by blood, but Amparo hoped their relationship would now bloom into true friendship. She wanted to be her daughter's confidante. She wanted to be her best friend.

Mariana sat down in the chair across from her mother and took her hands in hers.

"Mari, what are you doing home so early?" Amparo asked. "Where are Cata and Juli?"

"Mami, I don't know how to tell you this, so I'm just going to say it."

Amparo's brow furrowed in confused anticipation. The words tumbled out of Mariana's mouth.

"I'm pregnant."

Amparo dropped Mariana's hands. She stood up.

"No, no, no! No!"

She covered her face. She paced back and forth, feeling as if the walls around her were crushing her. Her desperation grew with each passing second. Her screams pierced the tranquil skies. Mariana sat motionless, watching as her mother crumbled before her into a fit of tears. She blinked back her own tears and kneeled down beside her mother. Amparo shook violently as Mariana reached out and tenderly rubbed her back. There was nothing Mariana could say or do for her mother. What was done was done. Amparo looked at her daughter and saw the burdens stacked high on her back. She was now truly a woman. Amparo held Mariana's face in her two hands.

"I didn't want this for you. I wanted you to have more than what I have."

Mariana tried to protest, but Amparo placed her finger over Mariana's mouth.

"It has nothing to do with him. Ay, Mari, unfortunately one day you'll understand what I'm trying to tell you. What do you want to do?"

"I'm keeping it."

Amparo wiped away her tears. She pulled herself up into her favorite chair and straightened her skirt. She closed her eyes and took a deep breath. When she finally opened her eyes, her heart ached at the plan she knew she would have to orchestrate.

"Let's call Antonio."

Mariana stood next to Amparo while she dialed the farthest corner of the country. Their silence was broken only by the harsh crackling voice on the other end of the line. Amparo spoke softly so her words would not run along the walls, jump out the windows, and multiply as they found their way to hungry ears. But her discretion was pointless. The man on the other end screamed for her to speak louder.

"I need to speak to Antonio Rodríguez! Tell him his mother needs to speak to him. I'll call back in two hours.

But please tell him not to call home. It's very important that he not call home. I'll call him. Thank you."

She hung up the phone. Mariana was shocked by her mother's boldness. Amparo felt pity for Mariana. Her daughter had no idea what she was in for.

"Get used to it. Let's get you some food."

Mother and daughter watched in silence as the clock ticked away the seconds. The house was empty except for Mariana and her mother; Amparo did not want any witnesses as she worked to weave Mariana's future. The maids scrambled out of the house when they saw the impossible list Amparo had created of the things that needed to be done. Time was of the essence. They had only a few hours before the boys would come home from school, and the girls would follow soon after.

As far as Amparo was concerned, Mariana had two options. The best one—and the one Amparo would pour her blood, sweat, and tears into—was to have Mariana marry Antonio by the end of the month. If a wedding was to happen, this left her with only twenty-one days to plan it. It seemed like an impossible feat, but impossible was nothing when it came to her daughter's future. The second option filled Amparo with dread. If Antonio did not marry Mariana, she would have no other choice than to have an abortion. Amparo knew of a doctor in Cali who specialized in discreet abortions. He had never lost a patient, nor had any of his patients ever been put in jail, but Amparo knew he was out of the question. Cali was too close to home. Amparo could not risk anyone finding out. Her best and only option would be to travel to the cold and unwelcoming mountains of Bogotá.

The clock struck one as Amparo walked down the hallway, Mariana following behind her. She picked up the phone and dialed. The phone rang and rang and rang. Finally, a worried voice picked up.

"Hello?"

"Hello, Antonio. It's Amparo Cabal Azcárate. Mariana needs to speak with you. When she is finished, please don't hang up, as I would like to speak with you as well."

Amparo handed the phone to Mariana. She walked down the empty hallway and locked herself in her bedroom. She kneeled before the crucifix above her bed and prayed Mariana would not have to carry too heavy a burden. She asked God to give her Mariana's pain. Her shoulders could bear it. Life had been cruel to her; she knew where to hide the sting of life.

"Hola…"

Mariana pushed the butterflies down her throat.

"Hola, mi amor."

Mariana felt Antonio's smile through the crackling phone line. His gentle voice caressed her ear.

"Mari, what's going on?"

The butterflies fluttered in her stomach again.

"I have to tell you something. I'm pregnant."

The line crackled as the endless seconds of Antonio's silence stacked one on top of the other. Her toes dug into the ground as she fought against the flapping wings of the butterflies that threatened to push her into despair.

"Will you marry me?"

The wind blew harder.

"Are you sure?" was all Mariana could manage to say.

"Of course. I love you. You love me. You're pregnant. It's clearly meant to be."

"Yes, *mi amor*, I'll marry you!"

Mariana's toes loosened their grip as the butterflies' fluttering wings slowly came to a halt.

Amparo came out of her bedroom. She knew by the smile on Mariana's face that her daughter would be married in a matter of days. Now the real planning would begin. Amparo took the phone from Mariana.

"Antonio, you need to get here right away. Tell Hernando your mother is sick. He'll let you leave without a problem. Don't say a word to anyone. Not your brothers, not your family, not even your best friend. Understand?"

"Yes."

"I'll take care of everything else."

The next day Antonio was on the bus that would bring him into the arms of the Cabal family, and into Mariana's bed.

Mariana came out of the bathroom wrapped in a towel. On her bed were a simple white dress, a string of pearls, and matching heels and silk stockings. Mariana was deeply touched by Amparo's thoughtfulness. The days leading up to Mariana's wedding had been heart-wrenching for her mother. The secrecy, the stress, and the constant lying had taken their toll. Her luminous eyes were shrouded in dark circles, her skin was ashen with exhaustion, and her temper exploded without warning. The sounds of screams and smashing plates serenaded the Cabal house in the days preceding Mariana's secret wedding. No one but Mariana knew the reason for Amparo's madness.

Amparo decided they would elope in Cali. But Mariana did not want to hide in Cali's anonymity. She wanted to share her love, if not with her friends and family, at the very least with the city that had raised her, but Amparo refused. Eloping in Buga would be impossible. There were too many prying eyes, too many family friends, and too many connections to people in high places. Amparo knew the only way their secret could remain theirs would be for it to hide in the corners of Cali. With a heavy heart, Mariana agreed to her mother's plan. She swallowed her desire to share the news of her wedding with her sisters, and she did not put up a fight when Amparo told her no one could attend the wedding. Mariana wanted to celebrate her new life, but her mother was mourning it before it even began. Neither tried to change the other's mind; instead they found a balance of happiness and grief, smiles and tears, and understanding and sacrifice.

Mariana placed the soft silk dress against her body and looked at herself in the mirror. Her worn blue jeans jutted out from underneath the lovely dress, and she stared at them. She wanted to start her life in those jeans. She let the dress fall to the ground. She liked how she looked in her blue jeans, with their worn-out knees. Her white cotton shirt seemed perfect for a wedding. She unbuttoned the first two buttons, smiling to herself, thinking, *Just to drive him crazy.* She slipped her feet into her leather sandals, grabbed a pair of scissors, and walked out to her balcony. The rosebushes were still in full bloom. Her eyes focused on a beautiful red rose. She cut it just under its petals, placed it behind her ear, and looked at herself in the mirror once again. This was how she would marry her husband. This felt right. This was how her life was supposed to begin. She was ready to be Antonio's wife.

Mariana opened her bedroom door, and just as her mother had promised, the house was empty. She walked quietly down the hall and out onto the cobblestone street. It was early morning, and Buga was stirring. Mariana waited on the same street where two months earlier her life had changed.

A light blue Renault pulled up beside Mariana.

"I heard you need a ride to Cali."

She looked through the window. There he was. Two months had not changed the shape of his eyes or the curve of his lips, but somehow he looked more beautiful than she remembered him. Mariana opened the car door, grabbed him by the back of his neck, and pulled him against her. Their lips grazed one another.

"Don't ever leave me again," she whispered.

He nodded. She kissed him ever so sweetly. Antonio felt the depth of her love in her kiss. He felt the circle of family envelop him. He wanted nothing more than to be inside of her at that moment, and feel the closeness of his child.

"Let's go get married," he whispered.

Mariana nodded. Antonio revved the engine and the blue Renault puttered down the street. The wind blew through Mariana's hair, and she felt the first inkling of freedom pierce her soul. Life was perfect.

Mariana and Antonio drove straight to the courthouse, just as Amparo had instructed them to do. They were giddy with excitement. Not even the harsh fluorescent light, the sweltering heat, or the constant stream of flies could dampen their mood. Their palms melted together as they waited to be called into the next room.

A short, pudgy man with a wrinkled red tie and ugly brown pants called their names. *Please don't let him be the one who marries us* was all Mariana could think as she entered the drab, windowless room. There, behind a stack of papers and countless coffee mugs, sat an old man with round glasses. He was bald as a baby's behind, but with a long blond mustache.

"You're here to get married, right?" the man asked without looking up.

"Yes," said Antonio.

"Do you have a witness?"

"No."

"Well, you need a witness."

"My mom didn't say anything about a witness."

Just as the words escaped Mariana's mouth, Amparo strode into the room.

"I'm their witness."

Mariana turned around and was amazed by what she saw. The decrepit and distraught woman of the last few weeks had vanished, and in her place was the woman Mariana had always known as her mother, the impeccable Amparo. She was dressed in a beautiful burgundy skirt and a matching burgundy silk top. Her hair was perfectly done, her makeup flawless. Mother and daughter smiled at each other. Mariana was overjoyed to have someone to share her wedding with. She knew Amparo would never admit to anyone that she had been there. She would take the secret to her grave. But the truth would unite them forever.

"Very well. Let's begin," said the magistrate.

And so it was there, among stacks of papers, wrinkled ties, and worn blue jeans, Mariana and Antonio were bound together as husband and wife.

chapter

FIVE

The silver moonlight bathed Antonio's imperfect face. His muscular arms wrapped around Mariana's body. She slid through his fingers like honey, slow and sweet. He kissed and licked every bit of her sweet body. She closed her eyes and lost herself in the infinite pleasure of Antonio's supple lips; she drowned in the wetness of his tongue and melted in between his teeth. He nibbled on her neck. His hands made their way behind her back and unsnapped her bra. A soft moan escaped Mariana's mouth and she opened her eyes, embarrassed by her boldness. He whispered in her ear, "Shhh…I like that." She giggled and relaxed back into her bed of bliss.

Antonio took in every inch of Mariana's naked body. He saw his wife, just as God had created her, for the first time. He memorized the shape of her small, round breasts, the soft pink shade of her nipples, and the patterns of the countless freckles that dotted her oddly shaped body. She was far from perfect, but she was his. Forever. Antonio's excitement overpowered his desire to memorize her. Antonio wanted to *know* her. He needed to be inside her. Slowly, he pushed Mariana's legs apart.

Mariana's heart raced. He was opening her, but she was not ready to be unlocked. She wanted to be explored, but Antonio was not interested in exploring. He wanted to conquer. The conquistador blood that lay hidden in his dark complexion, his almond-shaped eyes, and his black hair came to life with his desire. He pillaged and burned and thrashed inside Mariana just as his conquistador ancestors had done to the women in his family hundreds of years before him. The thrashing was quick and unmemorable; if not for Antonio's moans, Mariana would have mistaken their lovemaking for a cruel joke. Antonio collapsed next to Mariana, out of breath. He turned to her, sweat dripping down his face.

"That was amazing!"

"Really?"

"Yeah. Didn't you like it?"

"Y-yes, of course," she stammered.

A deep sense of pride overtook her. She was enough to make her husband happy. Her body was all he needed. She was all he desired. She realized that his happiness was more important than her need to be explored. They would have a lifetime to explore each other. Sweat trickled down their intertwined bodies as they lay naked in bed with the sheets tangled around their feet.

"Can I show you the house now?" she asked.

Antonio grinned mischievously. Upon their arrival at El Arado Mariana had begun showing him around the three-hundred-year-old home, but he had pushed her into the first bedroom he saw, thrown her on the bed, and stripped

PAOLA MENDOZA

her naked. Now that his desires had been satisfied, he was ready see his new home.

El Arado was the center of the Cabal family and a source of immense pride for every family member. It had been in the family since the conquistadors assaulted the New World. El Arado was majestic. Sugarcane fields surrounded the house as far as the eye could see. It was said that if a stalk of sugarcane grew in Palmira, it was the Cabal family's sugar. If sugarcane was the blood that ran through the family's veins, the house was their heart.

The house was a maze of fifteen bedrooms, countless courtyards, and a kitchen with a wood-burning stove that pumped out food for over forty people with ease. The family gathered for every meal in two separate dining rooms. The children always fought for a place at the grown-ups' table, rarely winning the privilege. But no one ever had to fight for a place to sleep. Each generation had added bedrooms to accommodate the expanding family, until finally the house had become a labyrinth of interconnected bedrooms, each with four doors. One door of each room led to the bathroom, another to the main hallway, and on each side were doors that connected to the rooms on either side. All fifteen bedrooms were connected, just as the family was.

Mariana showed Antonio the glorious courtyards, which overflowed with flowers of every color and the mango, guanabana, and lulo trees that had fed the Cabal family for generations. The high ceilings were made for the giants of the past whose spirits were said to still haunt the never-ending hallways. The terra-cotta tiles were worn down with age, but Mariana's grandfather Papá Carlos refused to change them.

Papá Carlos breathed life into El Arado. He was his parents' only surviving child; death had visited his family so many times while he was growing up that he'd lost count of how many brothers and sisters had died. But for Papá Carlos, El Arado bound father and son together. He promised his father on his deathbed that El Arado would be safe in his hands. Papá Carlos kept his promise until his own death. With Papá Carlos' dying breath, he asked his beloved son, Hernando Andrés, and his three sisters to keep El Arado safe for the next generation. Hernando Andrés promised his father he would protect El Arado until his dying breath, just as all the men before him had done.

Hernando Andrés took the reins of El Arado and steered it into a hugely profitable business. He doubled sugarcane production, made *panela* a staple of their business model, and introduced cattle and milk production. His three sisters were overjoyed with the constant flow of labor-free money. Hernando Andrés was happy to give his sisters what they wanted, because all he wanted was to work the land his father had left him.

Hernando Andrés and his family spent more time than anyone else at El Arado. His sisters and their families came for Christmas, New Year's, and Easter, but Mariana and her family spent every weekend and every holiday at El Arado. Everyone loved El Arado except for Amparo. As soon as the family car pulled up to the front of the house, Hernando Andrés ran out to the sugarcane fields and lost himself there, and the kids poured out of the car and ran like wild horses through the decadent house. Inevitably, Amparo was left alone to direct the women whose names she did not care to know in unloading the car.

Even though Amparo spent more time at El Arado than did her sisters-in-law, she was never allowed to forget that El Arado was not hers. No one owned El Arado, because El Arado belonged to every Cabal family member. Any decision regarding the house or the business was discussed among Hernando Andrés, his sisters, and his mother, Mamá Rosita. Five people, five votes. The Cabals were strong believers in democracy. Papá Carlos had instilled in his family the power of the majority because he despised communists. He hated the communists who reeked havoc in his beloved country, the men who made the mountains bleed red and the cities flood with tears. He spit on their ridiculous ideologies. He ran his family the way he believed the country should be run. There was no arguing once the vote was cast and the results were tallied. The vote was law.

The day Amparo revolted against the democracy of El Arado was no different from hundreds of days that had gone before it. Hernando Andrés was out in his sugarcane fields, and the children were riding horses or climbing mango trees. Amparo sat in the courtyard in the shade of her memories of her long-departed love, Camilo. It was an unbearably hot day. It was so hot the petals on the flowers in the courtyard had wilted into old ladies. Amparo had grown bored with her memories. She had reimagined her final kiss a thousand times, and she had attended her imaginary wedding to the point of exhaustion. She needed something different. She looked through the courtyard and out a window onto a flat piece of land. *What a perfect place for a pool,* she thought to herself. *I should ask Mamá Rosita if we can have one for the kids next year. Ay, Mamá Rosita will have to ask the three witches and convince Hernando Andrés to get his head out of his sugarcane for one second. It'll never get done.* She stared intently at the grassy field.

"Elvirita!"

The old woman came from around the corner. Elvirita had worked for the Cabal family almost as long as Hernando Andrés had been alive.

"Can you bring me a shovel?" Amparo asked her.

"A what, Señora?"

"A shovel! Bring me a damn shovel!"

"Sí, Señora."

"Bring it out there." She pointed to the grassy field.

Amparo rolled up her sleeves, put on a pair of sneakers, and pinned her hair back into a neat bun. She slammed the shovel into the ground. The feeling of the metal crushing into the moist brown earth filled her with power. Each pile of dirt she removed was an infidelity forgotten, a snide remark from Mamá Rosita put behind her, and a step closer to an unknown dream.

Elvirita watched with an open mouth. She did not know what to do. Should she go and tell Hernando Andrés that Doña Amparo had lost her mind? Or should she go and get her a glass of water? Or should she take the shovel out of her hand and dig the hole herself? Elvirita decided it was best to be a spectator in the telenovela that was unfolding before her.

Amparo did not say a word. She dug. She dug until her hands were covered in blisters and blood ran down her arms. Hernando Andrés showed up as he did every night, just as dinner was about to be served. The dining room was deserted. He looked out the window and saw Mario Andrés and Diego cheering and jumping, while Catalina and Juliana pointed and laughed at something on the ground. Intrigued, he went outside to see what the commotion was about. He almost had a heart attack when he saw Amparo digging a hole that was as deep as her waist.

"What are you doing?" he thundered.

The girls stopped laughing. The boys stopped jumping. Amparo climbed out of the hole.

"I want a pool. Get me a pool or I'll make it myself."

It was the battle cry that began the coup d'etat in the Cabal family. Against the wishes of Mamá Rosita and his sisters, Hernando Andrés installed a pool in the very spot where Amparo had begun digging.

Eight years later, Mariana floated on her back in the very same pool her mother had fought for. She was holding her husband's hand, the very same hand she herself had fought for. Mariana's honeymoon was perfection. She loved the fact that she was the first Cabal to spend her honeymoon at El Arado, but getting there had not been easy.

Hernando Andrés was furious over Mariana's elopement. When he first heard the news, his rage thundered through the streets of Buga. But his anger was a mask for the deep pain he felt at missing his daughter's wedding. He missed so much of his children's lives that he found comfort and joy in sharing in their special moments: baptisms, graduations, tennis championships, *fiestas de quince*, and, most important of all, weddings. Hernando Andrés screamed and yelled like a madman because he had failed his daughter by forcing her to elope. The only way he knew to express his shame was through fits of rage. As Hernando Andrés stormed up and down the hallways, mother and daughter played the parts they had tacitly agreed to play. Amparo wailed uncontrollably. Mariana remained unapologetic. And finally Hernando Andrés did the only thing he could do: accept Antonio as his son in law.

Mariana could see the pain in her mother's eyes when she offered Antonio and Mariana El Arado for a week. Her mother wanted her to visit the United States for the first time, or dance in the streets of Paris, or go to the bullfights in Spain. She wanted Mariana to feel the magic of the world. She wanted her daughter's breath to be taken away by the beauty of life. But what Amparo failed to understand was that Antonio took Mariana's breath away. Antonio allowed her to see the magic of the world. The United States and Europe were too ostentatious for their love. They wanted rough edges and simplicity and mangos. They simply wanted each other, in Buga, in Cali, or in El Arado. It did not matter.

Now Antonio's fingers loosened their grip around Mariana's hand. She lifted her head out of the water and followed Antonio's gaze. Elvirita was running down the gravel walkway from the house toward the pool.

"Señorita Mari! Señorita Mari!"

"Elivirita, what's wrong?"

"The phone. You're mother is on the phone!"

Mariana jumped out of the pool. She grabbed her towel, wrapped it around her skinny frame, and ran toward the house. Antonio was utterly confused. Why was everyone panicking about a phone call? What Antonio did not understand was that there was only one phone in El Arado. It was an old phone from a different era. A phone that had to be cranked in order to work, a phone that required yelling and pounding and echoes, a phone that was so impractical that no one would dare to use it unless it was an emergency. Mariana could count on one hand the number of times she'd heard the telephone at El Arado ring. So if her mother was on the line, something terrible must have happened.

Mariana grabbed the phone and brought it to her ear. She panted heavily as she spoke.

"Mamá, what's going on?"

Her mother's wails crackled over the phone line. Mariana's heart froze.

"Mamá, what happened?"

"*Ay*, Mari…Mari…"

"What? Did something happen to papi?"

Her mother cried even louder.

"Was there an accident? Is he…okay? Mami, please tell me he's okay!"

Mariana grabbed Antonio's hand. She felt her knees wobble.

"No, Mari, it's not that."

"Then what the hell is going on?"

"We've lost El Arado. El Arado is gone."

"What do you mean? I'm here right now. Everything's fine."

"Your *tías* sold it to Grupo Manuelita."

The words were like a punch to Mariana's stomach. She dropped the phone and doubled over. Antonio helped her to a chair. She sat in complete silence as the words sunk into her bones. *El Arado is gone.* She looked at the white walls around her. They pulsated with the blood of every Cabal for over three hundred years. The bone-white walls were *her* walls. They were her children's walls. She grabbed her stomach. *He'll never know El Arado,* she thought. She burst into tears. Mariana knew there was no point in crying, but the loss of three hundred years was far too painful to take without tears.

Mariana grabbed Antonio's hand. Her chest heaved as she caught her breath through her tears.

"We have to go back to Buga."

Antonio was confused.

"Why? We just got here."

Mariana blinked back her rage. Her anger silenced her voice. Unable to speak, she looked at his eyes and shot daggers filled with fury at him. It was the first time Antonio saw something other than love in Mariana's eyes, and it sent a cold chill down his spine. He acquiesced.

Antonio and Mariana returned to her home as the sun was setting over Buga. Mariana walked into a house that was filled with anger and grief. Her father screamed into the telephone and threw a glass of rum against the wall. As soon as the maid heard the glass shatter, she dutifully filled another crystal glass and, like a phantom, placed it next to him. Diego and Mario Andrés stood stoically next to their father. Amparo sat in the living room and stared out the window, tears streaming down her face. Esperanza, Catalina, and Juliana sat between their mother and their father, frozen in fear and confusion. The girls wanted to escape into their bedrooms, but just as drivers cannot avert their eyes when they pass a horrendous crash on the side of the road, they could not turn away from the carnage unfolding before them. Everyone was so caught up in their own drama that no one noticed Mariana when she walked into the house. She knew better than to speak to her father. Her mother was the only person that could answer the thousands of questions burning in her mind.

Mariana sat down next to her mother, but Amparo's eyes remained fixed on the horizon. Only when Mariana touched her mother's hands did she turn toward her daughter.

"Mari. I'm so glad you're home." She hugged her daughter close.

"What happened, mami?"

"Your aunts and grandmother sold El Arado behind your father's back. They've been lying to him for months. They took everything. Everything!"

Amparo turned back to the window. The sun reflected off her wet cheeks. She choked on her grief and shook her head in despair.

"Mari, we have nothing. Nothing..." Her voice trailed off.

"How could they do that? *Why* would they do that?"

Hernando Andrés spent the rest of his life and what remained of his fortune trying to figure out the answers to those questions. He never found out why his cherished sisters and his beloved mother not only sold El Arado behind his back, but never paid him his fair share of the sale. What Hernando Andrés *was* able to find out was that his sisters' husbands orchestrated the sale. The men pocketed most of the money without the sisters even knowing it. Hernando Andrés went to his grave never being able to forgive or prove the most damaging secret of all: Someone had forged his signature for the sale of his beloved El Arado.

Life knocked Hernando Andrés down, put his mouth on the curb, and kicked him in the back of the head. Within months of losing El Arado, he saw the new cattle business he had started in Los Llanos collapse in utter failure. The five hundred cattle he had invested his family's life savings into months earlier died of a virus no one had ever heard of. The virus spread so quickly that by the time Hernando Andrés received the news, not one cattle was left standing. The few friends he confided in rallied around him. They gave him hundreds and thousands of pesos to begin a new life. They lent him their hands, their minds, and even their hearts, but Hernando Andrés could not move beyond what had happened. He took their money and treaded the waters of the past. He spent it on lawyers and lawsuits, trying to get back his lifeline, El Arado. All the court battles, the lawyers, and the fights never resulted in answers or justice. His lawyers always seemed to conveniently drop his case the day before a trial was scheduled to begin. When he finally found a lawyer who believed in justice over bribes, the judges mysteriously refused to hear the pending case. His family and friends watched in anguish, but they were unable to help him as he spiraled down into despair. To Hernando Andrés, losing El Arado was like losing his soul. Without it he was nothing. His only refuge was in his dark office, where he searched obsessively for glimmers of hope to regain ownership of his beloved El Arado. The hours, days, and months he spent hunched over his desk were futile. El Arado was gone forever.

Friends and family thought Hernando Andrés was being irrational, obsessive, and foolish about El Arado. They were right, but he could not let go of his past for reasons no one would ever suspect. Hernando Andrés needed El Arado because he was paralyzed with fear without it. His entire life he had worked only at El Arado. He knew everything about El Arado's sugar. He knew about its soil, its machines, and its workers, but he knew nothing about the world outside El Arado. He was certain he would fail at any attempt he made to work outside its walls. The failure of his cattle endeavor was all the proof he needed. He masked his crushing fear with his obsession with justice. When Amparo begged him to go out and find work, he roared that he was working day and night. When she cried in his lap because the boys' schools had called, asking for their tuition, he calmed her by telling her he would borrow more money. Failing at favors was easier to take than failing at work. He could not bear the idea of finding out he was good for nothing. His fear kept him stuck in his past, unable to face the future or live in the present.

Months had passed since El Arado had been ripped from the family, and with each passing day life seemed to get harder. Amparo dreaded walking down the cobblestone streets of Buga. She hated the pity in her neighbors' eyes and the tongues that danced about as she walked by. The thought of being talked about in the past tense made the muscles in her back contort into one another like an anaconda killing its prey. She found no respite from the cruelty of the streets in her home. Every picture she saw, every bedsheet that rubbed against her skin, and every rose she smelled was a heartbreaking reminder of the life she'd once lived. El Arado haunted her and every corner of her cursed home.

Amparo was forced to accept the drastic changes that came with her poverty. Her stomach turned when she watched the chauffeur leave their house, never to return again. Her heart skipped a beat when they sold their car, and she shed a river of tears when she said good-bye to Dandaney, her maid of over fifteen years. She reached her breaking point on an ordinary Sunday morning. Without a maid for the first time in her life, Amparo was forced to clean her house on her own. She found peace in sweeping, she escaped her sadness while washing dishes, but when she kneeled down before the toilet she simply broke. Tears of humiliation ran down her face as she cleaned her family's shit and piss. She knew her time in Buga was over.

The loss of El Arado was a tremendous blow for Antonio as well. In Mariana's arms, Antonio had hoped to leave struggle behind. For a brief moment he was able to taste the sweetness of luxury and caress it with his fingertips. But he was crushed when it was torn from his grasp. Without El Arado, Mariana was just like him: another Colombian without a home, facing an uncertain future and leaving behind a painful past. Looking at Mariana was agonizing.

Her growing belly was a constant reminder of the doom awaiting them at the end of the road they were walking on. Every time he looked at her, he was reminded how cruel life was. So he stopped looking at her. He found his moments of relief when he was not with Mariana. While he was working he could forget the cruel joke life had played on him. So Antonio did everything in his power to not be around her. He got up to go to work before the sun rose and came home long after it had set. He took every job imaginable. He worked as a mechanic; he moved packages from one warehouse to another; he drove trucks, cars, and motorcycles across town and sometimes out of town, but the pesos he brought home were barely enough for food.

Amparo's heart was heavy for Mariana. She spent her days and nights alone, with nothing more than her growing belly to comfort her. Amparo, as she had in the past and as she would in the future, decided to help. She swallowed her pride and called a dear friend, Luisa Hoyos, and asked her to hire Antonio as her chauffeur. The next day Antonio was driving the Hoyos children to school, then taking Luisa to lunch with her friends and dropping her off at the social club for dinner. Mariana was thrilled because of the predictable hours and the steady income. Antonio was not happy about now having to spend hours each night staring at his broken dream, Mariana.

A few weeks into his job, Luisa asked Antonio to pick up her daughter after her tennis lessons. Antonio waited in the parking lot, as he had always had. He saw Manuela's blonde hair through the grated fence. He opened the back door, but when he turned to smile at Manuela, his eyes met Esperanza's. Esperanza immediately looked away. He knew exactly what that meant. Through clenched teeth, Antonio said, "Hello, Señorita Manuela. Hello Señorita...?"

"Esperanza. Nice to meet you."

He closed the door behind Esperanza. Antonio did not understand why Esperanza cared what a ten-year-old girl thought of her. He would have been more understanding if Esperanza had been with friends, but the fact that she was ashamed of her own brother-in-law in front of a ten-year-old girl made him finally understand that he would never be a part of Mariana's world. Even as broke as the Cabals were, they still belonged to a world that money could not buy, a world where last names mattered more than the pesos in your pocket.

Antonio quit the chauffeur job that night. He did not want to be part of a world that hardly disguised their hatred for him. Mariana was surprised to see him home so early.

"Hola, mi amor!"

"Hi. Is dinner ready?"

"No, but I can make something really quick."

"Why don't you have dinner ready?"

His voice thundered through the house.

"Mi amor, you're home three hours early."

"That's because I quit that piece of shit fucking job!"

"What? Why?"

"Because they think I'm a *burro* and they can treat me however they—"

"But you're their chauffeur!"

His eyes raged with fury. He spit out his words.

"And I'm your husband, so what does that make you?"

Antonio saw a flash of shame in Mariana's eyes. His heart broke. Even his wife could not accept him. He stormed out of the house. He did not come back that night, or the next. Two days later he came home just in time for dinner. Mariana and her mother were at the table when he walked into the kitchen. He sat down without looking at anyone and asked, "What's for dinner?"

Silence.

"What's for dinner!"

"Arroz con pollo."

"Perfect."

They ate in silence that night, and the next night, and the next, until words between Antonio and Mariana were as rare as cold days in Buga. Mariana was eight months pregnant when Amparo told her the family was moving to Bogotá.

"When?" was all Mariana managed to say.

"A few months after the baby is born. The boys are finally taken care of, and Cata and Juli will be done with school by then. You and Antonio are more than welcome to join us."

Mariana's heart sank. She had only a few precious months left with her family, and then she would be left alone. Over the past months Antonio had changed into a man she did not recognize. His warm, gentle smile had twisted into a permanent scowl. The man who only wanted to spend time with her had been replaced by a man who took every opportunity to be away from her. The man who could not keep his hands off her had turned into a man who could barely stand the sight of her.

Mariana knew she could not go to Bogotá. She knew she needed to mend her love where it had been born. In Buga.

"Thanks, mami, but we can't go to Bogotá."

Amparo knew Bogotá was an impossible dream for Mariana. She knew Mariana found herself exactly where she had predicted her daughter would be: heartbroken, lonely, and confused by the man her husband had become. Amparo cried until her eyes hurt, but she knew she could not take care of Mariana any longer. She was fighting for her own survival. She promised her daughter she would not leave until Mariana was ready to let her go. Mariana was not worried about motherhood; she knew her baby would be safe in her hands from the moment it left her womb. Mariana was more concerned with the mundane practicalities of life. Where were they going to live? Since their wedding, Antonio and Mariana had lived in her mother's home. Antonio made barely enough money to put food on the table. His jobs came and went like warm *arepas* in the morning.

She forced a smile onto her face.

"I think moving to Bogotá is a great idea. Everyone can start over." She wiped away her mother's tears. "But before you go, teach me how to make your empanadas."

Amparo threw her head back and laughed. Her deep, hearty laugh bounced off the walls and followed them into the kitchen, where they kneaded the dough for the empanadas.

That night Mariana lay in her bed and stared at the empty space where Antonio should be. She needed him to be her anchor during this storm, but he was nowhere to be found. She lost herself in a fantasy, only this time it was not Antonio or Evalina who saved her. In the maze of her imagination, she met her son for the first time. She saw his green-brown eyes, his heart-shaped lips, and his thick, wild black hair. His voice echoed through her mind. With each word he spoke, her fear slowly melted away and was replaced by love, forgiveness, and understanding. In her bed, protected by her mosquito net, she was able to forget the tears shed over the many nights spent in a panic about her future. She was able to forgive Antonio's insults, which were thrown at her with so much anger they slapped her across the face. She erased from her memory the countless dinners left uneaten. Once her body was filled with unyielding forgiveness, her son demanded to come into the world.

Gabriel Rodríguez Cabal was born on a rainy day in mid-November. The doctors were amazed that such a fat baby had forced his way out of such a skinny woman. His arms and legs were continuous rolls of fat that ended with tiny hands and feet sticking out like twigs on a scarecrow. The moment Mariana saw him, her heart melted with devotion. Their gaze locked, and they made a silent promise to protect each other from anything and everything that came their way. Mariana knew she would never have to face the world alone again.

The door to her hospital room creaked open. She looked up. Antonio was standing in the doorway, holding a bouquet of flowers. He smiled at her as he blinked back his tears. With the tilt of her head she motioned him to her. He sat on her bed and stared at his son. Not a word was spoken. The room was silent, and in the silence love was born. Antonio promised himself that he would be the father he had never had. To love his son the way his father had never loved him. He promised to give Gabriel the home he himself had always wanted but had never had. He knew he could not give Gabriel the life he had dreamed for him, but he could give him something better than what he was given.

Antonio looked at his son, wrapped in Mariana's arms, and the door to loving his wife was pushed open once again. Gabriel made him want to be close to Mariana. The baby made him want to try for something better than what he had.

Mariana saw the change in Antonio instantly. His smile resurfaced, his kisses returned, and his laughter filled their humble home. Mariana and Antonio moved into a home of their own three months after Gabriel was born. She was happy with what life had given her. Yes, her house was smaller than she would have liked. The kitchen was a relic of a forgotten past, and the constantly backed-up toilet sent her into fits of rage, but it was her home. She scrubbed the time-stained walls with as much dedication as she changed Gabriel's diapers. She swept the cracked tile floors in the morning and in the evening, before serving Antonio dinner on their flimsy dining room table with its mismatched wooden chairs. She spent her free time sewing curtains for the two small windows in their living room, hoping they would help her forget that they looked out onto a large brick wall. She covered the cracks in the walls with small terra cotta replicas of Colombia's finest homes.

Mariana found a peaceful balance between the sleepless nights spent with Gabriel and the never-ending good-byes with Antonio. The world melted behind Gabriel's eyes, and she found happiness with him. She got used to being alone with her son. With her family in Bogotá and Antonio traveling the country in search of money, the days flew by and the only other person Mariana saw was Gabriel, but those were the days she was happiest.

Unlike Mariana, who found peace in her new life, Antonio was tortured. The constant good-byes chipped away at his heart. He hated leaving little Gabriel, but he knew he had to go where the work was. He drove trucks filled with squawking chickens along the peaks and valleys of the countryside, through the city, and along the Atlantic and Pacific coasts. In good months he stayed close to home and sold refrigerators to his neighbors. At his lowest points, he navigated solitary rivers transporting packages that had no owners or final destinations but were pushed north by thousands of hands, their contents ultimately snorted into strangers' noses behind closed bathroom doors. No matter how many jobs Antonio had or how many days he spent away from his family, there never seemed to be enough money. Years passed with thousands of hours worked, and nothing changed. No matter how hard he tried, Antonio could not pull his family out of want. The crumbling apartment with its thin walls and broken toilet never allowed him to forget his failure.

Mariana looked at her son as he slept in her bed. She could still see the traces of the baby he once was. Four years of life had taken away his baby fat and replaced it with thin, muscular arms and skinny legs that protruded below his big belly. Mariana knew Gabriel would be a wonderful big brother to the little sister who was growing inside her. Just as Mariana had met Gabriel in her dreams, her daughter visited her nightly as well. She had not told Gabriel about his sister because Antonio did not yet know. It had been three months since Antonio had been home, and Mariana was thrilled at the thought of seeing him that night. Keeping her pregnancy a secret had been one of the most difficult things she had ever done. Mariana refused to tell Antonio that he was going to be a father over the phone. This time she wanted to see the joy in his eyes when he found out he was going to have a little girl.

The door creaked open and Mariana bolted upright. She quietly got out of bed and made her way quickly to the front door. Antonio placed his bags on the floor. He looked up and smiled at Mariana. She could not help but notice how tired he looked, and as she wrapped him in her arms she felt his bones poking through his skin. She sat him down on the couch and brought him a *tinto* and a freshly made empanada. She watched him eat in silence. She was convinced the daughter growing inside her was exactly what their marriage needed to rebound from the damage time had inflicted on their love.

"I'm pregnant!" she announced suddenly.

Antonio choked on his empanada. He turned to her, his eyes wide open.

"What?"

"I'm pregnant! Three months! I know it's going to be a girl! Can you believe it? A little girl!"

"You're sure?"

Mariana nodded her head excitedly.

"Yes, yes! I'm so sure! A little girl!"

"No, that you're pregnant!"

"Yes, *mi amor*! Yes!"

Antonio swallowed hard. The weight of the world came crashing onto his shoulders. He saw himself sinking deeper into the void of failure. Blinded by her excitement, Mariana did not see Antonio's devastation. That night, in the quiet darkness of his bedroom, with Mariana sleeping next to him and Gabriel sleeping on the floor, Antonio promised his unborn daughter she would not live a life of poverty.

Antonio was determined to start his own business. He believed the only way to find success was to be his own boss. He had spent his entire life toiling for others, and it had brought him to a dead end. So he hit the streets looking for inspiration, and he found it on a lonely corner, where he saw a banged-up, rickety old truck with two flat tires and a missing door for sale. He pulled out his checkbook and bought it without thinking twice. He saw how his new truck would transport live chickens over the mountain ranges and into the flat plains, filling his pockets with cash. But first he needed his truck to work. He bought new tires, had a brand-new engine installed, and welded on a scrap door from another truck. He bought hundreds of chicken crates and a cover for the back to protect the chickens. He moved at lightning speed. He worked on his truck every day, replacing, fixing, and adding things until finally the vehicle was ready to begin its journey.

Throughout their four years of marriage, Mariana had learned to let her husband run with his wild ideas. She knew that he was a free spirit and that when he felt trapped he lashed out in anger, in sadness, or by disappearing for days at a time. She'd learned that his far-fetched schemes tended to burn themselves out without her ever having to become involved, but his latest idea concerned her. He was spending money as if they had an infinite supply under their mattress. She saw him standing on the precipice of risk, ready to leap into the unknown. Mariana grabbed him by his shirt and tried to pull him back to the comforts of the known world.

"*Mi amor*, you can't do this right now."

"Mari, it has to be now."

"But we have to be responsible."

"I am. I promise. I am taking care of my family, Mari. I'm taking care of you, *mi vida*."

Antonio's words were coated with *arequipe*. Mariana did not want to bite into their sweetness, but they were too alluring, too scrumptious, too divine for her not to be taken by them. Mariana lost herself in the sweetness of his dream.

The morning their dream came crashing down to earth started out like any other. Three *arepas* were cooking on the stove; the *chocolate* was brewing while Mariana diced tomatoes and onions for the *huevos pericos* she was cooking. A loud knock at her front door startled her. She cautiously walked to the door.

"Who's there?"

"Open the door!" yelled a voice from the other side.

Antonio walked out of the bedroom half-asleep.

"What do you want?" asked Mariana.

Suddenly the door crashed open. Mariana screamed. Antonio looked at the two police officers and ran toward the open window in his living room. The two reached out to grab him, but Antonio managed to slip through their hands and jump out the window. Mariana screamed as Antonio crashed onto the cement below. She ran to the window and watched as Antonio lifted himself off the ground. His leg was hurt. She called out to him. He turned to her, saying, "I'm sorry, Mari."

Tears rolled down her face as she watched him hobble down the street. A police officer went barreling after him. Antonio ran as fast as he could, but it was not fast enough. Mariana saw her husband get thrown into the police car.

The days following Antonio's arrest stripped Mariana of her dreams and threw her into an unforgiving world of jail cells, corrupt police officers, and a legal system that took care of the rich and squashed the poor. Antonio's first offense had been writing hundreds and thousands of pesos in bad checks. To cover his debt, Antonio had agreed to be one link in the long chain that moved white bricks to the north. The police officers had shown up at Antonio's house not to arrest him, but to collect their customary bribe for ensuring the bricks would be allowed to pass by them. Fear and inexperience made him run—his biggest mistake. The police were furious they were not able to get their money. They were annoyed Antonio forced them to work on a hot Saturday morning, and so they were merciless in their punishment.

Antonio was placed in the worst jail in Cali. He was unable even to sit down in the overcrowded cell. Buckets of urine and feces surrounded him. Antonio did not eat for four days. He watched with longing as wives brought their husbands food. He wondered why Mariana had not come. He was starving, but he was too afraid to ask anyone for food. His hunger pangs were nothing compared to his worry, however. He worried that he had lost Mariana forever, but on the fourth day he saw her unruly curly hair towering above everyone else through the jail gates. Mariana pushed a heaping plate of rice, chicken, steak, and empanadas through the black iron bars.

"Mari, I'm so sorry."

"I know. I know. Antonio, it's bad. Really bad."

"How bad?"

"They're saying you're going to be here for five years."

Antonio's heart dropped to his feet. He reached out his hand and touched Mariana's stomach. She looked up to the sky, fighting back her tears.

"I've talked to my mom to see if someone can help us, but it's not looking good, *mi amor.*"

"Will you wait for me?"

Words eluded her. She tried to speak, but there was only emptiness. She nodded her head yes because that was all she could do. When it was time for Mariana to go, Antonio watched as she walked through the courtyard and out through the large metal gates. He looked down at the plate full of food. Even though he hadn't eaten in four days, his appetite was gone. He crouched down and placed the food on the filthy floor beside him. The grim vision of five years spent alone in a wretched jail cell knocked him to the ground. How was he going to survive five years of filth, five years of sleepless nights, five years of fear? He held on to the bars for support. His mind raced, trying to decipher how his life had turned out so differently than how he had imagined it. Growing up, Antonio had believed he was different from his father, better than where his mother came from. He knew in his heart that he was destined to live a better life than all of his brothers and sisters because he was special, yet here he was in a dank jail cell with hordes of criminals. His eyes welled with tears, his arms and legs shook uncontrollably, and his chest heaved with every breath.

A man whispered in his ear, "You better hold it together. It's the only way you'll survive."

Antonio had to survive for Gabriel, for Mariana, for his unborn daughter, and for the life he'd promised himself years earlier. The tears disappeared. His arms and legs relaxed. His breathing went back to normal. He sat on the floor, unfazed by the filth. He picked up his food and shoveled a spoonful of *arroz con frijoles* into his mouth. He was determined to survive.

A determination grew inside Mariana as well. She swore that Antonio would be home for his daughter's birth. She did everything in her power to have her husband released, but no matter how many doors she knocked on or how many tears she shed, no one was willing to give Antonio his freedom. With each rejection, Mariana's body fell further into neglect. Her mother begged her to move to Bogotá, but she could not leave her husband to rot in jail. Amparo moved heaven and earth and was miraculously able to have her son-in-law transferred to La Picota jail in Bogotá. Broken and dazed, Mariana packed up her twenty-two years of life in two suitcases and moved into her mother's dreary apartment in Bogotá.

Five years after the loss of El Arado, the Cabal family was still fighting their war with heartache and misfortune. Esperanza was recently divorced and living back at home with her mother and her infant daughter. The twins decided to find their futures where the sun shone brightest: Catalina had dreams of flying all over the world as a flight attendant and was knocking on doors in Cartagena; meanwhile, Juliana decided to try her luck in Cali. Mario Andrés and Diego were in military school, en route to the navy. The last loan Hernando Andrés was able to obtain ensured that his sons would finish school and at the very least have careers as naval officers. The fact that they left home at the ages of fifteen and fourteen almost killed Amparo. In Bogotá, Hernando Andrés gave up all hope and retreated into the abyss of fear his mind had created. His fear engulfed his entire being. Unable to even step outside, every day he sat in a chair staring out at the city, barely speaking a word, while Amparo and Mariana rose with the sun and worked whatever jobs came their way.

Bogotá's cold air seeped into Mariana's bones. The never-ending rain flowed as easily as Mariana's endless tears. Gabriel was the only thing that brought Mariana joy, and were it not for his constant questions about his sister, she would have completely forgotten she was pregnant. She slept only because Gabriel made her sleep next to him, and she ate only because Gabriel told her to eat. Eating was excruciating for Mariana. The acids in her stomach had created an ulcer the size of a plum, and she thought it was a miracle her daughter did not fall through the hole into her pit of sadness.

Andrea Rodríguez Cabal was born on an unusually hot December morning in the otherwise cold and gloomy city of Bogotá. Unlike her brother, Andrea was a sickly newborn. While Gabriel had been a mound of fat, Andrea was a tiny heap of skin and bones topped with a bundle of curly brown hair. Her yellowish, saggy skin hung off of her tiny body. The whites of her large brown eyes were as yellow as her skin. Andrea was so tiny Mariana was afraid she might break her. Unsure what to do, she did the only thing a mother *could* do: She gently brought Andrea to her breast and placed her nipple in her daughter's tiny mouth. Andrea spit it out and squirmed her tiny body deeper into her mother's arms.

"Come on...please."

Mariana put her nipple back into Andrea's mouth and squeezed a drop of milk onto her tongue. Andrea's milk-starved tongue soaked it up instantly. She turned her mouth toward her mother and latched on with so much power that Mariana knew that though Andrea might appear weak, she was a force to be reckoned with.

Andrea's strength was on full display for the first eight months of her life. The yellow tone of her skin disappeared within days of her birth, but with its disappearance a more sinister illness reared its head: Andrea's stomach worked backward. Instead of keeping her mother's milk inside her body, her stomach pushed it out of her, rejecting it like it was poison. It began as a trickle of milk dribbling from between her wrinkled lips, but by the end of her seventh day of life, Andrea's vomit splattered on the walls across the room from where she lay. No matter how much Mariana fed her daughter, her milk always ended up on the floor, on the walls, on her lap—everywhere but in her daughter's stomach.

Andrea was dancing with death. A few weeks after her birth, while she hovered between life and death, Mariana suddenly understood what her baby needed. In the quiet calm of the night, Andrea tended to keep her mother's milk inside her body. Mariana realized that what Andrea needed was stillness. She needed to be completely still in order to live. So Mariana made her daughter a chair that kept her perfectly still, and in her stillness Andrea began to embrace life. She slept in her chair, she ate in her chair, and she grew in her chair.

Gabriel stared at Andrea as she lay in her chair. She was skinny and wrinkly, with eyes so big she reminded him of a fly. This was not the sister he had pictured when he was told he was going to be a big brother. He wanted someone he could play with. Someone he could laugh with. Someone he could teach soccer to. But Gabriel couldn't even touch Andrea. Whenever his fingers came close to her, Mariana yelled, "Don't touch the chair!" Whenever he asked his mother when Andrea was going to get out of the chair, she always responded, "I wish I knew, *mi rey*." Whenever he asked, "Is she gonna be in that chair forever?" his mother's eyes welled with tears and his *abuelita* sent him outside to play. He wanted Andrea to get out of the chair so he could know what it felt like to be a big brother. He wanted his little sister to get out of the chair so his mother would stop ignoring him. He wanted Andrea to get out of the chair so life could go back to normal, but eight long months passed before Andrea could finally leave behind the chair that had saved her life.

As was Mariana's custom, she lay in her bed listening to the sounds of life bustling outside her window. She wondered what sounds Antonio fell asleep to at night. Did he hear cars honking and birds chirping, or just strangers breathing and doors slamming? She looked over at Gabriel, who was asleep next to her. She glanced at Andrea, asleep in the bassinet that her mother's church had given her, and realized she would share that very same bed with Gabriel, Andrea, and Antonio for the rest of her life unless she changed something. Antonio could not help her. Her mother had done everything she possibly could, her father was a walking ghost, and her brothers and sisters were trying to build their own lives. Mariana had made her choices, but her children's lives were just beginning. She knew she had to give them more than what Colombia could offer. She heard her mother's words in her head, as clear as the day she had spoken them to her:

I didn't want this for you. I wanted you to have more than what I have. Ay, Mari, unfortunately one day you'll understand what I'm trying to tell you.

Alone in a dark bedroom with her two children, Mariana finally understood her mother's words. She walked to her daughter's bassinet. Andrea was sound asleep in her chair. She was still skinnier than most babies her age, but she had done the impossible. She had survived. Mariana was overwhelmed by the need to hold her daughter. She scooped Andrea up in her arms and held her against her chest for the first time since she was born. Andrea snuggled into her mother's neck. She fit perfectly. Her breath danced down her mother's back, and shivers ran up Mariana's spine. She waited for Andrea to throw up. Seconds turned into minutes, and still Andrea slept peacefully in her mother's arms. Mariana had waited for this moment for eight months. She held her breath, closed her eyes, and saw her destiny. Mariana grabbed destiny by the neck, wrestled it to the floor, twisted its arm behind its back, and showed it where she wanted to go. Where she needed to go.

chapter

SIX

Mariana came to America with a pocket full of dreams. She had ten years of dreams stored up for Gabriel and Andrea. At ten years old, like every other Colombian boy, Gabriel loved to play soccer, but he loved to read even more. He fell in love with books because they allowed him to escape the cold corners of his house in Bogotá without ever having to leave his mother's side. Meanwhile, Andrea could not wait to get away from her mother. As soon as Andrea was able to crawl, she was constantly running away from her mother. She could not hold still for more than a few seconds. Mariana always knew where her daughter was because she left a trail of destruction behind her. She ripped through homes like a tornado. Mariana was always running behind her cleaning up, apologizing to strangers, and pulling at her hair in frustration, anxiety, and exhaustion.

"Mami, in school they told us that if we scratch our head too much it's because we have lice. Do you have lice?" Gabriel asked innocently one day after Andrea had destroyed the bathroom by pouring the shampoo and conditioner out on the floor and unspooling the toilet paper and tearing it into pieces, which she dropped on top of the pile of gunk.

Mariana laughed.

"No, *mi rey*. It's your sister. She drives me so crazy it's like I have lice."

"Andrea is a *piojo!*" Gabriel giggled to himself.

"Yes, she's my *piojito*."

They laughed hysterically. Andrea was just like those little bugs that burrowed in people's hair: so small, so unassuming, but impossible to ignore. Thus Andrea became *piojito* at age two, and by the time the family moved to the United States, she was a walking, talking, running six-year-old *piojito*.

Antonio and Mariana agreed there was nothing for them in Colombia. From where they sat, nestled in the Andes Mountains, their children's futures looked bleak. Gabriel and Andrea needed the vast plains of Montana to spread their wings, they needed the wetlands of Louisiana to plant the seeds of their futures, and they needed the redwood forests of California to help them reach for the stars.

From his dank jail cell, Antonio prepared for what he knew would be the most difficult journey of his life. He had nothing to offer his family besides the promises of the United States, and he would bet his life on it. Mariana took charge of all the preparations for his journey. She spent numerous hours in shady back offices, negotiating prices, departure dates, and boat rides through the jungles of Central America. She begged for guarantees. She needed to know Antonio would be safe, that he would get to the United States, that he would not be locked in some prison in the middle of some godforsaken jungle. But guarantees were impossible to come by. The only sure thing was the thousands of dollars she had to pay for Antonio's journey to *Gringolandia*.

Time was on her side. She had had five years to save up two thousand dollars. Five years to take every job that came her way. Five years to plot with her mother how she was going to get a tourist visa for the United States. Five years to become a woman. Five years of solitude had changed Mariana. Gone was the young girl who swooned whenever Antonio looked at her. In her place was a practical woman. A woman who was willing to risk everything for her children's future.

Mariana held Gabriel's and Andrea's hands as she waited in line. She was surrounded by hundreds of people who spoke languages she had never heard. Their voices created a sweet melody in her ears. Even the harsh fluorescent lights could not diminish the sea of beauty in which she found herself. Mariana had never seen so many different kinds of faces, in so many different shades. She marveled at the exquisiteness of her fellow passengers. Mariana's trance was broken only when the man behind the glass window called her to him.

Mariana's heart raced. She had been dreading this moment for months. She gripped her children's hands, her palms sweaty against theirs. In her head, she repeated everything her mother had told her to say. Amparo and Hernando Andrés' life before the loss of El Arado had been filled with memories in Los Angeles, Miami, New York,

Seattle—the list was long. They had spent so much time in the United States they had come to think of it as their second home. Mariana approached the counter, telling herself, *Don't let your hands shake when you give him the passport.* She smiled at the fat man behind the counter. His curly blond hair and blond mustache were exactly what Mariana had imagined the gringos would look like.

"Passport."

His voice was dull and uninterested. He was the exact type of immigration officer Mariana had prayed for. She wanted someone who was tired of his job, someone who would not ask too many questions. She handed him the three passports. Her hand was steady as he took them from her. He opened the small burgundy books and flipped through their pages. He stopped when he saw the large visa stickers.

"How long are you staying?"

Mariana panicked. She did not understand what he was saying to her. The words flew out of his mouth with such speed that she did not know where one began and the other ended. Her heart raced even faster. She did not want to bring any attention to herself.

"Slow. Please."

He let out a frustrated sigh.

"How. Long. Are. You. Staying?"

"Ah, two months." She reassured him by holding up two fingers.

"Where are you staying?"

Again his words took on a life of their own and twisted and turned into mush.

"Sorry. No understand."

Gabriel turned to his mother.

"He wants to know where we're staying."

Mariana could not believe it. When Antonio had left for the United States six months earlier, Gabriel had promised his dad he would know English the next time they saw each other—and there he was, a boy of his word. Mariana beamed. She turned to the man and said, "Uncle's house. In Los Angeles."

The man looked at Mariana. She kept her gaze strong and direct, as if she had nothing to hide. He looked down at the three passports in front of him. His fat fingers flicked through the passport pages again. He stopped at an empty page, grabbed the stamp from his desk, and slapped three stamps, one on each passport, onto the clean, crisp pages. He handed the passports back to Mariana. She smiled from ear to ear. She took both Gabriel and Andrea by the hand and sauntered into the United States with a new lease on life.

Gabriel was like a wild horse; Mariana could barely hold him back. Neither he nor Andrea had been able to sleep the night before they left. Mariana's harsh whispers had cut through the dark night, but their eyes stayed open until the sun rose. They tossed and turned in their beds, for different reasons. Gabriel was thrilled by the prospect of seeing his father. Andrea was excited about taking her first plane ride.

Gabriel knew his dad was just beyond the doors of the airport, and he wanted nothing more than to be in his arms. As soon as he walked through the doors, his eyes locked on Antonio. He ran so fast that he tripped and fell into his father's outstretched hands. Gabriel wrapped his arms around Antonio's neck and buried his face in his shoulder. He sobbed uncontrollably, trembling in his father's arms. Antonio held him close to his chest and rocked him from side to side. Mariana's eyes filled with tears. She had promised Gabriel for years that his father still loved him, but no matter how many times she said it, she knew he did not believe it until that very moment.

Andrea held her mother's hand, standing slightly behind her. She wanted to disappear. Andrea knew she was supposed to be excited to see her father, because that is what everyone asked her before she left Colombia: "Aren't you excited to see your dad?" Andrea had shrugged her shoulders at the question. She knew what it was to be excited—she felt it every time her mom bought her an ice cream, or when Gabriel let her play with him—but Andrea felt nothing when she thought about her father. For her entire life he had been an imaginary person. A person people always spoke about in the past tense, or with the disclaimer, "Imagine if your father was here." She never imagined him because she did not need to. He was a photograph on her refrigerator. He was the out-of-focus picture next to her mother's bed. Antonio was a constant presence in her life, but he never really existed. And that was how she liked it. She did not want to know him. His picture was enough.

Gabriel eventually stopped crying. Antonio put him down and patted his son on the head. He kneeled down in front of Andrea and smiled. Andrea hid behind her mother. She wanted him to go away. She wanted him to play with Gabriel.

"Andreita…"

Her back tensed. *Why is he calling me Andreita? No one calls me that.*

"I have something for you."

Andrea peeked at her father from behind her mother's legs. In Antonio's hand was a bright yellow square. Andrea was intrigued. She stepped out from behind Mariana.

"It's candy, like a *fruna*." Andrea reached out, swiped the candy out of his hand, and again disappeared behind her mother. He was surprised by her quickness.

"*Piojito*, give your papi a kiss and say thank you."

Mariana pushed her daughter toward her father. Before Andrea could turn away, Antonio pulled her into his arms and brought her to his chest. Antonio had waited six long years to hold his baby girl. Tears poured from his eyes. The sight of her daughter in Antonio's arms filled Mariana with joy. Mariana put her arms around her husband's skinny frame. She wept; he cried harder. Gabriel wrapped his arms around his mother and father. Finally, after six years, the Rodríguez Cabal family was together.

Mariana and the children arrived in Los Angeles at the beginning of summer, a perfect way to start their new lives. Andrea marveled at the heat waves that rose up from the asphalt. Gabriel was astounded by how big everything was. Mariana was amazed at how clean the streets were. They were all overjoyed to be away from the penetrating cold of Bogotá. But their joy did not last long. Mariana hated the solitary days spent in their tiny apartment on a nondescript corner. She tried to bring brightness and cheer to their dismal home, but nothing seemed to erase the sadness from its walls. The apartment was a tiny box with a cracked window and a steel door, which Mariana despised. The cold steel reminded her of the one thousand two hundred fifty-two times she had passed through La Picota's metal doors to see her husband in jail. Behind the apartment's metal door, Mariana felt as if she were locked out of her own life. Antonio convinced her that once the summer was over and the kids started school, she could start working.

With nothing to do, Mariana put all of her energy into cooking scrumptious meals. She spent hours in the kitchen preparing Antonio's favorite dishes. Every night she waited for Antonio to trudge into their apartment after a long day. She loved watching him eat a steaming plate of *arroz con frijoles*, a tender piece of chicken, and sweet plantains. She took such joy in giving him this small pleasure. Most of the time Antonio ate in silence. Mariana assumed it was because he was too exhausted to speak. She thought their silent moments spent at the dinner table were as romantic as their first months together in Buga. In their silences, Mariana fell deeper in love with him. But on the night she made him *ajiaco*, she stopped falling and began drowning.

"Mari…"

Antonio looked up from his steaming bowl of soup. She looked at him with pure love.

"Mari, you don't have to make me dinner anymore."

"What do you mean?"

"I didn't say anything before because I know you like to make me dinner, but I eat at work, and I just want to come home and go to sleep."

Mariana nodded her head. The wind had been knocked out of her. She felt Antonio pulling away from her once again, just as he had after the loss of El Arado. As Mariana sat across from him in an apartment the size of her balcony in Buga, in a country where she did not know a soul and did not speak the language, she realized he was a stranger to her. Mariana had been in the United States one month. Antonio had made love to her only twice. She kept telling herself it was because he was so overworked providing for his family, but as Antonio finished his *ajiaco*, reality began to crack Mariana's heart.

The next night Mariana did not make Antonio dinner, just as he had asked. The apartment was pitch black when the front door creaked open. Mariana pretended to be asleep as Antonio slid into their bed. She waited for him to reach out and touch her. Nothing. Reaching across the few inches that separated them in their bed was like reaching across the Atlantic Ocean and trying to touch the tip of Africa: impossible.

Antonio was lost in the depths of his failure. During the five years he spent in La Picota, the only thing that had kept him alive was the dream of the opportunities he was certain the United States would give him. He risked his life to get there. He took a job at a restaurant because it was a step toward his dream of a better future. At first he ignored the men at work when they talked about the fruitless years spent hunched over washing dishes and picking up plates after the gringos who didn't even notice they were alive. He refused to believe he was expendable.

Months had passed since his arrival in the United States. His English was nearly perfect. La Picota had given him the time to study English, and the streets of Los Angeles had given him the opportunity to practice. Antonio decided it was time to begin to chase his dreams. He knocked on the beat-up door in the back of the kitchen were his boss was always holed up.

"It's open."

Antonio pushed the door open with a smile. His boss glanced up at him, then returned his focus to his paperwork.

"What do you want?"

"How are you?"

"Fine."

Silence. Antonio cleared his throat.

"I wondering if I get new job. My family coming—"

"Look…"

"Antonio. My name is—"

"Yeah, okay. You're already a busboy. What more do you want?"

"I memorize menu, ingredients. I be waiter."

"That ain't happening."

"What you mean ain't happening?"

"You no job as waiter. You only busboy. Forever. Got it? I gotta get back to work. *Adios.*"

Antonio stared at him in disbelief and then spit out the words: "I quit."

Antonio knew he had made the right decision when the next morning he was hired as a busboy in another restaurant. This time he listened to the chatter of his coworkers, and he soon realized the only place for him in this world was washing dishes. By the time Mariana and the kids arrived, he despised his job, and hated himself even more.

Seven unbearable nights had passed since Mariana had prepared the *ajiaco* that broke her heart. Antonio and Mariana did not speak a word to each other until the night Antonio came home and quietly shook Mariana's shoulder. She woke up disoriented. He took her hand and pulled her into the bathroom. Her heart raced. He was taking her to the bathroom, the only place in their small studio apartment where they could have privacy. He wanted to make love to her! The butterflies that had been asleep in her stomach for years woke up with such force they almost knocked her over.

Antonio quietly opened the bathroom door and flicked on the light. He took off his shirt. Mariana devoured him with her eyes. He pulled down his pants. Everything was moving too quickly; she wanted to enjoy him. Before she could say anything, he slipped into the shower and disappeared behind the curtain. Mariana was not sure what to do. Should she follow him in? Or should she surprise him with her nakedness when he came out of the shower? Before she could decide, Antonio said the words that sent her life into a tailspin.

"Mari, I have some great news!"

She smiled. How many times had she heard him say that same sentence? She felt him coming back to her.

"What is it, *mi amor*?"

"I have an amazing job opportunity."

"That's great. What's the job?"

"It's a job that will get me out of the restaurant."

"See, I told you. You just needed to be patient."

Antonio stepped out of the shower. He grabbed a towel and dried himself off. Mariana lost herself in the droplets of water as they rolled down his back, arms, and stomach. He looked more beautiful than ever.

"Mari, the job is in Miami."

"Miami? So we're going to Miami?"

"Well…no. I'm going by myself."

"What?"

"Just for a few months. Once I'm settled, I'll send for you."

"No, no, no! You can't leave us here. We just got here!"

"It's only for a little bit.…"

"What am I supposed to tell the children? That papi is leaving us again?"

Mariana flew into a rage. She begged him to not leave her. Not to leave the kids. Not to leave Gabriel. She pleaded, she cried, she screamed, but it was no use. Antonio left Mariana five days later. She refused to say good-bye. Their thousands of good-byes had left her empty. She watched as he said good-bye to Gabriel. She watched as he hugged Andrea. Her eyes filled with tears as she watched him walk down the street and disappear around the corner.

In the apartment, on her bed, was a letter from Antonio. He promised he would send for her once he was settled in Miami. He assured her they would be back together in less than a month. She counted the money he had left her. Mariana had four hundred dollars to her name. With each passing day, Mariana's rage grew. She allowed her anger to fester for seven days, during which the mere thought of his voice sent fury shooting to every corner of her body. But after a week, her ire began to subside, and she longed for him again. She wondered how he was, if he was eating well. Finally, on the tenth day she called the number he had given in his letter. An answering machine picked up.

"I'm still mad at you, but I want to make sure you're okay. Call me back."

She waited for his call all day, but the phone never rang. The next morning she called again. Again the answering machine picked up. Finally, on the third day of trying to reach him, she lost her sanity. She sat next to the phone and called every twenty minutes for seven hours. Her mind spiraled down into the darkest of places. She was convinced he was dead. She grabbed the kids and went to see Alejo, the only friend to whom Antonio had ever introduced her. She pounded on his front door. Alejo was startled to see her. His beady brown eyes darted nervously around the room as he reluctantly let her in. The kids disappeared into the TV room to watch cartoons.

"Alejo, have you spoken to Antonio?"

"Yes."

"Where is he? Is he okay?"

"Mari, I'm sorry to...Look, Mari, he's not coming back."

"I know. We're moving to Miami."

"No, Mari. He's not coming back, and he doesn't want you to go there, either."

"What do you mean he doesn't want me to go there?"

"He says it's over, Mari."

"What?"

"I'm sorry, Mari. He told me he was going to talk with you."

"Where is he in Miami?"

"I don't know."

"Yes, you do! Where is he?"

"Just leave it alone."

"I have two fucking kids! I can't just leave it alone. I'm going to Miami."

"Please, Mari, don't."

Mariana looked at him with such contempt that his words ran back down his throat. Shame spilled out of his eyes and flooded his apartment, pushing Mariana out as she grabbed her kids and slammed the door behind her.

Mariana stumbled down the street in a daze. She stared at the strangers as they walked past her in slow motion. Car engines roared as they sped down the street. The sun set the black asphalt ablaze, forcing her to close her eyes. Mariana was lost in a world where she did not belong. She had been cast out to sea, with no one or nothing that could save her. The city sounds mixed with the beating of her broken heart, creating an opus of pure fear.

Gabriel and Andrea's screams pulled Mariana back to reality. Her eyes slowly focused on them as they jumped up and down, pointing at an idling ice cream truck and pleading. She needed time to think, and ice cream offered the perfect distraction.

Miami kept running through Mariana's mind as she watched the kids suck and slurp on their ice cream. She

knew she could change Antonio's mind. She just needed
to talk with him face-to-face. To get there, she needed to
make money. She needed to make money fast. Calling her
mother was out of the question; her father was sick, and
Mariana was afraid this news might kill him. Esperanza was
fighting her own battle without a husband, the twins had
just moved back in with Amparo and Hernando Andrés to
help take care of their father, and the boys were off fighting
a futile war in the backwaters of the jungle. Asking anyone
else for money in Colombia was impossible; because Buga's
gossiping tongues would make their to way to her mother.
Her mind raced in every direction until it finally crashed
into her salvation: empanadas! Her mother's famous empanadas were going to save her marriage.

"Come on, kids, we have to go the market!"

Mariana's first batch of empanadas was made by three
pairs of hands. Andrea kneaded the cornmeal, Gabriel
rolled it into balls that fit perfectly into his palm, and
Mariana chopped the tomatoes and onions and sautéed
the beef. Gabriel and Andrea watched with hungry eyes as
Mariana dipped the stuffed empanadas into the bubbling
oil. She gave Gabriel and Andrea each a steaming empanada. Their little mouths savored every bite, and for a few seconds their happiness made Mariana forget how completely
alone she was.

The next day Mariana rose with the sun and filled a tin
pan with the empanadas—her ticket to Miami. She woke
the kids and described to them how much fun they were
going to have because they were able to go to work with her.
Andrea shrieked with delight; she loved any new adventure.
But Gabriel knew something was not right. Mariana scurried around the house. She did not want him to see her
eyes. She did not want him to see the truth.

Mariana carried the empanadas as the kids walked along behind her.

"Remember, don't step on any cracks!"

Andrea jumped over one. Gabriel laughed at her.

"You stepped on it!" he told his sister.

"No, I didn't!"

"Yes, you did!"

"Mamá!"

"I'm not getting in the middle of it."

Mariana didn't know where she was going, but she put her faith in her destiny and walked on. After a few hours of walking aimlessly through the city, she stumbled upon a ragtag group of women. Their eyes looked past Mariana and focused anxiously on the cars behind her. Mariana approached them with a smile.

"Hello. Empanadas?"

Spanish jumped off a woman's tongue and danced into Mariana's ears.

"How much?"

"A dollar."

One of the women shook her head no.

"Two for a dollar," Mariana bargained.

"That's more like it!"

The empanadas flew out of Mariana's tin pan, and the dollar bills fell deep into Gabriel's pockets. Then a car honked and the women swarmed around it. Mariana watched, confused, as four women disappeared into the car. Those who were left outside pounded on the windows and begged to be let in. The car screeched off, leaving behind a pack of disappointed women. The women walked back to the street corner, their shoulders slumped.

"What are you guys doing?" Mariana asked.

A woman smiled and replied, "How long have you been here?"

"A month and a half."

"You're a little slow. If the gringos choose you, you have a job for the day."

"Really? How much do they pay you?"

"Around twenty dollars. Cash." The woman leaned close to her ear. "You have to leave them at home. They won't choose you if you if your kids are here."

As night fell over their shoebox apartment, Mariana asked Gabriel for the first of many favors. She needed him to take care of his little sister while she was at work. He looked into her eyes, and Mariana felt him searching for the truth. Then he whispered the words she'd feared the most.

"Mami what's going on with papi?"

"I don't know."

It was all she could manage to say. It was the truth. A truth he could handle, and a truth she could manage to say. A cloud of sadness enveloped Gabriel's eyes.

"But we're going to Miami," Mariana told him.

"When?"

"I don't know, but soon. Very soon."

Mariana knew the only way to take Gabriel's pain away was to get to Miami, and the only way to get to Miami was to work.

"When I leave tomorrow, you can't go outside. No one can come in. I'll leave breakfast and lunch in the refrigerator. No turning on the stove. Okay?"

"Don't worry, mami, it'll be fine."

She took his small hand in hers.

"Thank you, *mi rey*."

Mariana turned her back to Gabriel. She did not want him to see her cry. Gabriel turned his back on his mother because he did not want her to see him cry. In the shadows of their sadness, their tears found one another and danced together until the sun rose.

The next morning Mariana left the apartment. She shut the metal door behind her, suddenly grateful that it was made of steel. She placed her forehead against its cool surface and prayed it was strong enough to keep the world out. Every day, while Mariana cleaned houses, picked oranges, and sewed dresses, her mind constantly wandered to her shoebox apartment. Her employers complained that she never worked fast or long enough. As soon as the sun began to dip into the Pacific Ocean, Mariana was the first one packing up her things to leave. Her coworkers called her lazy, ungrateful, and stuck up, but Mariana did not care. Leaving her kids alone was heart-wrenching, but not being able to serve them dinner was unimaginable.

Mariana did not like how the blonde woman made her feel from the very beginning. Her blue eyes reminded Mariana of ice, and her thin, cracked lips were like snakes slithering across her face as she barked out orders.

"You and you!"

She pointed to Mariana and a few others. The drive was long, the workday even longer. As the sun began to set, Mariana asked the woman about leaving. She refused to let Mariana go. She locked the front door.

"You won't be leaving here until the job is done!"

Mariana looked at the pile of dresses that still needed to be sewn.

"That will take me all night."

The woman grabbed Mariana by her neck, dragged her to the sewing machine, and slammed her onto the chair.

"Well, you better get to fucking work, then!" She pulled her hair hard and whispered into her ear, "Got it?"

Mariana worked through the night without stopping. Her fingers moved in and out over seams while her foot tapped to the rhythm of what she imagined Gabriel and Andrea were dreaming about. Wherever she looked, she saw the cracks of her shoebox apartment and longed to be there. As the sun rose over the Santa Monica Mountains the monstrous woman finally unlocked the door. Mariana did not want to take the measly forty dollars the woman gave her, but she had no choice. She grabbed the money and ran all the way home. She ran faster than the buses that plodded alongside her. She ran between cars and dashed through crosswalks. She opened the door to her shoebox and almost fell to her knees when she saw Gabriel sleeping in a chair with his head resting on the dining room table. She picked him up in her arms. He was so big she was barely able to carry him. He opened his eyes and smiled at his mother's tear-streaked face.

"Mami, where were you?"

"Shhh, *mi rey*. I'm home."

"Do you have to go to work?"

"No, *mi rey*. No."

The next day, Mariana set out on the streets again, her tin of empanadas in her hands and Gabriel and Andrea at her side. Walking the long, desolate streets of Los Angeles, Mariana came face-to-face with her destiny once again. It grabbed her by her shoulders and pushed her in the right direction.

On any other day, the man digging through the trash would have been invisible to Mariana, just as he was to millions of others. The old man with curly gray hair and smooth black skin was a ghost who haunted the streets of

Los Angeles, an angel who lived because of what others threw away.

Mariana stared at the man in front her. She watched him intently as he leaned into the trash can. His hands pushed and prodded the discarded grime of people's lives. Mariana watched as his hands wrapped around an empty soda can. It glistened in the sunlight as he dropped it into his shopping cart, adding it to the hundreds of other cans the man had collected in the maze of trash of his beloved city. Mariana took in every detail of his cart. It was a moving sculpture. A piece of art. A broomstick pointed to the sky from each corner of the cart. From each stick dangled a clear plastic bag filled to the brim with hundreds upon hundreds of plastic bottles. The bags were like billowy clouds that helped the man float unnoticed through the city's solitary streets.

The old man pushed his massive sculpture slowly down the street, its hollow clinks bouncing off its plastic-laden clouds and landing in Mariana's ear. She felt the power of opportunity in her hands. She knew this was her road to redemption. In the city's trash, she would find her way back to love. The next morning Mariana pushed her newly stolen cart down a quiet street as the trash bags dangled down its side blowing in the wind. Andrea sat inside the empty cart, tapping her legs against the outside. The empty bags fluttered in the wind as Mariana approached her first garbage bin. Gabriel stood back and watched her, seething with anger. He was confused. He did not understand why his mother was digging through trash. He did not know where his father was. He wanted answers to his questions beyond his mother's constant "I don't know."

Gabriel watched his mother move her hand through the garbage and missed his father more than ever. He remembered the day Antonio left. Antonio had hugged and kissed Andrea good-bye on that hot, sunny day, as his mother looked on, her arms crossed in front of her. Then he had turned to Gabriel. He had hugged him tightly for a few seconds and then abruptly turned around. Gabriel had watched helplessly as his father had walked away down the sidewalk, and was overtaken by the urge to hug him one last time. He had screamed "Pa!" and ran after him. Antonio had turned around, and Gabriel had barreled into his father's unassuming arms, not wanting to ever let him go. He already missed him so much it hurt. Antonio had freed himself from Gabriel's grasp and whispered into his son's ear, "Take care of your mother and sister for me." Gabriel had nodded as his father kissed him on his forehead. Then Gabriel had watched him disappear around the corner.

As Gabriel watched his mother dig through the trash, thoughts of his father's disappointment raced in his mind. He knew his father would never have let his mother dig in garbage. Gabriel felt ashamed for failing. He wondered what Antonio would say when he found out he had not taken care of his mother. Would he punish him? Maybe he would let him off easy, and not let him go outside for a week. Or maybe he would be so angry he wouldn't let him play soccer for months. Gabriel fought back tears of anger.

Mariana felt her son's furious stare dig into her heart. No matter how much it hurt, she knew this was the only way. Her hands searched through wet newspaper and mushy scraps of food until her fingers wrapped around a silky-smooth aluminum can. She pulled it out and smiled to herself. She turned to Andrea and said,

"That's five cents we didn't have before."

Andrea giggled delightedly and kicked the cart in excitement. Mariana pushed the cart on to the next trash can. Gabriel did not move. She kept going. As long as she felt his angry stare, she knew Gabriel was with her. Every time she finished digging through a trash can she looked back to see where Gabriel was. He was always a few yards behind her with his arms crossed and his thick black eyebrows furrowed.

As Gabriel watched his mother hunched over trash cans, sweat pouring down her face, he wondered if his father meant he was supposed to take care of his mother even when he did not agree with her. He felt guilty watching her work so hard while he stood by and did nothing. He was confused about what he should do. He longed to ask his father for advice.

By the time the sun set, Gabriel had made his decision. There were six hands collecting cans instead of four. Six hands filled their cart with more than eight hundred cans daily. The twenty-five dollars they earned every day kept a roof over their heads and just the right amount of food on their table. Cans kept them afloat.

"Time for canning" was the children's wake-up call. Mariana was both amazed and heartbroken that they never complained when she told them it was time to go to work. They put on their work clothes and were out the door before she was.

The family canned in the sun, they canned in the rain, they canned on corners, they canned in alleys and at apartment complexes. Mariana made up games to make the time pass faster and to make the workload lighter. Andrea and Gabriel loved contests, and Mariana stayed up late into the night devising new ones for the following day. Some were as simple as guessing how many cans they might find in a trash can or how many cans they had at the end of the day, but their favorite was the race.

The race began with the family choosing teams. Most of the time it was Gabriel and Andrea against Mariana. Mariana would hang empty trash bags from the broomsticks at each corner of the cart. Each team had their designated bags. The goal was to collect as many cans as possible before lunchtime, and there was only one rule: Mariana had to be able to see the children at all times. Andrea loved digging through the same trash can as her mother. She laughed uncontrollably when they reached for the same can. She always managed to steal the can from her mother and run back to her bag, where she would triumphantly drop it in. The kids always had an advantage over Mariana when they found a Dumpster. Gabriel would jump right in and throw the cans out like a madman. Andrea picked up the cans and ran to the cart, laughing the entire way. Mariana fought hard for these small moments of happiness.

As the days turned into weeks, Antonio's silence was the only certainty Mariana knew. Every night after she put the kids to sleep, Mariana quietly snuck out of the house. On a corner a few blocks away from her apartment where the streetlights hummed incessantly and the music blared from the lonely, smoke-filled bars, Mariana called Antonio from a grimy pay phone. Every night she left him the same message.

"Antonio, I need you. The kids need you. We're barely making it without you. Please just call me back. Let's at least talk about everything. I still love you."

Mariana left Antonio the same message thirty times. As she was about to leave it for the thirty-first time, everything changed. Mariana dialed the same number she had dialed every night before, but instead of hearing a stranger's voice on an answering machine, she heard a recorded message that changed her life forever.

"This number has been disconnected. If you feel you have reached this recording in error, please hang up and try your call again."

She listened to the computerized voice tell her the only connection she had to Antonio was gone. Alone on a corner in a city that was not her own, with a dirty telephone to her ear, Mariana knew she had been abandoned. She felt her soul shifting. Her ten-year relationship with Antonio flashed before her eyes, and she saw the truth she had refused to see for so many years. Where she had once seen beauty, she now saw lies. Where she had once felt love, she now felt manipulation. Where she had once burned with desire, she now saw her own fear of rejection. Her anger exploded into a million pieces ignited by hate.

"You fucking asshole! I hate you! How could you fucking do this to me, you bastard?"

Mariana hit the receiver against the phone booth over and over until it crumbled to pieces in her hand. She dropped the shattered plastic onto the ground and walked away. Mariana thought of every single can she had collected in the month since Antonio had left. Each can she picked up was a reminder of Antonio's betrayal, but she had refused to see it. Now she saw everything crystal-clear. She saw his cowardice and his selfishness, but more important, she saw her own stupidity, fear, and insecurities.

Mariana made her way home and stepped back into her dark apartment. She could not look at Andrea and Gabriel. She did not have the strength to bear that pain. She quietly walked into the bathroom, her private sanctuary. Her thoughts wrapped around the enormity of what she was about to endure. She had to learn how to walk without Antonio, to breathe without Antonio, to dream without Antonio. She stepped into the steaming shower. The warm stream of water was like a whip lacerating her back. Her knees buckled as the weight of acceptance fell on her shoulders. She crumbled to the floor. Her salty tears mixed with the sweet city water and swirled down the drain. She lay there, perfectly still, with her eyes closed. The mere act of breathing was painful. Her mind spiraled down into its own labyrinth of fear. Darkness surrounded her as her body shivered uncontrollably. Suddenly, a flash of white light exploded around her. She froze. Every hair on her body stood on end. The sound of her breathing surrounded her. In the distance she smelled the sweet aroma of roses. She stood up naked and walked through the white light toward the roses of her childhood. The white light dissipated around her, and she was standing on her balcony in Buga. It was a warm, clear night. The moon was full and the stars looked like diamonds glistening in the sky. Mariana stood naked on the balcony, her hair dancing in the wind. She smiled at the familiar cobblestone streets below her. She turned to look into her bedroom and was shocked by what she saw. The bedroom she had grown up in was unrecognizable. The room had been divided into several bedrooms. Small single beds lined the dirty walls. The floors were destroyed beyond recognition. Stranger's clothes were strewn about the floor, piled on the tiny beds, and hanging from hooks in the makeshift walls. Her home was no longer her home. There was nothing left for her to go back to. Her old life was dead; she had to start anew. A life without Antonio. A life alone. A life where her mother could not save her from her choices. She knew staying in Los Angeles would hurt like hell, but going back to Colombia would kill her. Life as a single mother in Bogotá was a torture she had seen her sister Esperanza suffer through, and it was a torment she did not want to bear. She preferred to tackle the unknown in Los Angeles, because in its warm breezes she felt the caresses of possibility. She believed the hope of possibility for her children was worth the growing pains they would have to live through as a family.

Her realization brought her back to her body. Mariana pulled herself out of the bathtub and opened the door to the small living room. She watched Andrea and Gabriel sleep. She sat down next to her children and stroked Gabriel's long brown hair. He opened his eyes right away.

"What's wrong?" he asked.

"I need to talk with you and Andrea."

He sat up next to her. Mariana gently woke Andrea. Beads of sweat rested on her forehead. Mariana smiled.

"It's hot in here, right?"

Andrea nodded.

"*Piojito*, you need to wake up."

"We have to go to work already?"

"No, my love."

Andrea sat up in bed with sleep in her eyes. Mariana took a deep breath.

"I want you both to know that we're not going to Miami."

"I know...." Gabriel's voice trailed off into the dark.

"Does that mean we're going back home?" Andrea asked.

"This is home now."

"Good. I like it here,"

Andrea chirped.

Gabriel gave her a dirty look. They sat in the heavy silence. It said everything Mariana was unable to say.

"*Mi rey*, if he were to come back, would you want to see him?" Mariana asked Gabriel.

"Yeah. I wouldn't have to talk to him if he didn't want to. I just would want to see him, to make sure he's okay."

More silence.

"Andrea, if papi were to come back, would you want to see him?"

Andrea shrugged her shoulders. Gabriel looked at his mother. She seemed different. Their new home had changed her somehow.

"Mami, would you want to see him?"

"No, *mi rey*, not anymore."

Gabriel wrapped his arms around Mariana. He held her for a long time. Gabriel knew why his father had left. He knew that Antonio wanted to give them more than their little shoebox apartment, that he dreamed of living in a two-story house with a backyard and a pool with a diving board. He knew that Antonio dreamed of driving around Los Angeles in a red convertible instead of living with the constant stop-and-go of the city bus. Gabriel knew his father left so he could work day and night. He knew once Antonio had the big house, the car, and the pool, he would come back to them, and everything would be as it was before.

Mariana found tremendous comfort in Gabriel's embrace. His innocence protected her. His love gave her strength. His strength gave her faith. Andrea nestled in between the two of them and quickly fell back to sleep. Gabriel fought a hard battle, but eventually his eyelids were too heavy, and he too sank into a deep sleep. Mariana stayed awake staring at the ceiling until the sun rose. With the first light of dawn, Mariana felt a weight slowly being lifted from her shoulders. She had carried Antonio on her back for ten years. She had carried his lies, his schemes, his failures, and his impossible dreams. Her back had become his bridge to nowhere, but now that he was gone, there was room for her. She dug deep into herself and, for the first time, found her own dreams.

She started small. She wanted Gabriel and Andrea to go to school. When she walked them down the hallway toward their classrooms for the first time, the joy she felt was bigger than anything she had ever felt before. Her next dream was for herself: She wanted to work in a restaurant, away from the city's trash. The universe opened the door to her dream, and Mariana seized the opportunity with both hands. Mariana wanted a home, and six years later, with the help of her family, she found it in the solitary plains of the desert. But Mariana was blindsided by the horrors that lurked in the limbs of the Joshua trees and by the blood-stained secrets of the tumbleweeds. She watched in terror, helpless, as the desert slowly swallowed her dreams into its nothingness.

chapter

SEVEN

Little Quartz, 1993

"Ten. Nine. Eight. Seven."

You got this. Just hold on a few more seconds.

Andrea did not feel the pain anymore. Her body was numb to the blows that pummeled her back, her head, and her legs. She felt a knee slam into her stomach as she fell to the ground. She saw streaks of white sneakers as she ducked her head into her arms and covered her face, just like Rebeca had told her to do. A few kicks managed to slip through, and the salty taste of her blood touched her tongue. *Fuck! Not my face.*

"Three. Two. One."

Hands. Countless hands picked Andrea up off the ground and stood her on her feet. She stumbled, but the hands held her up. She was covered in dirt. The hands patted it away. Andrea wiped her lip. Blood stained her hand.

"Shit!"

"I told you to cover your face, *esa*."

Andrea looked up and saw Rebeca standing in front of her. Her brown eyes were outlined with thick black eyeliner, her burgundy hair was pulled back into a slick ponytail, and a black bandanna was wrapped around her forehead. If she hadn't been putting her large silver hoop earrings back in her ears, no one would have believed she had been jumping Andrea for the last thirty seconds.

"I told them to go easy on you, but shit, *vata*, you can take a beating."

"Fuck that—don't go easy on me. I'm down to go again. Right now! Let's go!"

"Chill. I'm just playing. Nobody went easy on you. You got the shit beat out of you. Look at your lip. Dreamer fucking clocked you hard."

Andrea wiped the blood off of her lip. She had waited six months to get jumped into 22nd Street. She had waited six months to finally have her gang become her family. She wanted to get jumped in on her sixteenth birthday because she wanted everyone to know how down she was. Rebeca was her best friend, and everyone respected Andrea because they respected Rebeca, but she wanted to earn her own respect. She wanted everyone to know that she was crazier than Rebeca. Ready to do whatever needed to get done for her new family.

"Come on, let's go celebrate!"

Rebeca and Andrea slid into the backseat of Casper's car. Casper had a joint in his mouth and passed it to Rebeca. She took a hit and passed it to Andrea. Andrea did not like getting high—she preferred drinking—but her lip and her back were throbbing and she needed to ease the pain fast. She inhaled deeply, and when she exhaled her pain left along with her breath.

"Where we going, Casper?"

"Lil' mama, I'm gonna take care of you tonight. Don't worry—tonight is your night. You got curfew?"

"Nah. I'm staying at Rebeca's."

"Cool. We gonna stay out all night, then."

Casper turned on the engine. The car roared down the street. The backseat vibrated as the bassline bounced to the beat of the blaring music. The wind blew through Andrea's wavy brown hair, danced on her face, and skipped over her lips. She looked out the window at the desolate, barren desert. She finally felt at home. When she had first arrived at Little Quartz at the age of twelve, the emptiness of the desert had scared her. She felt small and insignificant in its vastness. She knew there were secrets that were being kept from her in the red dust that surrounded her. Little Quartz secrets were as dark as the desert was vast. It was a town in the midst of a war. Gangs had infested its every corner. Crystal-meth skeletons walked the streets clacking their jaws amid the sounds of hungry babies and wailing mothers. Parents toiled day and night at the meat factory. They became killers of sheep, and their children became killers of one another. The fabric of Little Quartz was unraveling, and at its center was Andrea.

The City of Angels held Andrea in its wings until Mariana forced her into the bowels of the desert. Andrea begged her mother not move to Little Quartz. She was already nervous about starting the sixth grade in Los Angeles; the thought of starting school in a town where she did not know anyone seemed like a cruel joke. But Mariana saw the fangs of the angels who lived in the cramped apartments of Los Angeles, and she wanted a safer and more tranquil life for Andrea and Gabriel.

"But Mom, I don't want to leave LA!"

"*Piojito*, you'll like Little Quartz."

"I like it here!"

"I know, but you will like it there, too."

"I'll hate it! I know it's going to suck! My life sucks!"

Mariana watched as Andrea stomped into her bedroom and slammed the door behind her. She smiled to herself. Andrea's hips were filling out and her chest was coming in, but at the end of the day she was still just a stubborn little girl.

Andrea arrived at Sage Middle School a twelve-year-old girl who aced her classes without really trying, and she left four years later with a knife in her pocket, charcoal-black eyes, and an anger that consumed every part of her being. Life at home was a constant battle. The war that raged on the streets of Little Quartz exploded with ten times the fury in the Rodríguez Cabal home. Mariana and Andrea spontaneously combusted whenever they were in the same room. Andrea's only respite from the war was the quiet of her bedroom, but it was not enough to bring her peace. She had an internal ache that gnawed at her, and no matter what she fed it—alcohol, drugs, vicious fights, or stolen cars—it never went away. Her ache was dark. It was deep and all consuming. It was filled with pain. It lived in the shadows of her almost-forgotten father.

Rebeca was the only one who was able to dull Andrea's ache. Andrea first met Rebeca on her third day of school, when her worst nightmare was unfolding before her. Friends were grouped together and scattered around the black asphalt and dirt field of the school. Their circles were as impenetrable as walls of steel. Andrea was left alone on a bench with her face buried in a book.

"Hey, you gonna try out for the cheerleading squad?"

Andrea looked up and locked eyes with Rebeca. Rebeca had large brown eyes, which looked even bigger with the black charcoal eyeliner that outlined them. Her hair fell into perfect ringlets just below her shoulders, and her lips were outlined with burgundy lip liner. Rebeca's fingers were covered in bulging rings, and the *mi vida loca* tattoo on her hand confirmed what Andrea already knew. Rebeca was short and skinny, but her size was only a disguise. Andrea had seen many girls like Rebeca do the craziest things on the streets of Los Angeles, and she could tell Rebeca was one of those girls. Andrea swallowed back her fear.

"No."

"Why not?"

"'Cause cheerleading is fucking stupid."

"What's your name?"

"Andrea. What's yours?"

"My homegirls call me Flaca. Where you from?"

"LA."

"No, like where you from? Who you kick it with?"

"Oh, I'm not from anywhere."

"You down with Twenty-second Street? 'Cause this school rolls with Twenty-second. You better not be no fucking drifter."

"I'm down with Twenty-second Street."

"You down?"

"I mean I'm cool."

"Good."

Rebeca turned around and disappeared into a group of girls at the other end of the schoolyard. Andrea dropped her eyes back to her book, her heartbeat thundering in her chest. She tried to focus on the words in front of her, but the letters refused to make sense.

The next day Andrea sat in the back of the classroom, her face buried in her book once again.

"All you do is read, *esa*."

Rebeca sat down next to Andrea, and from that moment on their lives intertwined. They were inseparable. Wherever Rebeca was, Andrea was right there with her, and Rebeca never did anything without Andrea. Andrea needed Rebeca in her life because Rebeca dulled her internal ache. Rebeca needed Andrea in her life because she replaced the sister who had been taken from Rebeca years before.

Rebeca's sister was in jail, locked behind steel bars and concrete walls since Rebeca was six years old. Drugs, guns, and men had put her there. Rebeca's parents refused to walk her through the metal detectors and the pat-downs in order to visit her sister through a thick plastic window, where they could share stories by holding phones to their ears. Instead, her parents believed, their love could survive through letters and the collect calls that came every Sunday at four in the afternoon. Rebeca and her sister loved each other fiercely, but her sister's love was not able to change Rebeca's destiny.

Rebeca's parents moved out of the crack-infested streets of Los Angeles and, without knowing it, brought Rebeca into the crystal-meth labs of the desert. They wanted a life for Rebeca without gangs and guns and men who chased little girls. They wanted Rebeca to be a part of the American dream, but instead she became the American nightmare. Gangbanging wrapped its treacherous fingers around Rebeca's neck. Once it had her firmly in its grasp, it reached out to Andrea and began slowly choking her as well.

Now Andrea glanced over at her friend, at the other end of Casper's car. She was so grateful to have Rebeca in her life. The ache inside Andrea never went away, but she could not imagine what it would be like if Rebeca weren't there to dull the pain. Rebeca understood her. She knew what Andrea was feeling without her ever having to say a word. They spoke to each other in glances, in their silences. Rebeca took care of Andrea. She loved her for who she was, not for who she was expected to be. The pressure of the future did not exist with Rebeca. Only the gift of the present.

Casper's car slowly pulled up to a dark one-story house. Silhouettes of men with shaved heads and girls with big hair dotted the dusty front yard. Music blasted from the cars that lined the streets. Cigarettes and joints passed freely from person to person, and bottles of beer followed closely behind. Andrea's heart raced. So many battles had been fought with her mother over this very moment. Andrea wanted the freedom to do as she pleased, but Mariana hounded her with questions. *Who are you going with? Where are you going? Whose parents will be there?* She laughed at the thought. Parents did not exist here. Parents were at home, at work, or tucked away in the farthest corners of the world. Andrea pushed Mariana into the darkness at the back of her mind. She wanted her to disappear into the past. Tonight was the first night she could claim 22nd Street as her own, and she did not want her mother's ghost haunting her. Not tonight. Andrea opened the car door. Her feet touched the dusty pavement. She stood proud and flashed twenty-two across her chest. A silhouette spoke out.

"Where you from, *vata*?"

"Deuce Deuce! East-mother-fucking-side Twenty-second Street! What!"

The silhouettes turned and showered her with their love. Andrea felt their warmth surround her. An older woman with years of banging under skin approached Andrea. Tattoos covered her chest. The ink ran up and down her arms and twisted around her neck.

"You're real young to be claiming like that."

"I ain't that young, *esa*."

The woman laughed to herself and shook her head. She handed Andrea a beer.

"Don't forget the dead homegirls."

Andrea watched the woman disappear into the dark house. She opened the bottle of beer and poured some on the ground.

"Rest in peace."

"Andrea, Shorty's here, and he looks fine!"

Andrea looked where Rebeca was pointing. Shorty was leaning against the house. He had a cigarette in one hand and a forty-ounce beer in the other. His brown pants were perfectly ironed with crisp creases down the middle, grazing his flawless white sneakers. His flannel shirt was buttoned at the top and flowed open, allowing his white tank top to shimmer underneath. Andrea loved the way his tank top accentuated his perfectly flat six-pack. He was a mystery to Andrea, but from the moment she saw his ice-blue eyes, she knew she wanted him. Andrea did not want to waste her time. She walked over to him and tapped him on the shoulder. He turned around. His smile told her all she needed to know.

"How you doing, Andrea?"

"I'm good."

"What happened to your lip?"

"Nothing. I got jumped in today."

"Where you from, *vata*?"

"East-side Twenty-second Street. Fuck drifters."

"You look good when you say that." He caressed her cheek. "Let's go inside."

Andrea nodded. He grabbed her by the hand and led her into the smoke-filled house. Music blared from an unseen stereo. It was dark, but Andrea could make out the bodies that rubbed up against one another in the hallways, on the couch, and in the doorways. Shorty navigated his way through the half-naked bodies and stopped in front of a door at the end of a lonely hallway. He opened the door and turned on the light. A large bed was in the center of the room. The walls were covered in drawings of faces and unknown places. Black graffiti marked the four walls as his dominion. REST IN PEACE was etched in black on one wall, and shout-outs to homies who were locked behind bars kept count of the fallen soldiers. The door clicked closed behind them, and Andrea turned to Shorty. For the first time, she saw the thin lines around his eyes and the heaviness that comes from burying too many friends. She saw the years of pain stacked on his back. Soft music filled the room and drowned out the outside world. He led her to the bed and sat her down.

"I haven't stopped thinking about you."

"Really? Does your girlfriend know that?"

"I don't have a girlfriend."

"That's not what I heard."

"You heard wrong, baby. Come on, you haven't thought about me?"

"A little."

"Just a little?"

Andrea nodded.

"Well, a little is better than nothing."

He lightly kissed her neck.

"You smell good." He kissed her again.

Andrea kept still. His lips slid down her neck as his hands slipped up her shirt. Her breath skipped over itself. She closed her eyes. He grabbed her breast and pinched her nipple and a bolt of lightning shot through her body. Pleasure and pain twisted into each other. She felt the world spin as he laid her down on the bed. He rubbed against her, and she moved along with him. His fingers worked the zipper and button of her jeans with ease. She felt his fingers dig inside of her. Her tightness squeezed them. He explored while her world expanded. His words fell into her ear.

"Baby, are you still a virgin?"

The answer got lost in Andrea's throat. She closed her eyes and nodded. His breathing turned into panting. His body felt harsh. His touch was rough. He rubbed harder. Andrea tried to pull the words from her throat. She begged herself to have the strength to say, *Stop. No. Enough.* But she did not. He slid her pants down and pushed her legs open. She prayed for him to stop. She prayed for something to stop him.

Suddenly, three loud shots pierced the silence. The window shattered and glass rained down on them. The sound of a car skidding around a corner. Silence. Then screams. Screams from the outside world. Shorty's voice broke through the cries.

"Are you okay?"

"Yeah."

More screams. He scrambled to his feet and ran toward the screams. The sound of women wailing poured in through the broken window. Andrea's hands shook with fear. She struggled with her pants. Rebeca rushed through the door.

"Casper was shot!"

"What?"

"A blue truck drove by about twenty minutes ago. Really slow, but they didn't do shit, and then they came back. Come on. Dreamer knows whose truck it is. We're all going now."

Andrea looked at the broken window. Her body froze. Her limbs were glued to the bed. Her mind raced with questions. What if Shorty hadn't laid her down on the bed?

What if she hadn't been inside the house? Time folded into itself as Rebeca slowly pulled Andrea off the bed and led her back through the smoke filled house.

Outside was chaos. Women stared off into nothingness. Girls cried. Men seethed with anger. Police cars invaded the front yard, their red and blue lights bounced off the tears on the faces of those gathered. Casper's body was sprawled on the ground, one arm poking out from underneath a white sheet. He lay in a pool of blood. Police officers spoke to stone faces. No one knew anything. No one saw anyone. No one spoke. The color of the car was a mystery, the passengers anonymous. The police tried to break through the silence, but the code of the street was to take care of your own. Revenge was sweetened with blood, not with snitches. One by one everyone disappeared into the night. The police watched them go with their secrets toward their own future graves.

Shorty slowly walked toward Andrea and her stomach clenched. Her palms were sweaty as he wrapped his arm around her and whispered into her ear, "You and Rebeca should go. I don't want you guys to get picked up because of curfew. These fucking pigs are looking for any excuse to lock everyone up. We're gonna meet up at McAdams Park at midnight."

"Okay."

"Stay off the street until then."

He kissed her on the cheek and went into his house. Andrea turned to Rebeca, and their thoughts collided in midair. How were they going to get home? Casper had driven them there. They looked around. All the cars were gone; everyone had scattered. They were alone.

"Come on, let's just kick it here with Shorty," Rebeca said.

Andrea grabbed Rebeca's hand and shook her head, and Rebeca understood her silent plea. They turned their backs to the pool of blood left by Casper's body and walked off into the desert. The night was clear. The stars shimmered in the sky. They walked in silence. Rebeca could not escape the faces of all the friends lost, all the friends buried. She saw their smiles and heard their laughter. They walked close to her in the crisp desert air. Andrea thought only of Casper. Death had never before visited her doorstep. She had never felt its cold hand brush against her. Their silence was interrupted by the howls of the coyotes that roamed the desert night.

"Andrea, we should go to my house. Kick it there until we gotta go to the park."

"Can we stay around here? I just feel like walking."

"But the cops are—"

"Let's just stay off the main streets. Please."

The truth was, Rebeca wanted to stay in the darkness of the night, too. She wanted to walk with the ghosts. She wanted to live in her pain so her revenge would be even sweeter.

"Okay. But we have to be at McAdams by midnight."

"For sure."

They avoided the red and blue lights of police cars chasing drug dealers and gunslingers. They walked in the shadows of the slithering snakes and the prowling coyotes, reminiscing about Casper. They kept him alive through their memories of him. They laughed at his drunken escapades and his dirty jokes. They remembered his dreams of being an artist. They smiled at his kindness. Both girls were so lost in the memory of Casper that they did not notice the small red car driving slowly behind them.

The car's headlights were turned off, and two shadows shifted back and forth in the front seat. It snuck up quietly on the girls. They kept laughing. They kept walking. The car sped right toward the girls and came to a screeching halt in front of them. Andrea and Rebeca froze in mid-step as the passenger door swung open and Gabriel stepped out onto the street. Andrea's heart sank. *No, not now!* she screamed to herself. She did not want to see her brother's green-brown eyes glistening in the night. Now was not the time for him to try to be her big brother. The driver's side door opened and Mariana jumped out of the car as well. She looked like a crazed animal ready to attack. Andrea saw the black under her eyes. Her hair was sprinkled with white, and her hollow cheekbones hardened her face. The two weeks Andrea had spent away from Mariana had changed her mother.

The day Andrea had run away was the day her life began to transform. It started off as a normal afternoon. Andrea came home from school and turned on the television. The telenovelas made her forget the world around her. As she watched, the sun dipped into the Pacific Ocean. Before she knew it, Mariana was walking through the front door. Exhausted from work, Mariana dragged herself into the living room. Mariana was used to seeing Andrea lounging on the couch, staring at the television set, but when she walked into the kitchen her rage exploded.

"Andrea! What is this?"

"What?" Andrea asked, annoyed, eyes glued to the television.

Mariana stormed into the living room and slammed off the TV.

"Mom! What are you doing?"

"Why isn't the kitchen clean?"

"Oh, God, I forgot, okay?"

"No, it's not okay. I work all day, and all I ask is that when I come home to cook *you* dinner, I want the kitchen clean."

"Not this again!"

"Why can't you do this one thing for me?"

"I forgot!"

"How can you forget? All you do is watch TV!"

"What else am I supposed to do? You don't let me go out when you're not home! And you're never here—"

"Because I'm working!"

"Get a better job! Oh, wait, you're too stupid to do anything but cook."

Mariana raised her hand and slapped Andrea hard across the face. Both mother and daughter were shocked into silence. It was the first time Mariana had hit Andrea. The closeness of Mariana's breath repulsed Andrea. Her mother's smell was like rotting corpses, her touch like shrapnel. Andrea needed to get away.

"I'm going to Rebeca's."

"No."

"Why not?"

"Because I said so."

"But you're home now!"

"I don't fucking care. Get out of my sight!"

Andrea stormed down the hall and slammed her bedroom door. She dove onto her bed and buried her head in her pillow.

"I fucking hate you! Why are you such an evil bitch? Fuck your house. Fuck your rules...."

She stopped abruptly. She lifted her head off of her pillow. She got out of bed. She grabbed her backpack and emptied its contents onto the worn blue carpet. She opened her closet and grabbed her favorite clothes. She filled the backpack to the brim with clothes, her journal, her makeup, and her toothbrush. Only the essentials. The time had come for her to run away. She had been toying with the idea for a long time. It was a fantasy she thought about often. But now was the time. She needed to escape. She needed a place where she could rest, a place where she could let her guard down. A place that felt like home. She climbed out the window, chasing her freedom. Once her feet hit the concrete she ran and never looked back. Home was in front of her. Home was wherever she made it. Home was anywhere without Mariana.

Andrea's freedom was spent on people's couches, in people's cars, and hiding at Rebeca's house. Mariana stopped by Rebeca's house almost every day, and Rebeca told her the same thing every time: "Andrea ain't here."

"Please let her know I'm looking for her. I just want to know she's okay."

"I haven't seen her since she ran away."

As the lies jumped off of Rebeca's tongue, Mariana shot daggers from her eyes. She wanted nothing more than to slap the smirk off of Rebeca's ugly face. But there was nothing Mariana could do. The police wanted proof. A mother's instinct was simply not enough. Mariana took to the streets. Every night she scoured the desert, the mountains, and the ditches. She saw the ghosts of so many girls wandering through the night that the fear of losing Andrea pushed her to the edge of an impossible choice.

Now, before Gabriel was able to grab Andrea, she turned around. She ran away from the little red car. She ran for her freedom. Her arms and legs pumped and her chest heaved, but she was no match for Gabriel. He was beside her in seconds. She closed her eyes. *Run faster!* she commanded herself. Her legs twitched with the effort. Gabriel reached out and grabbed her by the wrist. Andrea pulled away, refusing to give up. She refused to lose.

"Leave me alone! I'm fine. I'm taking care of myself."

"Shut the fuck up, Andrea! Just stop. Right now. Stop!"

"Fuck you!"

Gabriel knew he had to stop her. He slowed down and trailed her from behind. Andrea's heart raced. She was outrunning him! Suddenly he wrapped his arms around her tiny waist and tackled her to the ground. They crashed onto the concrete sidewalk, their bodies smashing into each other and coming to a grinding halt. Rebeca screamed as they wrestled. She jumped on Gabriel's back. She scratched and pulled and hit him, but he refused to let go of his sister. Mariana approached from behind. She grabbed Rebeca by her hair and threw her halfway across the street, roaring, "Stay away from Andrea!"

Gabriel picked Andrea up off the ground. She was limp in his arms. She did not have the strength to fight. She cried as her eyes met Rebeca's. She was a pile of broken bones. Rebeca sobbed uncontrollably and reached her hand out to Andrea like a toddler searching for her mother, and Andrea's heart broke. The world was crushing Rebeca. Andrea was leaving her quivering and shocked on the asphalt street.

The car door closed, the hollow sound rattling the cracks in Andrea's heart. Inside, the only sound was the hum of the car's engine. Andrea stared into the night sky. The idea of going home crushed her. She felt Mariana's oppression slowly wrapping around her neck and suffocating the life out of her, and she knew she would not stay home for long. Freedom had tasted too good to have it yanked away from her. Her thoughts ran in endless circles. Nothing made sense. Her eyes were heavy from the tears, from the running, from the sadness that pulsated in her body. Sleep. She needed sleep. At least in her dreams she could escape Mariana.

The little red car did not stop at their home. Instead, it drove through the mountains and into the valley and stopped in the heart of the City of Angels. The roaring planes overhead woke Andrea from her slumber. The lights confused her. The lights confused her. The traffic disoriented her. Her words broke the silence.

"Where are we?"

Mariana did not say a word. Gabriel was too scared to speak. Andrea read a sign overhead: WELCOME TO LAX.

"Why are we at the airport?"

"You're leaving."

"What?"

"You have a ticket to Colombia."

Colombia was a strange place to her. A place where her memories began. A world where people only existed in crackling, delayed phone calls. A country where outsiders claiming to be family lived.

"Why?"

"Because you're going to live there."

Silence.

"For how long?"

"We're going to try it out for a year. If you don't like it, you can come back."

"Are you guys coming?"

"No."

Silence. Shock. Confusion. The car stopped. Mariana turned around.

She handed Andrea her passport. Andrea opened the small burgundy book with the word *Colombia* etched in gold across the front. She stared at the picture of herself as a little girl. She was so far removed from that awkward smile, those excited eyes, and the perfectly braided pigtails. She was a stranger. Mariana gave Andrea a small plastic card that Andrea had never seen before. She looked at it and read the words *Green Card, Legal Alien.*

"This is your green card," Mariana said. "Don't lose this. It's the only way you can come back. Understand?"

A flood of memories roared into Andrea's mind. She remembered how her mother had suffered over that piece of plastic, how they'd prayed for amnesty every day. When Andrea asked her mother what it meant, Mariana told her it meant they would be able to have a home someday. It meant they would move out of their cockroach-infested apartment and into a house with three bedrooms and a backyard. She told her amnesty meant they could see their grandmother and their cousins. Amnesty would bring them happiness. So Andrea had prayed alongside her mother every day. They burned candles and they stayed on their knees for hours, until finally a small envelope came in the mail. Amnesty brought them little plastic cards. Amnesty was sending Andrea back to Colombia.

"Who am I going to live with?"

"Your Tía Esperanza. You'll be living with your cousin Valentina. She can introduce you to her friends. It will be fun."

Andrea sank into the backseat. *Fun* was not the word she would use to describe going to a place where she did not know a soul. *Fun* was not the word she would use to describe starting all over again.

"What about my stuff?"

"I packed a suitcase for you."

Andrea turned her head. She did not want to look at her mother. A packed suitcase in the back of the car meant a plan had been made. A plan was being executed. Mariana clearly did not want her. So she would do just as her mother wanted. She would not be around. Gabriel drove the car around the airport terminals that were bridges to the other side of the world. The car stopped at a red light. They were approaching her terminal. This was Andrea's last chance to create the life she wanted, and not live the life her mother expected her to live. Andrea quietly unbuckled her seat belt. Her fingers slowly wrapped around the door handle. She kept her eyes on Gabriel and her mother. She waited for her opportunity. Finally it came. In the blink of an eye, she pulled the door handle. Nothing happened. She tried again. The door remained shut. Gabriel slammed on the brakes. Andrea rammed her shoulder against the door but it stayed closed. Andrea slid across the backseat and desperately tried to open the other door, but it didn't budge.

"Andrea, you're not going to be able to get out," Mariana said.

She frantically pulled and pushed the door. She tried to roll down the power windows, but they didn't move. She slapped the window over and over. Mariana's calm voice cut through Andrea's panic.

"*Piojito*, you're going to Colombia whether you like it or not. Please don't make it hard for us. Trust me—I know what I'm doing."

Through her tears and anger Andrea whispered the words "Fuck you." Those were her words of resignation. Those were the words that ended their war. The car settled back into silence. As they parked the car, Mariana turned to her daughter once more.

"Andrea, if you run, we will catch you. The police know you're coming. All I have to do is make one phone call, and every single cop in Los Angeles will be looking for you in seconds. They won't put you in jail. I've told them that no matter what, you must get on that plane to Colombia. They agreed to help. In fact, they were eager to help. So please, let's make this easy."

Andrea stared out the window. Mariana hoped her daughter believed her. She hoped Andrea did not run off into the night because her only recourse would be to run after her. Mariana looked at Gabriel, and they got out of the car. Gabriel opened the back door and grabbed Andrea by her arm, holding her tight. Mariana grabbed her other arm. They walked her through security and led her to her boarding gate. She was their prisoner. Mariana never let her go, too scared at the possibility of losing her. But Andrea was broken. Too confused to run. Too hurt to think.

No one said a word. Their silence was heavy. A voice crackled overhead.

"Passengers on flight 1442 to Bogotá, Colombia, this is your final boarding call."

Gabriel stood up. He couldn't look at his sister. He mumbled, "Take care of yourself."

He wrapped his arms around her, enveloping her tiny frame. Memories of their childhood flashed before his eyes. He remembered how they had collected cans in the streets of Los Angeles until they found sanctuary at school. Mariana kept collecting cans on her own until she found a job in a restaurant. Restaurant work paid better than the cans from the street, but it came with a price: Gabriel and Andrea were left alone once again. Those hours spent alone with Andrea were the best memories of his childhood.

Andrea had hated being locked in the apartment while their mother was at work. She had convinced Gabriel to sneak out to the park a few blocks away. The park was huge; the grass seemed to spread out forever. Andrea and Gabriel quickly found their favorite corner of the park—the baseball fields. A group of ragtag kids played baseball there every day until the sun went down. At first Gabriel and Andrea just watched from the stands, both wishing someone would ask them to join. Until finally, after weeks of just watching, Andrea stood up.

"*Piojito*, where are you going?" Gabriel had asked her.

"To play baseball!"

He had watched as Andrea walked up to the oldest boy. She tapped him on his side; she was too small to reach his shoulder. He turned around, and as Andrea spoke to him, Gabriel's heart raced with excitement. He didn't take his eyes off of her. She pointed to Gabriel. The boy shrugged his shoulders and turned back around. Andrea screamed, "Gabi, we can play!"

Gabriel ran off the bench. He had been waiting for weeks to throw a ball, pick up a bat, run around the bases, but he had stayed on the bleachers because he was too scared to ask to play. He did not want to hear the word *no*. He did not want to feel unwelcome, not good enough, an outsider, all the feelings he had felt since arriving in his new home. All the feelings he had felt since his father left.

Gabriel picked up an old, beat-up glove and slid his left hand inside. It felt big and clumsy on his hand, but he liked its roughness. Someone tossed him a baseball. He opened the glove and stuck out his hand. The ball fell right into the sweet spot of the glove and a surge of happiness raced through his body. He fell in love with baseball the moment he caught that ball.

After that day, Gabriel and Andrea played baseball every evening after school with the group of ragtag kids. Gabriel was a natural. His hands wrapped around the end of the bat, his back elbow pointing directly behind him, his chin tucked into his front shoulder. He stepped into his swing as if he had been playing baseball since he learned to walk. Soon Gabriel was playing better than all the kids in their group. Without knowing it, Andrea had given Gabriel the gift that saved him from himself. When Gabriel played baseball, he could forget the nagging questions about his father. He could forget how much he missed his *abuelita*. He could forget all the worries about money, food, and rent. He was grateful for Andrea's impatience that day. As hard as it was for him, Gabriel was saying good-bye to Andrea because he believed sending her back to Colombia was his gift to her. He hoped he was saving her from herself.

Gabriel released his sister and sat down, his eyes welling with tears. He looked at the ground and waved his mother and sister away. Mariana took Andrea by the arm and led her to the door of the Jetway. She hugged Andrea. Andrea stood with her arms at her sides. Cold. Emotionless. Her mother's arms felt like they were sucking the breath out of her. Finally Mariana let go. Andrea refused to look at her mother. She did not want to give her the satisfaction of connection. Mariana sighed in resignation as Andrea turned around. Her fingers grazed the Jetway wall, her last connection to home. She walked alone toward an uncertain future in an unknown city. With each step her heart grew heavier with anger.

Andrea sat in the airplane with her shoulders hunched forward and her hands tucked between her legs. She stared out the airplane window. The plane backed out of the terminal. The people in the waiting room became smaller and smaller. The plane rumbled down the tarmac, faster and faster. The wheels lifted off the ground. The plane lifted into the night sky. Andrea mumbled to herself: "Fuck you,

Mom." Mariana had abandoned her just as her father had, and now she was left to survive in Bogotá alone, shivering and stunned. Andrea's eyes filled with tears. *No,* she told herself, *No tears.*

chapter

EIGHT

Bogotá, Colombia

The glass doors slid open and the cold air rushed past Andrea's face. A sea of people spread out before her as they clutched one another, stood on their tiptoes, and searched for their loved ones. People yelled out to the passengers as they passed through the glass doors and into the cold air of Bogotá.

"Juan Carlos! Juan Ca *mi amor*!"

"Mami!!!!! We're here."

"Diego! You've gotten fat!"

Their voices mixed with the roar of airplanes, car horns, and screeching tires. Bogotá pulsated with life. Andrea scanned the faces of the strangers before her. There was uniformity in the sea of people: mostly short, with various shades of brown hair and brown complexions. The women had bright red lips. The men wore black shoes. The girls wore tight jeans. The boys wore jean jackets. Andrea's baggy pants and flannel shirts would not go over well here.

Andrea looked for Tía Esperanza. She knew it was a pointless search. Pictures lied, and time had erased her *tía*'s face from her memory. Bogotá's frosty air slid down her neck. She shivered as it made its way into her bones. She had forgotten the piercing cold of Bogotá. Andrea felt like an outsider wrapped in the chaos of the city where she was born. Ten years away had given her hips and filled out her chest, but had left her empty of the heartbeat of her homeland.

"Andreita! Look at her, she's so skinny, just like Mariana! Andrea!"

Andrea locked eyes with Tía Esperanza and the memories came flooding back to her. Days spent licking her lips, waiting for the *arepas* to be grilled to perfection. Road trips through the luscious mountains, passing makeshift roadblocks of rope and rocks. *Novenas* spent in cold living rooms with *buñelos* warming her hands.

Tía Esperanza waved her arms frantically. Her red-tinted bob bounced up and down excitedly. Her large eyes darted back and forth, searching for a path toward the front. Tía Esperanza exuded elegance. Esperanza screamed out Andrea's name and pushed herself through the sea of bodies. Within seconds she was at the front of the crowd, wrapping Andrea in her arms. Andrea fell against her *tía*'s chest as Esperanza held her tight. Andrea tried to pull away, but Esperanza refused to let her go. Unsure what to do, she hesitantly hugged her back.

Esperanza had found luck one bright Sunday afternoon six years earlier on the corner of La Septima and Eighty-fourth Street. Her daughter, Valentina, had begged her mother to take her roller-skating at *la ciclovia*. Esperanza had agreed not because she wanted to but because it was something Valentina could do for free. Money was not only tight; it was practically nonexistent. Esperanza had been fighting with her ex-husband since Valentina's birth ten years earlier. But no matter how much she begged or screamed, he refused to help. He said the apartment he gave her was enough.

Esperanza's spirit had been crushed. Her beauty was slipping away, and she had become her own worst nightmare: a single mother without any potential suitors. That day, as Valentina rode her roller skates in the distance, Esperanza walked in a haze of self-pity. Her haze blinded her to the man standing on the corner. She walked right into him.

"Watch where you're going!" the man shouted. He turned around, annoyed, and was shocked by what he saw: a tall, voluptuous woman with the most beautiful white skin and dazzling long dark brown hair. "Oh, I'm sorry. I didn't mean to yell at you."

Esperanza sensed his interest right away. She pushed aside the haze.

"It's okay. It's my fault."

"My name's Roberto. What's yours?"

"Esperanza Cabal."

"Esperanza, has anyone ever told you that you're beautiful?"

Esperanza smiled flirtatiously. They stared at each other. Suddenly Valentina grabbed her mother's hand.

"Mami, let's go."

Esperanza saw the disappointment in Roberto's face. She refused to lose him that easily.

"Roberto, this is my daughter, Valentina. I was just going to drop her off at her father's house."

"I'm going to see my dad?" Valentina asked, confused. She could not remember the last time she had seen her father.

"Yes."

"Oh. Well, in that case, I'm going to have drinks at La Rosa if you'd like to join me," Roberto said to Esperanza.

"Sure. I'll see you there in a bit."

Esperanza's determination paid off. Roberto fell in love with her in a matter of weeks, and they were married within the year. Without planning it, Esperanza was restored to the glory of her years in Buga. The years she had spent suffering as a single mother in Bogotá were forgotten in the comforts of Roberto's home. Roberto was generous with his vast wealth. He let Esperanza buy a home for her mother and father, he let her send money to Mariana the few times she would accept it, and he let Andrea come stay at his home not as a houseguest but as a daughter.

Now Esperanza said to her niece, "*Ay*, no, Andreita, you're way too skinny. What is your mother feeding you up there? And these clothes—they're so big. Why are you wearing such big clothes? Vale, look at her. You're very pretty, but we need to put some meat on your bones! Vale, you remember your cousin Andrea, right?"

Andrea's cousin Valentina stood next to her mother. Andrea was shocked by what she saw. Valentina looked just like her own mother, Mariana. Her hair was wild and unruly, a chaotic frizz. Her skin was as white as snow and sprinkled with freckles, which dotted her entire body. Her small brown eyes where shy but intense. If not for her thick lips and her small pudgy nose, she would be the spitting image of Mariana.

Valentina leaned forward and gave Andrea a kiss on the cheek.

"Of course I remember my *prima*!"

Andrea's memories of Valentina danced in her mind. She remembered a rare day when the sun shone bright in

Bogotá and the crisp air disappeared behind the Eastern Cordillera. The family had taken a bus to the outskirts of the chaotic city, toward the rolling green mountains. She and Vale were riding a donkey together. Suddenly the donkey refused to take another step. Frustrated, the girl holding the reins dropped them and picked up a stick. She hit the donkey on the behind. It took off, running through the pastures at lightning speed. The girls screamed as the donkey raced around corners and avoided head-on collisions with trees and passersby. No one could stop the infuriated donkey. His age and his exhaustion finally brought him to halt on the other side of the hill, far from their screaming mothers. Andrea laughed at the memory.

"Are you hungry, Andrea?" Esperanza asked.

"Yeah, I'm starv—"

She stopped herself. *Not in English, Andrea.* She flipped the switch to Spanish. Suddenly her tongue was heavy. It felt clumsy in her mouth. It tripped over itself as she pushed the words past her lips.

"Yes, very hungry."

Tía Esperanza took off down the crooked, cracked sidewalk. The girls followed behind her.

"Come on, let's get you something delicious. I'm glad you haven't forgotten all your Spanish. With me you can only speak Spanish, because *no espik inglish*! But you can speak English all day with Vale if you want; she speaks it perfectly."

Andrea looked over at Vale for help. Tía Esperanza spoke so fast her words became jumbled in Andrea's ears. Vale smiled at her.

"She said she doesn't understand English but I do."

"Okay. Cool."

"No. No. No," said Esperanza. "No English when I am here. Okay?"

The girls nodded their heads. Vale rolled her eyes behind Tía Esperanza's back. She looked at Andrea. They shared a smile.

Cars zoomed in and out of the parking lot. They swerved around people, suitcases, and idling cars without ever missing a beat. It seemed like a thousand and one accidents waiting to happen. Tía Esperanza tapped on the window of a dark blue SUV that was parked just outside the chaos. The driver's door opened and a short, stocky man with curly black hair and round glasses stepped out. He rushed to the passenger side of the car.

"Is that your stepdad?" Andrea asked her cousin.

"No. That's William, the chauffeur."

Andrea watched as William scurried around the car, opening doors, lifting suitcases, and smiling, all the while agreeing to whatever Tía Esperanza wanted. While William opened the passenger door for Esperanza, Andrea jumped into the backseat of the car. She grabbed the door with one hand and pulled it toward her. The door did not move. She grabbed the door with both hands and again pulled it toward her as hard as she could. It shut with a loud *thud*. Andrea looked to Valentina for explanation.

"It's bulletproof."

"The car?"

"Yep."

"Why do you have a bulletproof car?"

"Girls, Spanish please," said Esperanza from the front seat.

"Andrea wants to know why we have a bulletproof car."

"Ahhh...don't worry about that. It just makes Roberto feel better. Right, William?"

"Yes, Señora. Don't worry, Señorita Andrea—you're safe. I won't let anything happen to you."

He smiled at her through the rearview mirror. She smiled back at him, unsure of what she needed to be kept safe from. Andrea looked out the window as William eased the SUV into the pandemonium of the Bogotá streets. She pushed the button to open the window, but it did not move.

"Windows don't go down in bulletproof cars," Valentina explained.

"Oh. Thanks."

Andrea looked out the window toward the city where she would spend the next year of her life. The deep green mountains reached up to the sky, a constant reminder that the sprawling concrete jungle was not meant to be there. Graffiti covered the half-crumbling walls along streets that were littered with dogs, piles of trash sitting next to half-empty trash cans, and potholes so big mattresses had been thrown inside them. The people's way of doing the job their government could not do.

Tía Esperanza's voice bounced around inside the fortified car and random words landed on Andrea's lap. Their meaning was inconsequential. The SUV stopped at a red light, and Andrea stared at a girl about her age who was standing in the middle of traffic, wearing a sweater that was two sizes too big. The sweater had been white at some point but was now the color of midnight. Her jeans were frayed at the bottom, and so long that they covered her shoeless feet. The girl clutched a clear plastic bottle to her chest. Andrea watched as she brought the bottle to her lips and inhaled deeply. Her eyes darted about. She made eye contact with Andrea. Andrea looked away, uncomfortable for having intruded in the girl's private moment.

BOOM! BOOM! BOOM! The car window thundered. Andrea snapped her head toward the sound. The girl laughed hysterically, her voice seeping through the steel doors.

"Don't look so scared, girl. You got some spare change?"

"Too bad this car isn't street-kid-proof. Just ignore them, Señorita Andrea. They're just high and crazy," said William.

William put the car in gear and continued down the arteries of Bogotá. The one-story cinderblock buildings gave way to high rises that towered above the wayward buses and snarls of traffic.

"We're almost home, Andreita," said Esperanza.

"The traffic here sucks," Valentina chimed in.

"*Ay*, Valentina. I hate it when you talk like that."

A cart filled with flattened cardboard boxes and broken side panels and pulled by an emaciated donkey passed their stationary SUV. A hunchbacked old man held the reins in his wrinkled hands. Every few seconds he smacked the protruding bones of the equally old donkey with the leather leads. The donkey's pace never changed. The old man never complained. He slowly swerved in and out between the immobile cars. He was the only thing that moved in the gridlock. Andrea chuckled at the irony.

They crept forward slowly until Esperanza said with genuine excitement, "Andrea, we're here! You're home! William, we'll get out here. Park the car in the lot."

Andrea stepped out of the car and took in her new home. She liked the deep red brick the ten-story building was made of. A sweeping marble staircase welcomed her into the lobby. A man in a gray suit sat behind an elegant counter made of marble and deep cherry wood.

"Good afternoon, Señora Esperanza, Señorita Valentina."

"Hello, Juan Pablo. This is my niece Andrea. She is going to be living with us for the next year."

"Welcome, Señorita Andrea."

Andrea smiled at him. He smiled back, then returned to watching his small black-and-white portable television. He seemed so young. He reminded her of Gabriel. The women walked toward the opulent garden, which overflowed with luscious trees and lavish flowers. The fountain gave the lobby a tranquility that made one forget about the madness just outside the glass doors.

"Andreita, the good news is that we live on the top floor," said Esperanza. "The views are spectacular. The bad news is that sometimes the electricity goes out and you have to walk up to the tenth floor."

"It happens like once a week," Valentina added.

"But if you're carrying anything really heavy, you can ask Juan Pablo or the other one—I forget his name—to help you with your stuff. Oh, and before I forget: You live in Los Rosales. That's what the neighborhood is called. Okay?"

"Yes, Los Rosales."

They waited for the elevator. When the doors opened, they saw that William was already inside with Andrea's suitcase. They all stepped into the cramped elevator. Tía Esperanza spoke as fast as the elevator was slow. The words flew past Andrea. The Colombia of Andrea's memories was not the Colombia she found herself in now. Bulletproof cars, chauffeurs, and marble floors were what Hollywood dreams were made of. Her Colombia was cold cinderblock houses warmed with *arepas* and *chocolate* and late nights spent with her *abuelita* while her mother worked. The elevator doors opened and snapped Andrea back to her new Colombia. Tía Esperanza's heels clicked on the tile floors, and the orange pink glow from the setting sun shone through the skylights above them.

"Tía, how's *abuelita?*" Andrea asked.

"She's very excited to see you! She'll be coming in from Barranquilla this weekend."

Andrea had forgotten that the cold of Bogotá had sent her *abuelitos* chasing the sun. El Valle was an impossible reality for them, so instead they had settled on Barranquilla, a town full of strangers that was drenched in sun.

"Is *abuelo* coming, too?"

"No, *piojito. Abuelo* doesn't like it here."

"Why?"

"Who knows."

But Esperanza knew. After moving to Bogotá, her imposing father had become a walking skeleton. At first no one understood why he refused to leave the house, but with time everyone realized he *couldn't* leave the house. As soon as he stepped through the door, his hands trembled, his eyes went wild with fear, and his chest heaved ferociously as he gasped for air. With each passing year Hernando Andrés' fear ate a little more of him, until the father they had all known and loved was gone, and in his place was a stranger who never spoke. They had hoped the sun and the breeze of the Atlantic Ocean would bring back his vitality, but he was too far gone by the time Esperanza was finally able to buy her parents a home.

Tía Esperanza dug through her purse, searching for her keys.

"Your *tía's* are coming, too. Everyone's very excited to see you. Your uncles send their love from where ever they're stationed now. I can never find my keys. William, check to see if you have them. Someone is always home, so you don't need keys, but if for whatever reason no one is home just look under the mat. They'll leave you a pair of keys. Gloria! Gloria! Open up. It's me."

She rang the doorbell incessantly.

"Gloris! Hurry up!"

The door swung open.

"Hi, Gloria. This is my niece Andrea. The one I told you about. Is her room ready?"

"Yes, Señora. Hello, Andrea. Hello, Valentina."

"Great. Please get them something to eat. I'll be right back."

Esperanza passed Gloria as she held the door open for her. She disappeared down the hall. Andrea smiled at Gloria. Her simple cotton dress, with its cheap lace collar and see-through apron, made her seem much older than she was. Her hair was carefully braided into small, thin braids that sprouted from the top of her head. Her dark black skin was striking. Her sweet, honey-brown eyes radiated a history of women caring for other women's children, cooking dinners for strangers, and pleasing husbands who were not their own. Gloria smiled back at Andrea.

"Gloria is the best cook in all of Bogotá. Right, Gloris?"

"Not really."

"She's been cooking since she was, like, eight, and she's a genius. What do you want to eat, *prima?*"

"What is there?"

"Gloris?"

"Steak, chicken. *Pinchos.*"

"Ohhh, *pinchos.* You like *pinchos,* Andrea?"

Andrea shrugged her shoulders. Unsure of what pinchos were, but too embarrassed to ask, Andrea looked down at the floor, wishing she could disappear into its cracks.

"You don't know what a *pincho* is?"

Andrea shook her head no, still too self-conscious to look up from the ground.

"It's beef on a stick. Or chicken on a stick."

"So it's like a kebab, I guess," Andrea said.

"*Kebab.* I like that word. If you don't want that, there's chicken."

" Ummm…a kebab, I mean a *pincho*, is fine."

"Gloris, two *pinchos* with rice and plantains, please," said Valentina. "Come on, Andrea, I'll show you the house."

Andrea watched Gloria disappear behind a large wooden door. She turned and followed Valentina down the long hallway, the beautiful white marble of the floor sparkling beneath her feet. The floors were accented with colorful Turkish rugs. Valentina disappeared behind a wall, and Andrea followed her into a very large living room. Leather couches, silk curtains, and artwork in gilded golden frames abounded. Bouquets of fresh tropical flowers made the room smell of sweet caramelized sugar. Antique clocks and statues of Jesus and the Virgin Mary accentuated the grandiosity of the towering walls and elegant columns.

"I never use this room; it's too stuffy. They use it when they have their parties."

Valentina opened two glass doors at the other end of the living room. Bookshelves lined the walls, filled with neatly organized books. A small desk sat facing a large window, which overlooked the tall, nondescript brick buildings of Bogotá. Next to the desk was an overstuffed leather couch overflowing with pillows of different colors, shapes, and sizes.

"My mom has this thing with pillows. She brings them back from all her trips."

"What about the books?"

"They're Roberto's, but he never reads in here. He's always in his bedroom. This is his office, but I use it when my friends come over. My mom likes for us to hang out here so she can watch us through the glass doors. Especially with the boys. She'll walk by, like, every thirty minutes, and she never lets them stay longer than two hours. Come on. "

They walked down another hallway, which looped back around to the front of the apartment.

"That's the kitchen. Gloria's room is in there if you ever need her."

Valentina opened the door at the end of the hall and said, "This is your room."

A twin bed sat underneath a large window. The white lace bedspread reminded Andrea of a dollhouse. A small desk stood across from the bed. Paintings of beautiful landscapes hung on the walls. The closet at the end of the room stretched the entire length of the wall.

"I have a TV in my room, so you can hang out there whenever you want. It's right next door. You want unpack your stuff? I'll help you."

Unsure of what she would find since her mother had packed for her, she wearily unzipped her suitcase. Andrea's clothes were folded into perfect squares. In the center was a piece of white paper with her name written on it. Andrea picked it up. She instinctively traced her finger around the perfectly written *A*. As a child, Andrea had adored her mother's handwriting. She had wanted to write as beautifully as her mother did and would stay up for hours tracing her mother's handwriting over and over, trying to perfect the curvature of the *A*'s and the graceful *S*'s. Andrea felt a pang of longing in her heart. Suddenly her bedroom door swung open.

"Girls, Roberto is here. Come say hello," Esperanza said.

"She never knocks, so get used to it," Valentina whispered.

Andrea left the letter on the desk as she walked out of the room, and the two girls scurried down to the other end of the hall. Valentina pushed open the door, Andrea following closely behind. The marble floors gave way to lush white carpet. The moonlight shone through enormous windows that covered one entire side of the bedroom. Roberto sat in a plush leather chair, looking like a king on his throne. A few feet in front of him was a large-screen television. He sat with the remote control in one hand, entranced by the evening news. His jet-black hair was perfectly in place, and his long black mustache emphasized his thin lips and crooked yellow teeth. The sun had kissed his skin and hidden his age under its bronze color.

Roberto had traveled a long, difficult road in order to be able to relax in front of his television. His father had died unexpectedly when he was only ten. Roberto was the oldest, the strongest, and the smartest, which meant that he was the one who carried his family of seven on his tiny shoulders. The burden of his family had been heavy. There were many nights when food was a luxury. He always said it was his mother's tears that gave him the strength to move the impossible mountains of opportunity.

Roberto had built a small empire selling chickens to housewives and grandmothers. His salesman's wit mixed with his dictatorial authority filled his bank account with enough pesos for his mother and all his brothers and sisters. But chickens were a finicky lot. They liked predictable surroundings, quiet homes, and warm temperatures. If they didn't get what they liked, they simply keeled over and died, by the thousands. The imminent possibility of their deaths hung over Roberto every minute of every day. He felt his childhood hunger pangs always lurking around every corner.

The only place he was able to push away the fear of hunger and his mother's tears was in front of his television set.

"My love, this is Andrea. Mariana's daughter."

"I know who Andrea is, Esperanza." His words cut through the air like acid.

"How are you, Andrea?"

"I'm fine. Thank you. And you?"

"Give him a kiss hello," Tía Esperanza whispered in Andrea's ear, pushing her toward Roberto.

Andrea walked to Roberto, bent down, and kissed him on his cheek. He barely moved. Valentina followed closely behind her. Roberto did not take his eyes off the television. The girls stood in awkward silence for a few moments.

"We're going to go keep unpacking," Valentina finally said.

"Okay, Vale. Don't stay up too late; you both have school tomorrow."

The girls disappeared into Andrea's room, where two trays of steaming food were resting on the desk. The silverware was placed on linen napkins, and a tall glass of fresh passion-fruit juice accompanied each meal. Valentina grabbed a tray, sat down on the floor, and dug into her food.

"I start school tomorrow?" Andrea asked her cousin.

"Yeah. You're going to La Candelaria. Mmm…these *pinchos* are so good."

"That's where you go?"

"No, I go to the English School, but that's a bilingual school and your mom didn't want you to go there. She said she wanted you to practice your Spanish, not your English."

"Great, so I am going to be by myself."

"No, I have some friends there, Las Buenaventuras. Are you gonna eat?"

"In a bit. Are they in my grade?"

"No, younger. Luisa and Monica. They're both really nice, and they love La Candelaria. So you'll be fine. Your uniform is in your closet."

"I have to wear a uniform? Fucking great."

"All schools have uniforms. Don't let your food get cold; it won't be as good. I gotta go do my homework."

"Wait, Vale. Was Roberto mad or something?"

"No, why?"

"He just seemed a little…I don't know…"

"Cold. He's always like that. Trust me, you'll know when he's mad. 'Night."

Valentina closed the door behind her. Andrea looked at the *pinchos* on her desk. Her stomach was growling, but she could not bring herself to eat. Rebeca came rushing to her mind. It seemed only a few hours ago that she had been walking in the desert hand in hand with her best friend. Now she was completely alone. She looked at the letter from Mariana. She grabbed it and ripped it to pieces. The last thing she wanted to know about was her mother. She dropped the shredded letter into the trash can, and the ache in her heart grew heavy, so heavy that it pulled her to the ground. She lay motionless on the red-and-yellow Turkish rug, feeling as if she were falling into the ache in her chest. The deeper she fell, the lonelier she felt. The thought of school terrified her, and the idea of putting on a uniform infuriated her. She closed her eyes, hoping the darkness might ease the throbbing in her chest.

Andrea felt a tap on her shoulder. She looked up and saw Gloria's face smiling at her.

"Señorita Andrea, why did you sleep on the floor? And you didn't eat your dinner; you must be starving. What you do want for breakfast?"

Gloria's Spanish flew out of her mouth at a rapid-fire pace. The words became jumbled in Andrea's head.

"Slow, please. Breakfast? What time is it?"

"It's six thirty in the morning. You have to get ready for school."

Gloria emphasized her words with exaggerated hand signals.

"I got it. I understand," Andrea answered.

Gloria helped Andrea up off the floor. She opened Andrea's closet, which was empty except for a blue-and-white checkered skirt, a dark blue V-neck sweater, and a few bone-white button-down shirts. Gloria laid the sweater, the skirt, and the shirt out on the bed. She grabbed a pair of dark blue socks out of the drawer and a pair of bright red shoes from the closet. Andrea stared at the shoes, horrified.

"I have to wear *those* shoes?"

"They *are* pretty ugly," Gloria admitted.

"I can't fucking believe this."

Gloria disappeared into the kitchen. Andrea went to the bathroom, where she stepped into the shower and let the steam engulf her. Her ache was heavier than it had ever been. She felt as if she were drowning from the weight of it, unable to catch her breath, unable to run away from it. She needed quiet. She needed stillness. The pounding water refused to give her relief. She needed to focus all her energy on functioning like a normal sixteen-year-old girl. She washed her hair, lathered the soap and cleaned her body, and shaved her legs. Her movements were quick and mechanical until the razor accidentally nicked her shin. She watched as her blood trickled down her leg. Its crimson red mesmerized her. A flash of silence momentarily calmed her. She held the razor in her hand. It was light in weight, but heavy in possibility.

Andrea needed more than just a flash of silence. She needed to quiet her ache. She took a deep breath and pressed the razor into her shin, then dragged it across her leg. A sharp pain shot up her leg as her skin slowly tore open. She kept cutting. Suddenly there was stillness. She stopped. Her leg throbbed. The pain pulsated throughout her body. The ache inside her disappeared as her external pain grew. She relished the calm, staring at the blood as it oozed out of the cut, which was long as her finger, a perfectly straight line. The blood dribbling down her leg was comforting. It was beautiful. It was hers. She held the razor tightly in her hand, grateful that she finally held the key to unlocking herself. Grateful for her newfound secret.

Andrea stared at her red shoes as she walked through the front gates of La Candelaria. They reminded her of her secret. They gave her the strength she needed to walk across the muddy parking lot and into the small school. The classrooms were flimsy white Fiberglas buildings with green tiled roofs. Each room had a large window with a matching green or red windowsill. The classrooms surrounded a large grassy courtyard. Groups of girls of all ages, all in red shoes, sat scattered on the grass. The littlest ones ran up and down the roofless corridors, screaming and laughing at one another. Andrea's heart sank. She was surrounded by girls. *It's an all-girls school! Could this get any fucking worse?*

As she walked she felt the girls' stares burn into her back. She saw her room number on a green door. She opened it, entered the room, and quickly closed the door behind her. She shut her eyes and began falling into her ache.

"I hate it here, too."

Andrea's eyes snapped open. A girl with a long brown mane of hair that hung to her waist, pearly-white skin, and deep black eyes sat in front of her at a shabby wooden desk. She was hunched over, writing obsessively in a small black journal.

"My name is Maria Neyla, but they call me Mané. You're Andrea. They told us you were coming, a girl from the United States. Sucks for you."

"Sucks for you, too, then."

"No, I meant the United States part."

Andrea grabbed a chair across from Maria.

"That's Mayita's desk."

Andrea grabbed the chair next to it.

"That's Natalia's."

She walked to a desk on the other side of the room.

"That's Carolina's."

"So what desk is free?"

"This one." She pointed to the desk next to her. "Don't look so scared. Trust me, *gringa*, you don't want to sit next to any of these girls. I'm the best bet you got here."

"If you're my best bet, then I'm in deep shit."

"You're in La Candelaria; you're deeper than shit. You're in hell."

Andrea walked over to the empty desk next to Mané. She settled down into the hard wooden chair just as the classroom door swung open and a sea of blue sweaters rushed toward her.

"Do you speak Spanish?"

"Where did you live in the United States?"

"What's Los Angeles like?"

"What neighborhood do you live in?"

"Do you have a boyfriend?"

Mané did not look up from her journal as the barrage of questions slammed into Andrea. Nor did the girls make any attempt to acknowledge Mané's presence. A deep voice with feigned authority cut through the sea of blue and sent the girls scattering toward their desks. Once the girls dispersed, Mané whispered into Andrea's ear, "César hates the gringos, but don't let him scare you."

César walked toward the front of the room. He wore dark brown pants and a light blue shirt. He tried to cover his bald head with the few pieces of brown stringy hair that remained, but it was futile. His face was as flat as a pancake. His glasses constantly slid down the bridge of his nose. He was short. He was fat. He was mean.

"Ah, well, look who we have here. The already famous Andrea from the United States of America. Andrea, what's your last name?"

"Rodríguez."

"Rodríguez what? In case you didn't know, here in Colombia we use two last names."

"Andrea Rodríguez Cabal."

"Thank you, Señorita Rodríguez."

"Cabal."

The class erupted in laughter.

"Okay, Andrea Rodríguez Cabal, this is a history class. We discuss Colombian history here, but I am sure you don't have a clue about Colombian history, because why would they teach that in the United States? So in order for you to still be able to participate in class, I'll ask you questions about the parallel history of the United States. So we will all be learning together. Make sense? As an example, ladies, what year did Colombia get its independence?"

Everyone's hand shot up in the air except for Andrea's and Mané's. César pointed to a tall girl with blonde hair.

"Eighteen nineteen."

"Easy question, of course. Andrea, now you know when Colombia became Colombia. So tell us, when did the United States become the United States?"

Andrea swallowed hard. She did not have a clue.

"Do you need me to repeat the question in English? Because believe it or not, I do speak English."

She shook her head no. She looked down at her desk. Andrea wanted to disappear once again into the cracks in the floor. Mané pushed her journal slightly toward Andrea. On the upper corner, written in the clearest of handwriting, was the number 1776.

"Seventeen seventy-six," Andrea blurted out.

"That's right. Now, that wasn't so hard. This is how we'll be running class, so everyone can participate."

The rest of the class was a blur. César asked Andrea questions incessantly. Mané helped when she could, but most of the time Andrea shrugged her shoulders, remained silent, and dug her finger into her freshly cut secret. The searing pain that shot through her body made her ignorant silence tolerable. César relished her moments of silence. Watching Andrea shrink behind the large shadow of his knowledge delighted him.

"Ladies, tomorrow we will discuss how the FARC came into existence. Please read chapters five and six. Have a good day." He tapped Andrea's desk as he walked out. "Welcome to Colombia, Andrea Rodríguez Cabal."

Andrea was so furious she did not say another word in class for the rest of the day. She refused to eat the rice and the beige slop the women in the cafeteria served her for lunch. She needed her space from the babbling girls and their constant stream of questions about the United States. She left them in the cafeteria and walked out to the courtyard where Mané was sitting alone, lost in her journal. Andrea figured at the very least the other girls would leave her alone if she was sitting next to Mané. Mané barely lifted her eyes when Andrea sat down next to her.

"I'd rather starve then eat that shit," Mané said.

"Yeah, it looked gross. How long have you been here?"

"Since kindergarten."

"What?"

"I've been in the same class with those same girls since I was six. We haven't had a new girl join us since the third grade."

"No wonder they're so excited. I thought it was just me."

They both laughed.

"You'll stop being a novelty by next week. Don't worry."

"I can't wait. Hey, I wanted to ask you, around what year did the FARC thing happen? You know, what César mentioned class was going to be about tomorrow."

"In the fifties."

When she got home Andrea stormed into Roberto's office and looked at the shelves full of books. What she needed had to be there. She scanned the books' spines, not exactly sure what she was looking for, but certain she would know when she found it. *Great,* she thought. *Everything is in Spanish.* Reading was going to take her twice as long. But she pressed on. She recognized some titles, but most of them were completely new to her, until she happened on *The World Encyclopedia*. To her astonishment, Roberto had four different sets of Encyclopedias. She pulled out the volume from each set that dealt with the United States. She turned to the sections on the 1950s and started the slow and arduous task of reading in Spanish and translating what she was reading into English notes. She grabbed a piece of paper and titled it "USA 1950s."

"Hola, Señorita Andrea," Gloria said, interrupting her research. "How was your first day at school?"

"It sucked, Gloria. I hate it."

"Lots of homework?"

"Exactly."

"Do you want something to eat?"

"Yeah, I'm starving. I'll make something in a second."

"I'll make it for you. What would you like to eat?"

"Right, umm…whatever."

"I can make you anything you want. What are you in the mood for?"

"I don't know, hamburgers."

"Anything else?"

"French fries, I guess. Thanks."

"My pleasure."

Andrea took notes on the historical highlights of each year from 1950 through 1970. By the time Gloria came back with her hamburger and french fries, Andrea had filled five pages with facts. Gloria placed the food on the table and turned to leave.

"Wait. Gloria, do you think you can help me?"

"Sure. What do you need?"

"Choose any year from the first three pages of these notes, and I'll tell you what happened in that year."

"I think it would be best if Señorita Valentina helped you with that."

"She's not here. Please, just thirty minutes. I have to know this for tomorrow. Please."

"It's just…Andrea…I have to get back to work."

"I'll help you with your work once I'm done."

"No. I mean, thank you, but that's not a good idea."

"It'll only take ten minutes. Please."

"Andrea, it's not that…I mean…I can't…I don't know…how to read."

Andrea was stunned into silence. The blood rushed to her face. Gloria's eyes stared at the ceiling as she fought back tears.

"Oh, I'm sorry. I mean…okay…I'll…I'll just practice on my own."

Gloria rushed out of the office. Andrea felt like the air had been punched out of her lungs. She picked up the sheets of paper and stared at the words. Their rough edges hurt her eyes. She felt their distance and their power in her hands. Andrea owned words; Gloria was owned by words. She shuddered at the thought, then pushed it to the back of her mind. She needed to focus. She paced back and forth for hours, studying and memorizing. The sun dipped behind the Bogotá River, on the other side of the city. Andrea repeated the words she owned. Valentina asked her the questions she needed to know and gave her the answers that hid in the shadows of her memory. She memorized nineteen years of history in one night. Finally she collapsed in exhaustion, frustration, and exhilaration.

"*Prima*, you're going to do great tomorrow."

"I hope so. I just need that asshole off my back."

"We can talk to my mom about it. See what she can do."

"No, it's okay. Hey, how long has Gloria been working here?"

"Like three years."

"How old is she?"

"I think nineteen or twenty. Why?"

"Just curious."

The next morning on the bus Andrea hid behind her five pages of notes. The brutal hoses that kept the progress of black people back, the vicious dogs that bit at the heels of equality, and the man born as Martin and lost as King in the twenty years of history she had just discovered mesmerized her. The forty minutes she spent on the rattling bus as it maneuvered around chaotic traffic, over broken bridges, and on dirt roads that threatened to become rivers of mud with the next rainfall flew by.

At school, Andrea sat down next to Mané in the otherwise empty classroom.

"Mané did you do the homework?"

"I skimmed through it. It's basic shit."

César strolled into class. The girls followed behind him. Andrea tapped her leg to the rhythm of her nerves. César stood in front of the classroom, his chest puffed up like a rooster claiming its territory.

"Pop quiz, ladies. Put your books away. I'll ask the question and then call on someone to give me the answer. We'll start off easy. Year and date of *el Bogotazo*? Ana María."

"April ninth, 1948."

"Good. Andrea, can you name an important event that happened in the United States in 1948?"

Andrea blinked back her disbelief. The sound of her heart pounding thundered in her head. She thought to herself, *Shit—1948, 1948. Fuck, what happened in 1948?"*

"Andrea? Nineteen forty-eight?"

Crumbling and defeated, Andrea shrugged her shoulders. She'd studied 1950 to 1970 not 1948. César's sneer of triumph seared Andrea's pride.

"In a letter to his mother, how did Ernesto 'Che' Guevara describe Colombia? Maria Neyla?"

"He said he thought a revolution was going to happen because the countryside was in revolt and the army couldn't stop it. He basically said it was a horrible place to live. Police with machine guns everywhere. Cops always asking for people's papers, violence all over the place. Sounds exactly like how we live today."

"Not exactly how we live today, Maria Neyla. Andrea, enlighten me on 1952 in the United States."

Andrea could not keep the smile from her face.

"Eisenhower was elected president."

César raised his eyebrows in shock. He loved a challenge.

"Thank God you at least know that. What about 1953?"

"The Rosenbergs were executed."

"Why?"

"They were convicted for giving secret information about the atomic bomb to the Russians."

"The Russians. The communists. Natalia in what year and why would you say the FARC was created?"

"The FARC was created in 1964. They came from the communist movement. They said they represented the poor people in the countryside and they believed in land reform, but in reality they're just drug dealers who want money and power."

"Natalia, I'm talking about historical facts, not personal opinions."

"Andrea, the most important historical moment in the United States in the 1950s?"

"I think I would say it was Rosa Parks. She started the bus boycott, which lead to black people having equality in the South."

Andrea talked about *Brown v. Board of Education* while César ranted about Manuel Marulanda and the Seventh Guerilla Conference. Andrea discussed the assassinations of Malcolm X and Dr. Martin Luther King Jr. while César raged about the Patriotic Union and the disappearance and the massacre of its four thousand members. Andrea spoke of Armstrong setting foot on the moon while César decried the crumbling of millions of dreams with the loss of Gaitán and Galán.

At times Andrea's knees buckled or her grip loosened, but she stood firm for more than an hour and a half. She was battered and bruised, but she survived the battle of César. Mané turned to Andrea, astonished.

"Andrea, that was fucking amazing!"

"I hope he leaves me alone now."

"Don't worry; he will. Girl, we gotta go celebrate!"

"Celebrate? Where?"

"La Tienda de Tuta."

chapter

NINE

Andrea pushed open the wooden door to La Tienda de Tuta. Cigarette smoke filled the dimly lit room. Candles sat on rustic tables. Empty stools were scattered about. Men hovered over the women who leaned against the walls, each with a hand on one hip, the other hand holding a drink. Their laughter cut through the music while their hips instinctively swayed in sensual figure eights, luring their partners onto the dance floor.

Andrea, Valentina, and Mané sat in an empty table at the end of the room. Andrea crossed her arms over her chest. Her brow furrowed as she took in the room. Valentina reached under the table and rubbed her leg.

"*Prima*, don't look so mad."

"I just…I can't believe I let you convince me to wear this."

"Mané, she wanted to wear these jeans that were big enough to fit that fat guy over there."

Valentina pointed to a tall man at the other end of the bar. The fat from his stomach hung over his pants, and his jawline was lost in the rolls of fat around his neck.

"I told her she needed to wear something that showed off her figure. She has an amazing body. She shouldn't be hiding it. Look, *prima*, I don't know what the gringos like, but here men like to see a woman's body."

"Fuck what men want, Andrea," said Mané. "But I can only imagine how ugly those big-ass pants must have been!"

"So ugly!" Valentina agreed.

"I haven't worn tight pants in like two years," Andrea said. "I feel gross."

"You look fine. Come on, let's get some drinks," Mané said.

"Mané I don't have a fake ID."

"Why would you need a fake ID?"

"*Prima*, we can drink here," Valentina explained. "Nobody cares. What should we get? Rum? Aguardiente?"

"It's her first night out in Colombia. Aguardiente *mija*!"

A clear glass bottle was placed on the table, along with three shot glasses. Mané cracked open the bottle and poured the crystal-clear liquid into Andrea's shot glass.

"You're not really Colombian until you get drunk on aguardiente, dance salsa with a Caleño, and fuck a Colombian. So tonight at the very least you get to check one off the list," Mané said, raising her shot glass. Valentina and Andrea did the same.

"*Prima*, may your first night out in Bogotá be incredible!" Valentina added.

Andrea brought the shot glass to her lips. The clear liquid smelled of black licorice. Andrea loved black licorice. She downed the entire shot in one fell swoop. The aguardiente slid down Andrea's throat, instantly setting her insides on fire. Her body contracted with shock. She coughed violently. Valentina and Mané burst out laughing.

"It's time for another one," Mané announced.

Unable to speak through her fit of coughing, Andrea shook her head no.

"Trust me. If you drink another one right away, the rest of the night they'll go down like water."

"Really? I never knew that," Valentina said.

Mané's eyes shot daggers into Valentina for her naïveté.

"Just have another one, *prima*," said Valentina, ignoring Mané's look. "We'll take care of you. Don't worry."

Andrea grabbed the shot glass. Without her even thinking about it, the aguardiente disappeared down her throat. She shivered in disgust but embraced the lightness in her head. She closed her eyes. She was surrounded by music. The song was unfamiliar, but the rhythm felt like home.

"Vale, what kind of music is this?"

"Merengue. You just kind of march in place and move your hips," Valentina answered.

"You wanna dance?" Mané asked.

"No way," said Andrea.

"After a couple more drinks, you'll be dancing on the tables, *prima*," Valentina told her.

Three more shots appeared on the table. The girls drank them as if they were drinking water. Andrea's head spun. Her tongue, which for the last few days had been weighed down by the awkward twists and turns of Spanish, was light and nimble with the taste of aguardiente. Her tongue enjoyed the ride of rolling her *R*'s. She uncrossed her arms and fell into the comfort of her body. She crawled out of her ache. She enjoyed the music blaring overhead. The singers sang of places Andrea had never heard of, telling stories from a history she was unfamiliar with.

"Vale, what's this song?"

"This is Colombia, *prima*. It's called *cumbia*."

She closed her eyes and breathed in the rhythm that surrounded her. The music pulled at something inside her, and she found the warmth of home as the *gaitas* danced with their interlaced melodies. The drums beat to the rhythm of her heart. The singer's soulful voice wrapped around Andrea's hips and rocked them to the words of her heartbreak. Andrea disappeared into the sounds of her ancestors. She heard the cries of her African grandmothers and grandfathers as their chains dragged on the cobblestone streets of Cartagena. She saw her Wayuu brothers and sisters slaughtered by the viruses her Spanish mothers and fathers gave them. History boiled inside her. It was both familiar and foreign to her, just as Colombia was.

She opened her eyes and saw Mané tapping her fingers to the beat on the thick wooden table and her heart sank. Rebeca flooded her mind. She wondered what Rebeca was doing. Was she wandering the desert alone? Dancing in a dark corner of an abandoned house with a man whose name she did not know? Was she as drunk as Andrea? Was she missing her so much it hurt? Andrea slowly sank back into her ache and wrapped herself in its blackness. Its thickness held her hips in place. The music flooded her with the painful sting of loneliness. She needed to escape.

"Vale, I'll be right back."

Andrea stumbled outside. Bogotá's chilly air fell upon her. Her eyes focused on the kids on the corner as they sold gum and cigarettes to passersby whose jeans cost more than they would ever earn in a year. She laughed at the stupidity of it all.

"*Mamita*, you look lonely. I can take good care of you tonight."

A short man with dark skin and even darker hair stood in front of her. His wrinkles were full of worry, his eyes blackened by the cruelty of life. Andrea muttered under her drunken breath: "Fuck you."

"Oh, a *gringa*. Perfect. I teach you Spanish and you teach me English."

She slurred the *F* as it fell out of her mouth, and the *U* stuck to the *CK* as she spit it out. Her body swayed back and forth. An arm came from behind her and grabbed her around the waist. She forced her eyes to focus on Mané's beautiful porcelain face.

"Mané!"

"Andrea, you make friends wherever you go, don't you?"

"Well, with that pretty face, how could she not?" said the man.

"Have a good night," Mané said to the man.

"Come on! We can all have a fun time tonight," he answered

"Any night with you would be far from fun. Good-bye," Valentina said as she joined them on the sidewalk.

The girls watched as the man walked away down the lopsided sidewalk.

"Let's go before you get us into real trouble," Mané said to Andrea.

"I don't want to go home," Andrea told her.

"We're in Colombia. We're not going home until the sun rises," said Mané.

Valentina sat Andrea down on the cold concrete. Mané sat on one side of her, Valentina on the other. They used their bodies to hold her up. Mané pulled the bottle of aguardiente from her black overcoat and gave it to Andrea.

Andrea took a long swig from the almost empty bottle. Valentina grabbed the bottle and took an even longer swig. Andrea looked up to the sky, which was shrouded in clouds. She looked around her. Cars surrounded them.

"Where are we?" she asked.

"It's my after-party spot," said Mané. "No one will bother us here. I know the parking attendant. He's cool. We just have to give him some of our *guaro*. And we can stay as long as we want."

"*Guaro?*"

"*Ay, prima*...Short for *aguardiente*," said Valentina.

"*Guaro*...I want more *guaro*. Please."

"Andrea, why is your Spanish so shitty?" asked Mané.

"'Cause after my dad left, my mom only spoke to us in English. She needed to practice her English, so no Spanish in the house."

"Where did your dad go?" Mané asked.

"I don't know. He told my mom he got a job in Miami, and then he never came back."

"Never?"

"Nope. Asshole just left us. But I don't really care. I mean, I never really knew him, so fuck him! Give me some more *guaro*. Please."

"How old were you when he left?'

"I was six. My brother was ten. I haven't seen the fucker since."

"Your dad can join my dad in the fucking-asshole club," Mané said.

"What did the asshole do to you?" Andrea asked.

"He left my mom when she got cancer."

"That's fucked-up! Is your mom okay?"

"Yeah. For now."

"I don't talk to my dad, either," Valentina said.

"Really, *prima*? Why not?" asked Andrea.

"I don't really know. My parents got a divorce when I was really small. I call him all the time, but he never calls me. He just never wants to talk to me."

"Well, fuck him, too," Andrea cried. "Fuck dads! Who needs them, right? If they don't want us, well, we don't want them. It's their loss. They probably have miserable lives, anyway. They're all fucked-up and old and unhappy wishing they were with us, but we don't want them. So fuck them and their shitty lives."

With each word Andrea's voice cracked with the years of pain she had stored in her heart. Her tears twisted around her hatred, her pain, and her unanswered questions. Her tears fed her ache, making it grow darker and bigger. It was on the verge of swallowing her whole.

Valentina protected Andrea from the darkness that threatened to drag her down. She carried her cousin home and placed her in her bed, watching over her until her tears ran dry.

"*Prima*...I have to tell you something," Valentina said.

"What, Vale?"

"I know where your father is. I heard my mom talking about it with Abuelita."

Silence. Andrea felt herself sinking into a hole that was blacker than night. The silence screamed. She dug her fingernails into Valentina's hand. She was falling into the deepest part of her ache. A dangerous place.

Andrea stumbled out of bed toward the bathroom.

"*Prima*, where are you going?" asked Valentina.

"I think I'm gonna be sick."

Valentina stood up.

"No. I'm fine," Andrea told her. "Just go to sleep."

"But—"

"I'm cool. Good night."

Andrea locked the bathroom door behind her. Her eyes landed on the razor resting on the clean white tiles. She grabbed it. Her breath quickened as she stared at its sharp blades. She looked at her smooth caramel skin, searching for the perfect place to meet her savior once again. She pressed the razor against the top of her wrist. Her heart pounded and her breathing grew shallow; her hand shook as she slid the razor across her wrist. She watched as her blood fought its way out of her body. Suddenly in the darkness there was light. In the silence there was sound. She stopped falling into her ache. She lay on the cold tile floor of the bathroom, shivering.

Time seemed to stop inside the bathroom walls, but somehow reason prevailed. Andrea meticulously wiped away any evidence that might reveal her secret. She cleaned the razor until its edges sparkled in the light and placed it just as she had found it at the shower's edge. Bloodstained tissues were flushed into the bowels of the city. She tied a wide yarn bracelet around her wrist, making sure her secret would stay secret.

Andrea stepped out of the bathroom ready for sleep. She did not want to sleep alone, so she curled up alongside Valentina. Andrea's dreams wrapped her in memories of her childhood. Her grandmother's laugh enveloped her. Her mother's off-key singing comforted her. Her brother's smile reassured her. Hours later, her eyelids fluttered open. Sunlight filled the room. A silhouette sat on the edge of her bed. She wiped the sleep from her eyes and was shocked by what she saw: Her *abuelita* smiled at her. Andrea wrapped her arms around Amparo. Time had changed her. Her body felt fragile in Andrea's arms, and her brown hair was now white as snow. Her skin was like sandpaper, and her hands bore the brown marks of age and worry. But her grandmother's smile was the same smile she remembered. Amparo laughed in delight, her laugh bouncing from the ceiling down the hall and out into the streets of Bogotá, just as Andrea had always remembered it.

"Abuelita!"

"*Piojito!*"

They rocked in each other's arms, searching for the years they had lost. Amparo took her granddaughter's face in her hands. The little girl she had helped raise was still alive in the corners of Andrea's eyes. Amparo found her in the soft pink lips she loved to kiss. But she also saw the heavy years lived in the creases around Andrea's mouth. She saw the sadness of the past in Andrea's hunched shoulders. She saw the confusion in her eyes.

Andrea laid her head in Amparo's lap, just as she used to do when she was a small child in need of soothing. Amparo's long fingers stroked Andrea's hair. Andrea found comfort in each stroke. Each caress reminded her of her childhood.

"Andrea, what's wrong? You have *mamitis*? You used to always get *mamitis* when your mother worked too much. You want to call her? We can call her."

"No, it's not that."

"*Mi amor,* what is it, then?"

"Abuelita, you know where my dad lives?"

"Yes, Andrea. I do."

"Why didn't my mom tell me he was here?"

"*Piojito,* she didn't know. She doesn't want to know anything about him. She's asked us not to tell her anything."

"How long has he been here?"

"A couple of years, I think."

"Have you spoken to him?"

"No."

"Do you know—"

"I don't know anything about him. I don't want to know anything about him."

"Where does he live?"

"Close by. Your *tía* knows a lot more than I do. We can ask her if you want to see him."

"Excuse me," Andrea said suddenly. "I have to go to the bathroom."

The bathroom spun in circles as Andrea turned on the water. Its coldness felt good on the palms of her hands. She splashed her face with it. She wanted to wash away her fear and watch it disappear down the drain. She wanted the thoughts of her father to go back to where they lived, in the quiet corners of her almost forgotten memories. But he was alive now. He was no longer a faded picture on a refrigerator or a strange man who once gave her candy in a distant airport. Father and daughter were breathing the same air, in the same city. His proximity burned her. She dug her finger into the cut on her wrist. The pain shot through her arm. Her brain screamed for her to stop, but her heart begged her to dig deeper. She stared at herself in the mirror. She knew she needed to put out her father's fire. She dug her finger deeper, and finally the bathroom stopped spinning. She had made her decision. She stepped out of the bathroom.

"Abuelita, I want to see my dad."

"Okay, *piojito*. We can arrange that."

"No, I want to see him today."

"What do you mean, today?"

"I mean I want to go to his house right now. My *tía* knows where he lives. I want to drive to his house and knock on his door. I want to talk with him right now."

"You're sure?"

"Yes. And I want you and Vale to go with me."

"Okay."

The next hour was a whirlwind of emotions and a flurry of action. Showers were taken before the water even had the chance to heat up. Not a word was said over the *arepas* and *chocolate* Gloria served. As soon as the last bite was eaten, Valentina, Amparo, and Andrea walked out of the house, fully aware that change was in the air. The car sped them through Bogotá's chaotic streets toward the answers Andrea had been chasing her whole life. With every stoplight Andrea's heart pounded harder. A tornado of questions swirled inside her. What did his house look like? What type of neighborhood did he live in? Did he live alone? Did he have another daughter? Would he remember her? Would he want to see her? Her stomach was filled with butterflies that pushed her heart to the brink of exploding. Suddenly the car stopped.

"We're here, Señorita Andrea," William said.

Andrea looked out the window. The white, two-story building William was pointing to was a dirty, run-down apartment building. The windows were long rectangles that covered the entire front side of the building, sheer white curtains hanging behind their dirty glass. An ugly brown fence surrounded the house. The maroon door added a touch of sadness to the building. *He left us for this?* Andrea thought to herself.

"*Prima*, do want us to go with you?" Valentina asked.

"No, just wait for me here."

Andrea's feet felt heavy on the sidewalk. She focused all her energy on peeling her feet off of the sidewalk and placing them in front of her, one at a time. Each step toward the house was an effort in concentration. As she approached the somber maroon door, she felt a thick and impenetrable wall rise up inside her. Her butterflies suddenly turned into angry wasps that swarmed in her stomach, threatening to burst out of her mouth and attack everything in sight. Andrea's finger pushed the small yellow doorbell. As she heard footsteps behind the door, her eyes glazed over with a look as far away as the moon. The swarm of wasps grew even more ferocious. The door opened. Father and daughter stared at each other. They were complete strangers to each other, but their blood bound them together. His greenish-brown, almond-shaped eyes, which were the mirror image of her own, stared back at her. In their eyes two worlds, two social classes, and two countries collided. They stood in silence, lost in their familiarity. Finally Andrea spoke.

"I'm your daughter, Andrea."

Andrea watched as each word landed on Antonio. She saw his face transform at the realization that the young woman before him had once been the little girl he sacrificed so much for. She saw the few memories they shared flash before his eyes. Suddenly Antonio pulled her into his arms. Andrea did not move; her arms dangled at her sides.

"Andrea! Andrea, I can't believe it's you! How long have you been here? Where are you staying? For how long? Tell me everything. Come in. Come in."

"No. I'm fine. Thank you."

"You can't stay out here, it's freezing. Please, come in. Who are you with?"

"My grandmother."

"Amparo? Where is she?"

"She doesn't want to come in."

"Well, you didn't come here to stand outside. So please, I'll make you something to drink. To eat. Come in."

Andrea's curiosity was stronger than her pride. She hesitantly stepped into the house. It was a small studio apartment with a full-size bed, mismatched furniture scattered about, and a large TV in the center of the room. It reminded Andrea of their first apartment in Los Angeles. She casually searched the house to see if she existed in her father's world. There was not any proof of her on the walls. She glanced toward his bed. There were a few newspapers stacked on top of one another, but she was nowhere to be found. Her eyes followed him as he walked into the kitchen. Andrea felt as if she were being crushed by the silence that filled the house. He opened the refrigerator, where two faded pictures hung from the door. One was of Andrea as a baby, sucking her thumb as Gabriel held her in his arms. Next to the baby picture was another photograph. It was of one of the only memories she had of her father. Gabriel, Andrea, and Antonio were at a baseball stadium, each wearing a blue baseball hat. Andrea sucked on a lollipop with a huge smile on her face, looking directly at the camera. Antonio and Gabriel screamed in delight as they watched the game, ignoring the camera.

Antonio's eyes caught the same photograph. *So much time has passed*, he thought to himself. How many times had he thought about Andrea and Gabriel? How many times had he wished things had been different? He had wanted to find his children, start over, and make up for all the wrongs, but he didn't know where to begin. When he had finally realized his mistake, his family had already moved from their little shoebox apartment. His shame kept him from searching too hard. Now life was giving him the gift of another chance.

Antonio closed the refrigerator door. He could not bear the silence any longer. Their conversation was an awkward dance of one-word responses, uncomfortable silences, and unexpressed feelings. With each question Andrea became more and more angry. She did not recognize herself in the shadow of her resentment. She felt marooned in a storm of unrecognized emotions. She was filled with a rage that paralyzed her. She wanted to run out of the house, but at the same time she did not want to leave her father's side. She wanted Antonio to hug her again, even though she was completely repulsed by him. She felt like a crazed animal that needed to attack its prey. She needed to taste blood. She had to do what she came to do.

"So, you haven't told me what you're doing in Colombia," Antonio said to her.

"My mom sent me here."

"Why? Is everything okay?"

"I don't know. Why don't you ask her/"

"I will."

"How are you going to talk with her?'

"I'll call her."

"You have our number?"

"No."

"Oh, that's why you never called. You didn't have our telephone number. Now it all makes sense."

"How's your brother?"

"He's a lot bigger since the last time you saw him."

"I am sure he is."

"How long has it been now? Ten years since you last saw him."

"It's been a really long time."

Complete silence. Andrea glared into her father's eyes.

"Andrea, I'm very sorry for everything."

"For what?"

"For not being there. For leaving. For everything. But I want to make it up to you. I know I really can't be your father anymore."

"I don't need a father."

"I know—look at you. I mean, you're practically all grown up. Look, I won't try to be your father, but I was hoping I could at least be your friend."

Andrea's insides twisted and turned and tightened around her heart. Her breath escaped her. Her arms tingled with an uncontrollable fury. He was telling her what he wanted instead of asking her what she wanted. The time had come. Andrea needed the answer to the question she had been asking herself for ten years.

"Why did you leave?"

The air was instantly sucked out of the room. Andrea held her breath while she waited for the answer she prayed would free her.

"Andrea...because...I was...irresponsible."

The word *irresponsible* hung heavily in the room. It rang loudly in Andrea's mind and stunned her heart. It made the wasps swarm ravenously in her stomach as her hands shook with rage. Of course he was irresponsible! That was obvious. Andrea needed to know why he did not call, why he never wrote on birthdays or Christmas. She needed to know what the world had offered him that was so much better than her.

Antonio stood in silence, unsure what else to say. He placed a glass of freshly squeezed orange juice on the counter. Andrea stared at it. She did not want anything from him.

"I have to go," she told him.

"Why?"

"Because."

"Wait, Andrea. Where are you staying? I'd like to keep on talking with you."

"No."

"Please, Andrea. Let's start over. Start fresh."

"No!"

Andrea turned around and walked out the door. Her ache was again raging inside her. The hidden hopes she'd held on to in the corners of her heart were gone. In their place was the darkness of her ache. She stepped into the car, looking fragile and broken. Amparo saw her pain.

"*Piojito*, what happened? What did he say?"

"Nothing. I don't want to talk about it. Let's go home, please."

Silence.

"*Piojo*—"

"I don't want to talk about it!"

"Okay."

The car pulled out into the chaotic Bogotá traffic. Valentina grabbed Andrea's hand and whispered in her ear, "We don't need them, *prima*. Remember, we don't need them."

Andrea nodded. It was true she did not need her father, but it was not a need she was looking to fill. She wanted to fill a yearning. A yearning she could not find the words to explain, a yearning that controlled her, a yearning she was looking to escape. She knew there was only one person who yearned as she did: Gabriel.

She had not called home since arriving in Bogotá, and the telephone felt heavy in her hand as she reached out to touch home. Gabriel's voice crackled over the phone line.

"Hello?"

"Hey, Gabi."

"Andrea? Is everything okay?"

He had stopped calling her *Piojito* when she'd started painting her eyes with charcoal-black eyeliner.

"Yeah, everything's fine. I just wanted to say hi and see how you are doing."

"I'm good. Mom's not here; she's at work."

Growing up, Gabriel and Andrea had been inseparable. Each was all the other had while their mom was at work.

"I figured she would be. I actually wanted to talk with you."

"Oh, okay. What's up?"

But adolescence had turned them into strangers. They barely said good morning and good night to each other. Gabriel did not understand Andrea's rage. Andrea did not understand Gabriel's constant need to be good.

"I went and saw Dad today."

"How did you find him?"

What they did not understand was that Andrea's rage and Gabriel's perfectionism came from the same place: the hole their father left when he abandoned them.

"He lives in Bogotá. A few blocks away from me."

"How does he look?"

For years Gabriel had dreamed about his father. He wondered if he would recognize him on the streets. He wondered if he looked like his father.

"I don't know; the same, I guess. He has a lot of gray hair."

"What did he say?"

Andrea never dreamed of Antonio. She never thought about him. She tried to pretend he never existed.

"He asked about you. He wanted to know how you were. I told him you were good."

"What else did he say?"

Brother and sister never talked about their father. Silence was easier to bear than rejection.

"He wants to keep on talking."

"Are you going to?"

For years, Gabriel had wanted nothing more than to see his dad.

"I don't think so, but I was calling to see if you want his address."

Gabriel's silence was heavy.

"I don't know," he finally said.

Gabriel was an adult now. His grown-up eyes saw the world differently.

"Well, if you want it, just let me know."

"Okay. Thanks for calling."

"Yeah, of course."

"How are you doing out there?" Gabriel asked.

"Good. I like it. It's different."

"Nice. Well, take care of yourself. Miss you."

"Yeah, me, too."

Andrea hung up the phone. Her yearning was still there. Her questions were still unanswered. So she did the only thing she could think of to do: She fulfilled her yearning with a nonstop stream of aguardiente and secret cutting. Her scars lay hidden under the countless yarn bracelets she refused to remove. She spent every Friday and Saturday night at La Tienda de Tuta, in Mané's parking lot, or lost in the depths of Tía Esperanza's fully stocked bar. Andrea was drowning in her ache. Her only salvations were the liquid black licorice she gorged on and the secret ritual she performed in her bathroom. Six months passed in a blur of Friday and Saturday nights spent over porcelain toilets and blood-soaked tissues. Andrea stripped away the gangster she had become in Little Quartz. She traded in her baggy pants for jeans that hugged her slender hips and shirts that teased the world with her perfectly rounded breasts. Instead of fighting on the streets, she went head-to-head with César in class. She stopped running from cops and started running toward salsa clubs. She ran wildly and freely until the day she smacked headfirst into Colombia's war.

It was a Sunday afternoon like any other. Roberto was watching television. Esperanza was sketching the world as she saw it from her tenth-story window. Valentina was curled up on her bed, cooing with her newfound love. Andrea was bored, and boredom was never a good thing for her. Boredom made her restless, and restlessness made her look for adventure. She found the adventure she was looking for on the kitchen table, in Tía Esperanza's shiny black half-open purse. Andrea's eyes zeroed in on her car keys. She snatched the keys and snuck out of the apartment.

Andrea's slender body nestled perfectly into the driver's seat. She turned on the engine and eased the car seamlessly into the chaos of the city. Cars were all around her. The grace with which she flowed between buses, taxis, and bulletproof cars hid the truth: that she had never driven. It was as if Bogotá's unwritten rules were written inside her. Andrea felt the power of true freedom for the very first time alongside the black smoke billowing from buses and the luscious green mountains that surrounded her. Her hands and feet had the power to drive her anywhere she wanted. She had the ability to escape; adventure and freedom were at her fingertips. She looked over at Mané.

"Mané, where do you want to go?"

"I don't know."

"We can get out of the city. Go to the countryside."

"Yeah! Let's do that!"

Andrea looked over her shoulder to change lanes, a maneuver that was too complex considering her inexperience. The car drifted ever so slightly while she searched for an empty space between two wayward buses. Suddenly the car smashed into the sidewalk. The sounds of steel curling over itself, concrete being crushed, and shrieking rubber screamed from the front of the car. Andrea slammed on the brakes. Andrea looked over at Mané, her eyes filled with fear. Andrea could not bear to get out the car. She was too afraid to see the damage. Other vehicles swerved around the unmoving car, and horns blared around them. Strangers hurled curses at her through their closed windows. There was not a lie she could invent that could save her, so she did the only thing she could think to do: drive home and wait for her punishment.

Andrea left the keys exactly as she had found them, then locked herself in her room and awaited her imminent doom. A few minutes later, Andrea heard Tía Esperanza walk down the hall and open the front door. The clinking of Tía Esperanza's keys played the song of her demise, and her heart sank into a pit of doom. Minutes passed that felt like hours. Andrea heard the front door open again. She took a deep breath and braced for the worst. Her bedroom door swung open. Esperanza's eyes were crazed with rage.

"What did you do to my car?"

"I-I-I...took it—"

"You took my car?"

"Yes, ma'am."

"Why did you take my car?"

"I don't know....I was bored...."

"Jesus Christ! Do you know what could have happened to you, Andrea? Are you stupid? What did you hit? Please don't tell me you hit someone!"

"No, no…I just hit the sidewalk."

"What am I going to do with you?"

Andrea stared at the floor. She had been here before. How many times had Mariana yelled at her? How many times had she seen that same frustrated look in her mother's eyes? Andrea felt a twinge of guilt as she looked at Esperanza.

"Andrea, I want you to tell Roberto what you did."

"What?"

"Yes, get up right now and go tell Roberto what you did. Now!"

Esperanza's finger pointed the way toward her punishment. Andrea slowly stood up, giving her aunt time to change her mind. But Tía Esperanza was resolute. Andrea walked down the long solitary hallway toward Roberto's bedroom. Large paintings of Christ's crucifixion hung from the walls, and she felt his eyes looking down on her in pity. An ominous glow seeped from underneath Roberto's bedroom door. Andrea was filled with dread. She rarely spoke to Roberto. A daily hello and good night were the only words they exchanged, but Roberto's presence was felt in the entire house, throughout the entire day. His anger exploded without warning or prejudice; his insults knew no boundaries. Andrea had witnessed Roberto's wrath as it took down Tía Esperanza, Gloria, and, on rare occasions, Valentina. She placed her hand on the doorknob, prepared to be next in his line of fire.

She found Roberto as he always was: sitting in his leather chair, watching the nightly news, not a hair out of place. His clothes were impeccable.

"Excuse me, Roberto, can I talk to you?"

"Yes, of course."

He did not look at Andrea. His eyes were glued to the television. Andrea started to speak and quickly stopped, her voice cracking with emotion. Her eyes welled with tears. Roberto turned to look at her. Andrea was stunned to have Roberto's complete attention. He turned off the television, and Andrea saw his harshness melt away. He looked at her, and she felt he was seeing her for the first time. She burst into uncontrollable tears.

"*Mija*, what's wrong?"

"I did something I shouldn't have done."

"Okay, well, I'm sure it can't be that bad. Not bad enough for all these tears."

His words were kind. She could not stop her tears. He took her hand in his and stroked it as tenderly as a mother caressing her newborn baby.

"Roberto, I took Tía Esperanza's car, and I crashed it into the sidewalk."

"Why would you do that?"

Andrea shrugged her shoulders. She could not explain to him her burning desire to be free. Her need to be impulsive. Her want for adventure. Her longing for an escape from her ache.

"Andrea, you know what you did was wrong."

"Yes, sir."

"I love having you stay in our house, but if you do something like this again, you will have to leave. Understand?"

"Yes, sir."

Roberto turned away from her. It was times like these that made him miss his father. He had been only ten years old when he died, but he still had vivid memories of his father's kindness. He remembered what an understanding father he was. Roberto's life rarely presented opportunities for such kindheartedness, but he cherished those brief seconds when he was able to be like his father. It made him feel close to him. It reminded him that there was a time when life had been so much simpler. There had been a time when he was carefree, happy, and innocent of the pain life brought. The loving memories of his father also brought with them a sense of loss. Roberto flicked on the television again to numb the pain. He lost himself in the war that was raging in the countryside. Andrea was unsure what to do. She watched the talking heads passionately argue whether peace could ever exist with the FARC. Would peace talks end the decades-old war, or further strengthen the rebels who threatened to tear the country to pieces? The men in ties screamed about things Andrea had heard of only in passing. Los Pepes, ELN, the personalized jail of the world's most-wanted man was an embarrassment to the country. A plane exploding in mid-flight was the country's latest nightmare. The bombardment of blood and death sent Andrea to her room. Esperanza followed right behind her.

"Andrea, don't think you're getting off that easy. You're grounded for a month. The only place you can go is to school. No phone, no going out, no nothing for an entire month. Understand?"

"*Sí*, Señora."

Andrea's days ticked by as slowly as thick, sweet honey dripping from a spoon. School was her only distraction from the monotony of homework, warm dinners, and melodramatic telenovelas. The only thing worse than the boredom was the solitude of the apartment. The house was almost always empty except for Andrea and Gloria. Andrea was forced to bounce back and forth between the two television channels Colombia had to offer. One day, overwhelmed by the nonstop news of Colombia's countless deaths, robberies, and political scandals, she turned off the television and went upstairs to play a game of pool—anything to ward off her boredom. As Andrea chalked her pool cue she heard the faint sound of music coming from the laundry room. The song intrigued her; it was different from the orchestral sounds of merengue or the easy grooves of salsa. This music had wind blowing through its rhythms and soul pulsating in its melody. Andrea peeked her head around the wall and saw Gloria standing in front of a large sink. Clothes hung from clotheslines all around her as her hands dunked and scrubbed to the rhythm of the music that blared from the small metallic radio on the windowsill. Gloria twisted the water out of the flimsy piece of cloth in her hands, then draped it over a clothesline. Andrea stared at the white cotton underwear Gloria had just washed. The underwear hanging on the line was hers. A knot twisted in her stomach. Gloria placed another pair of Andrea's underwear on the clothesline, and shame pushed Andrea back behind the wall. Images of Mariana cleaning other people's houses flashed in her mind. She remembered watching Mariana on her hands and knees, scrubbing other people's toilets. She remembered thinking as a child how disgusting her mother must have felt. She remembered the boredom of having to play alone in corners of rooms that were bigger than her whole house. She peeked back around the wall. Gloria was washing a pair of jeans.

"Gloria?"

"*Ay!* Señorita Andrea, you scared me half to death!"

"Sorry. I was just curious, what kind of music is that?"

"It's *currulao* from El Pacífico."

"That's where you're from?"

"No. I'm from Northern Cauca. A little village called La Toma. But we listen to *currulao*, too."

"I like it."

"I bet you you're the only *Rola* listening to *currulao* in all of Bogotá!"

"How long have you lived here?"

"A few years."

"You go home a lot?"

"Once a year, for Christmas. I go and visit my kids."

"How many kids do you have?"

"Two."

"Wow, you're so young. How old are you?"

"Twenty-four."

"How old are they?"

"Nine and six."

"Who do they live with?"

"Their dad."

"That's nice. What are their names?"

"Kevin and Francia. Are you ready for dinner, Señorita Andrea?"

"No, I'm fine, Gloria. Thank you."

That night Andrea's mother haunted her dreams. Mariana never spoke; she just watched. Her eyes took in everything. Andrea spent the whole night running from her mother's watchful eyes. The next morning Andrea woke up restless. Her ache was darker and heavier than usual. She trudged through her classes, barely speaking to Mané. César did not faze her. All she could think about was her mother. She arrived home exhausted. Gloria opened the door for her.

"Hola, Señorita Andrea. How was school?"

"Fine. Is anyone home?"

"No. I was waiting for you to get home because I have to go run some errands."

"I'll come with you."

"Sorry, Señorita, but you can't leave the house."

"Come on. It's just to the corner."

"Señora Esperanza said you couldn't leave no matter what. Sorry."

"Fine. Can you get me some ice cream, then?"

"Of course."

"But can you get the Santa Lucía one? You know, from the guy in front of the grocery store."

"Yes, of course, raspberry, I know. There's some food on the stove if you're hungry."

Andrea went to her room and threw herself on her bed. She never knew boredom could be so exhausting. She closed her eyes for what seemed like a second. Suddenly a thunderous boom rattled the house. The windows in the entire apartment shook uncontrollably. The entire city fell silent. Then it erupted in the chaos of sirens, horns, and screams. Andrea sat frozen in her bed, unsure what was going on. When the phone rang, she answered it in a daze.

"Hello?"

Esperanza's voice was frantic.

"Andrea, thank God you're home. Who's with you?"

"No one."

"Where's Valentina?"

"I don't know."

"I need you to call David and see if she's there. If she's not, then I need you to call all her friends—"

"Tía, what's going on?"

"A car bomb went off a few blocks from the house. Everything is going to be okay, but listen to me: Don't leave the house, and don't let anyone in, no matter who they say they are. Okay? I'll be home as soon as I can. Don't leave the house, Andrea! Call all of Valentina's friends right now!"

Andrea waited alone in the house for hours. Her only company was the television, with its vile images. *Why, why,*

why? screamed a woman as she tore at the twisted and charred wreckage of a car in the hope of finding her young daughter. Broken glass and pieces of wrecked cars carpeted the street, which was dominated by a large rainwater-filled crater where the bomb had exploded. Andrea's heart dropped when she saw the grocery store and a charred Santa Lucía ice-cream cart behind the crater.

Slowly, her family trickled in. Valentina came home first, then Roberto, and finally Tía Esperanza. They waited all night for Gloria, but she never came home. Andrea was devastated. With the sunrise began a new day. But her mind was stuck in the past. She knocked on Roberto and Esperanza's bedroom door. Roberto wiped the sleep from his eyes and slowly opened the door.

"What's going to happen to Francia and Kevin?

"Who's that, Andrea?"

"Gloria's kids."

"I'll take care of it. Don't worry. Go get some sleep."

Andrea could not sleep. For the past six months she had been living in a haze of aguardiente. Certain words lived in her periphery—*FARC, Los Pepes, peace talks, ELN*—but they meant nothing to her until death knocked on her door, shaking her out of her privileged ignorance.

chapter

TEN

Andrea's hands disappeared into the soapy water, her fingers wrapped around a pair of her underwear. She pulled the underwear out of the water and stared blankly at the light blue cotton. She watched as the iridescent bubbles slowly dripped back into the warm water. Andrea looked out the small window next to the sink. The tall brick buildings were familiar to her; she knew them well. They were all the same: a doorman in a drab gray suit, sparkling marble floors, elevators that led to houses with impeccable furniture and the maid's room adjacent to the kitchen. She wondered what was beyond the sea of redbrick buildings.

Andrea's hand caressed the old transistor radio in the windowsill. Did everyone's house have a radio like this one? She turned it on. A man's voice cooed from its tiny speakers. She smiled to herself and remembered Gloria's voice: "*I bet you're the only Rola listening to currulao in all of Bogotá!* Andrea closed her eyes. Gloria had been buried that morning. She tried to imagine the details of her funeral: a small wooden casket carried by her son, Kevin, her husband, and her brothers. She imagined Gloria in a white cotton dress, with her hair wild and beautiful, just as it had been in life. She wanted to believe that Gloria's home was between beautiful mountain ranges and rivers whose soothing water eased everyone's soul, both living and dead. She imagined music ringing out of the church, the *currulao* offering Gloria's family a certain comfort that only it could give. She pictured Gloria's honey-brown eyes living on in Francia as tears spilled down her cheeks. She envisioned Kevin's boyish face wrinkled with pain and worry, already looking far too old for his nine years of life.

The music stopped. Andrea snapped out of her daydream.

"Señorita Andrea?"

Andrea looked at Sirley. She stood motionless among the damp, hanging clothes. She was wearing the same cheap cotton dress Gloria had worn. Her short hair was pulled into a tight bun at the back of her head. Her skin was as black as midnight, matching the color of her eyes. She had a large scar from her ear to the bottom of her lip. She had arrived to the house yesterday, the same day Gloria's body was delivered to her family.

"Señorita Andrea, I should wash those."

"It's okay, Sirley. I'll wash them."

"But—"

"I don't want you to ever wash my underwear. Okay?"

"Yes, Señorita—"

"And you don't have to call me that. Andrea is fine. Where are you from?"

"Excuse me?"

"Your accent is different from everyone else's. Where are you from?"

"A little town called Riosucio, in El Chocó."

"Where's that?"

"On the Pacific Coast."

"Where *currulao* comes from?"

"Yeah."

"How long have you been in Bogotá?"

"I just got here a couple of months ago."

"Why did you come?"

"I-I had to."

"What do you mean, you had to?"

"We had to leave. They made us go."

"Who?"

" The men…*Ay, Señ*— I mean Andrea, I don't really want to talk about it. What would you like for dinner?"

"Nothing."

An awkward silence filled the washroom until Andrea asked, "Sirley, what happened to your face?"

Sirley's hand instinctively touched her scar. She looked at her feet, unable to speak.

Finally, she answered: "I don't want to talk about it."

Andrea turned back to the soapy water and dunked her underwear again. As she scrubbed it against the ribbed plastic sink, she watched her bracelets move up and down her slender wrist, exposing the corners of her silky-smooth scars, secrets she also did not want to talk about.

Andrea hung her underwear on the clothesline.

"Good night, Sirley."

The next morning Andrea waited for the school bus on the corner as usual. The sun shone radiantly on the morning dew as it kissed the flowers that had sprung up from the cracks in the sidewalk. Andrea watched the people around her. The welcoming sun brightened their usually dim faces. Their gaits as they crossed the street were looser, freer, and more open to the world around them. Their freedom was contagious. Andrea crossed the street, enjoying how her body moved under the Bogotá sun. She kept walking. She continued up the steep hill, cars zooming by her in every direction. In the distance she saw a beleaguered bus, its four wheels too small for its heaviness. Andrea wanted to ride that bus, so she hailed it. It did not matter to her that it was going in the opposite direction of her school. Andrea pushed the bus fare through the small opening in the clear plastic wall that protected the driver from his passengers. As she did so, she noticed that the driver had created an entire world behind his plastic wall. A large rosary hung from the rearview mirror. Stickers with slogans of love, Jesus, and peace reminded passengers that God was watching their every move. The *vallenatos* that blasted from behind the plastic wall perfectly complimented the driver's red velvet seat.

Andrea walked toward the back of the bus. She sat down in an empty seat next to a cracked window. Her seat was not made of red velvet. The wire coils threatened to burst through the black tape that held the worn plastic seat cover together. Andrea did not know where she was going, but she figured a window would help her decide. In starts and stops, the bus took her south. She watched as the city changed from beautiful brick buildings into nondescript, grimy structures. She passed large plazas filled with people and pigeons. The pigeons ate while the people sold blankets, sweaters, food, and jewelry. A childhood memory floated through Andrea's mind. The memory was blurry, almost as if it had never happened. She saw Mariana and Gabriel sitting on two small stools. She was on a pink blanket next to her mother. Andrea remembered stacks of books in front of her. She saw her mother taking money in exchange for a book. Then the memory disappeared as quickly as it had come. She stared back at the plaza, wanting to walk in the footsteps of her memories. She turned to the person next to her.

"What neighborhood is this?"

"We're coming up to La Candelaria."

The irony did not escape Andrea: She was ditching La Candelaria school only to end up in a neighborhood called La Candelaria. It seemed like a sign. She jumped off the bus and breathed in La Candelaria's magic as she wandered its steep, meandering streets. The cobblestone roads were so narrow that cars were barely able to fit on them. They were so unlike the wide and far-reaching arteries of the rest of the city. The narrow streets, street dwellers, and students kept the magic of La Candelaria alive. There was not a building in sight that stood more than a few stories tall. The red bricks that dominated the rest of the city did not exist there. The houses were made of thick adobe walls, the roofs of deep red tiles. The outside walls were painted in purples, whites, and blues. The windows were tall and thin, with wooden shutters from a bygone era. The streets were filled with children on their way to school, men on their way to drive the wayward buses of the city, and women going north to cook and clean for other women's families. Andrea walked up La Candelaria's hills while everyone else walked down. She was in no hurry, with no final destination in mind. She walked until an archway that led into a small plaza welcomed her.

The plaza was filled with people. Black blankets were scattered about, with bracelets, earrings, and necklaces for sale. Men with dreadlocks sat next to their merchandise as

-women with long skirts and even longer hair made jewelry. A woman with a guitar strummed a song. On the other side of the plaza, a man on stilts with a white painted face and a red nose entertained a small group of vendors. At the center of the plaza was a large, waterless fountain. Young men and women sat on its edge reading, smoking, or sleeping. Andrea walked toward the fountain. She sat and watched as life unfolded around her. She smiled at a young couple kissing on a bench. She wondered if her mother and father had held hands here, if they had kissed here, or if their love had died here. Andrea watched the strangers around her until her eyes landed on a young man sitting on the other side of the plaza in front of her.

He had caramel-brown hair that hung just above his shoulders. His beard was trimmed close to his face. His jeans were torn at the knees. His sneakers were worn on the outside. *He drags his feet,* Andrea thought to herself. He looked like the hundreds of other young men Andrea had met in Bogotá: a mix between Che in his younger years and the grungy gringos they loved to hate. He held a book with bent corners and a half-ripped cover. It seemed to be the only thing that existed to him. Andrea was intrigued by his mystery. She wanted to know what he was reading. She wondered what his name was. Why was he sitting alone? He must have felt her questions bouncing off his leather jacket, because he lifted his eyes and looked right at her. Andrea's breath escaped her. His eyes were the color of the green emeralds pulled from the depths of the Muzo mine. They transfixed her. Andrea watched him walk toward her, his feet dragging, just has she had imagined. He sat down next to her and Andrea breathed in the faint smell of coffee and cheap cologne.

"Next time you ditch school you should have a change of clothes in your backpack. You'll fit in a little more."

His voice was gentle, with a hint of sadness. He sounded like the wind. Andrea blushed. She looked down at her feet, too embarrassed to make eye contact. He followed her eyes, caught a glimpse of her red shoes, and burst into laughter. His laugh was boisterous, reminding Andrea of her grandmother's laugh. She grabbed at the fleeting sound and held it close to her. It was warm. It was kind. It was safe.

"Those are the ugliest shoes I've ever seen," he said when he stopped laughing.

"I know. I hate them."

"The girl with the fucked-up shoes. That's how I'm going to remember you."

"No!"

"You better tell me your name quick, before 'girl with the fucked-up shoes' is engraved in my mind forever!"

"Andrea!"

"Just in time. I'm Santiago. Where are you from?"

"From here."

"Not with that gringo accent."

"I'm from here, but I grew up in Los Angeles. You?"

"Born, bred, and raised here for generations. No one in my family has ever left this shithole we love so much. I'm going to get a beer. You wanna come?"

"Sure."

Andrea followed Santiago as they climbed to the top of a forgotten hill through narrow streets and steep stairways. Neither said a word. Santiago knew every bar, every neighbor's hardships, and every newborn in all of La Candelaria. His great-grandfather had come to Bogotá to escape the Thousand Days' War, while his great-grandmother had run from blood-soaked bananas. Their story began by accident on a corner of a forgotten street on a forgotten day, but ended with eight children and twenty-four grandchildren. Santiago came from a family of intellectuals who bled red, not for the Liberals, but for the communists who were changing the world. The blood of writers, musicians, teachers, and poets pumped through Santiago's veins while he studied anthropology.

Santiago finally stopped at a dilapidated yellow house. Andrea was completely out of breath, while Santiago had barely broken a sweat. The windows had mismatched shutters in different shades of green. A single lightbulb hung from the ceiling.

"It's the cheapest beer and the best *pandebono*. You can thank me later."

"Well, thank fucking God we did all that exercise, then," Andrea replied.

Santiago did not flinch. Andrea was impressed. No one in Bogotá could stand Andrea's filthy mouth. Andrea had become another person over the course of the six months she had been living in Bogotá, but her cursing was one thing she was not willing to change.

They sat down on flimsy metal chairs and Santiago ordered two beers. Andrea hated beer, but she could not bring herself to tell him. She did not want him to think she was a bourgeois girl from the north, a *gringa* requiring special treatment. She wanted to be accepted into his world without prejudice.

"So, Andrea, *la gringa*, what are you doing in La Candelaria in your school uniform?"

"So, Santiago, the Rolo, what are you doing in La Candelaria reading all by yourself?"

"Escaping."

"Me, too."

"From what?"

"I'm not sure yet. You?"

"A woman."

"Ah...I see. Did you lose her?"

"Not yet."

"Good luck with that."

"Thanks."

Their conversation flowed as easily as the cheap beer in front of them. They laughed more than they spoke. Their skeletons walked out of their closets and sat down at the table with them. Andrea told Santiago about her father. Santiago told Andrea how the love of his life, Rosa, had recently left him for another man. They laughed at the stupidity of tears and the need for aguardiente. Santiago confessed that he was a horrible dancer. Andrea admitted she cried too easily. He warned her of his sensitivity. She told him about her tendency toward melancholy. He corrected her constant misuse of *tu* and *usted* and she corrected his mispronunciation of his *O*'s in English. She told him about Gloria's death. He told her how at times he felt the only way to escape his broken heart was to walk toward death. Their confessions lasted until the sun began to dip to the other side of the earth.

"We should go. I'll take you home."

"It's cool, don't worry about it. I can get home by myself."

"Sometimes you're so Colombian, but sometimes you're such a *gringa*. Come on."

"Is that a compliment or an insult?"

"I don't know. It's the truth."

As they stumbled down the narrow stairs, their arms, hands, and fingers twisted and intertwined. Santiago hailed a bus while Andrea rested her head on his shoulder. It was a simple gesture, but it was Andrea's way of letting Santiago know she wanted more from him than just laughter and confessions.

Santiago walked Andrea to the door of her building. He kissed her on the cheek and told her good night.

"Santi, do you live close by?"

"No. I live in La Candelaria."

"What? Why did you come all the way here, then?"

"*Gringa* moment."

"Sorry," she said. "Listen, I'm going to have some people over next week. My *tía* is going to be out of town. You should come."

"Maybe. I'm supposed to see Rosa. So I'll keep you posted."

"Sure. No problem. You can bring her if you want."

"Cool. Good night."

"'Night."

Andrea floated up the marble stairs of the lobby. The butterflies in her stomach kept her walking on clouds all the way upstairs and into her bedroom. She lay down on her bed and stared at the ceiling. She reimagined her favorite moments shared with Santiago. She smiled at the memory of the constant tug-of-war between his hair sliding in front of his eyes and his hand brushing it away. She thought his half-eaten fingernails were sweet. She melted at the memory of Santiago biting his lower lip as he listened to her confessions. She drifted off and dreamed sweet dreams of Santiago.

The days leading up to Tía Esperanza's trip were a whirlwind. She was leaving for her first art exhibition abroad. Tía Esperanza's loneliness had pushed her into the joys of colors, textures, and canvases. She conversed with shadows and shapes like they were old friends. She made love with her fingertips to the grains of stretched canvases. Now colors had forged her road to Spain so she could share her secrets with strangers. She kissed Andrea on the cheek when she left, her car keys gripped tightly in one hand, Roberto's hand in the other. Andrea watched Tía Esperanza pull out of the parking lot and drive down the street toward the airport. She loved when Tía Esperanza and Roberto left her and Valentina alone in the apartment. She treasured not having to answer to anyone.

Andrea quickly began to transform the apartment. On the black granite countertops, she set out the alcohol: rum, vodka, whiskey, and her favorite, aguardiente. She made mix tapes filled with salsa beats, merengue, and Spanish rockathons. She pushed the couches against the walls so people could dance. She rolled up the carpets to hide the evidence from her aunt. She gave Sirley the night off. Two hours later, Esperanza and Roberto's apartment was filled with cigarette smoke, blaring music, and sweaty bodies. Valentina was in a corner, lost in the hands of her boyfriend; meanwhile, Mané was the queen of the pool table. With a never-ending cigarette in the corner of her mouth and a pool cue in her hands, she challenged anyone to try to dethrone her. Andrea slid through conversations and past sweaty bodies. She grabbed drags of cigarettes in between the hellos and good-byes of friends. She enjoyed orchestrating everyone's fun, but she never took her eyes off of Santiago.

Santiago had surprised Andrea when he rang her doorbell that night. She had called him twice since they met, but she was left waiting on the other end of a phone that never rang. For seven nights she had dreamed of him and his emerald-green eyes. She heard his voice whisper his secrets into the winds of her imagination. She felt his hands wrap around her hands as he walked her out of her dreams and into the radiant sun of her bedroom. For the past seven days, Andrea had awakened from her sleep with the desperate desire to hear Santiago's voice. Every morning was a battle not to call him. Andrea was being sucked dry by Santiago's indifference. His rejection was crushing her.

Andrea thought a bolt of jealousy might shake Santiago into noticing her. She began circling Santiago by way of his friends. Her smile lured a scrappy friend into her arms. A song of primal love blared through the speakers, and she held his friend close as their bodies moved in unison. She caught glimpses of Santiago as she twirled on the dance floor. He clutched a bottle of rum to his chest as his friends surrounded him, never even glancing her way.

Andrea pulled Mané into the bathroom.

"This better be important," Mané told her. "I got twenty thousand pesos on that game, and I'm kicking Diego's ass."

"Mané, I'm totally into Santiago."

"So why are you in the bathroom with me?"

"He's not paying attention to me."

"Make him pay attention to you."

"I'm trying. I don't know what else to do."

"Andrea, you're too smart for these stupid games. Just tell him you're into him."

"But I want him to make the first move."

"Andrea, stop the bullshit. Stop being such a girl. You like him. Tell him. See what happens."

"And then what?"

"See if he's into you."

"And if he's not?"

"Just don't cry."

"Great. Thanks, Mané."

As Andrea walked toward the dance floor, she saw Santiago walking in her direction. She surprised herself by reaching out her hand and stopping him, her boldness born of her desperate need for his attention.

"I haven't seen you all night," she said to him. "Come dance with me."

"Sure."

She placed her hand in his and her heart melted. He wrapped his other hand around her waist and rested it in the small of her back. She felt her knees go weak. Santiago guided Andrea slowly around the dance floor. He was shy in his movements. Andrea gently brought him closer to her. He in turn pulled Andrea closer to him until they were dancing so close their cheeks brushed, their bodies melting together. No one led, no one followed. Andrea whispered into Santiago's ear, "Santi, let's get a drink."

Out on the terrace, they breathed in the fresh night air. The night was crisp and the air felt good against Andrea's sweaty body. The night sky was clear, with a full moon. Andrea realized she had come to love the typically cold Bogotá nights. She poured two shots.

"Now or never. Cheers," Andrea said, toasting.

"I vote for now. Cheers."

The rum slid down their throats as easily as water.

"Santi, I have to tell you something."

"What's up?"

"I-I think you're really amazing."

"Um. Okay. Thanks."

"What I'm trying to say is...I-I like you. I'm really into you."

Silence.

"Look, Andrea...you don't want...I'm really...I'm... I'm...broken right now."

"So am I."

Andrea took Santiago's small hand in hers and their fingers intertwined. It was a perfect fit. His palms were damp with nerves. Hers were warm with desire. She looked into the eyes that had taken her breath away only days before and saw the depth of his pain. He quickly looked away, unable to let her in. She took a step toward him, walking on a plank of vulnerability. His rejection would kill her. His love would save her. Her body trembled with the fear of both.

Santiago allowed himself to see Andrea for the first time: her large brown eyes, her perfectly arched eyebrows, her thick lips. As he looked at her, he became enchanted. He ran his fingers through her hair and pulled her close to him. His lips gently kissed hers. Their breath quickened with their longing. Their tongues tasted each other's sweetness. Their desire slid down their throats and led them into Andrea's bedroom. Santiago left a trail of wet kisses on her neck while his hands discovered the perfection of her breasts. Andrea slipped out of her shirt and stood exposed before him. He took in her beautifully large nipples. He was in awe of her supple brown skin. His fingers caressed the curves of her waist. He whispered into her ear, "You're so fucking beautiful."

Andrea felt beautiful. She felt her beauty transform her into a woman. She walked across her room no longer a girl, but a woman who led Santiago to her bed.

Santiago laid her down on the white sheets and slid off her pants. The room filled with the smell of her earthy wetness. He kissed her breasts. Andrea moaned in pleasure. His fingers discovered her wetness. Waves of pleasure and pain pulsated through her body. His tongue discovered her neck, her ears, her stomach, and then slowly made its way down between her legs. His tongue touched the center of her womanhood. Its wetness sent waves of shock through her body. His tongue moved slowly, seductively, inside her, outside her, touching every part of her. She was wild with desire.

"Santi, I want you inside me."

He pushed her legs open, gently pressing the breath out of her to make room for himself. She dug her fingernails into his flesh, sharing her pain. He tenderly pushed and pulled inside her until she opened to him completely. Until she was finally his.

Santiago made love to Andrea cautiously, slowly, and finished quickly without warning. Andrea was confused. It all seemed to end too soon. He lay down beside her while he caught his breath.

"Sorry."

"About what?"

"Come on, you're gonna make me say it? Normally I have a little more control."

"It's okay. I liked it."

"*Ay*, Andrea, we've been honest with each other since we met. Don't start bullshitting me now."

"Well, I wouldn't really know the difference."

"What do you mean?"

"That was my first time."

"Ever?"

"Yeah."

Silence filled the room. Andrea waited for Santiago to speak, but he disappeared into his thoughts. She watched as he fought a futile battle against the tears welling in his eyes.

"Andrea, I've been carrying around this tightness in my chest for the past five months. And no matter where I go or what I do, it's always there. It kind of controls me. I can't get rid of it, you know. It's like she's always with me 'cause the pain is always with me. I don't see anyone else. I don't notice anyone else. It's been just me for the past five months."

They sat in silence for a long moment, until Andrea asked, "You haven't slept with anyone since you and Rosa broke up?"

"No."

They both lay perfectly still in the heavy silence surrounding them. Neither was sure what to do with the responsibility that had been laid at their feet. Andrea was suddenly, inexplicably overcome with laughter. Santiago looked confused, which made her laugh even harder. She fought to compose herself.

"Santi, let's go get something to eat. I'm starving."

"Wait. What was so funny?"

"Life. Life is fucking hilarious."

"Yeah, I guess so, *llave*."

"*Llave*? Did you just call me a key?"

"Yeah."

"Why are you calling me *llave*?"

"It's like when gringos call each other *dude*."

"Um...Okay?"

Santiago watched as Andrea's naked silhouette moved to the window and peered out. The orange glow of the street lamp kissed the nape of her neck seductively; its shadows caressed the curves of her backside. Andrea did not need to see Santiago to know he was lost in her body. She felt his eyes memorizing her curves and imperfections. She felt Santiago slowly falling for her.

chapter

ELEVEN

Andrea lay on Santiago's bed, entangled in his arms. The sheets twisted around their feet as they melted into each other, their bodies fitting together perfectly. Andrea's mouth ended where Santiago's began. He ran his hand through her hair; she gently bit his shoulder; he ran his nails down her back; she buried her face into his neck, inhaling his sweet smell; their eyes found each other just as their waves of pleasure overtook them. Andrea's moans mingled with Santiago's panting as they fell into each other's sweaty and exhausted arms. She looked at him. After two months, he was no longer afraid of her penetrating gaze, her loving caress, or her passionate kisses. Santiago and Andrea rediscovered the joy of kissing with each other's lips. They reignited the excitement of holding hands. The daily fog of living was lifted when they looked into each other's eyes.

"Santi, what are thinking about?"

"How beautiful the moonlight makes you look."

"Thanks. You, too."

"I look beautiful? Not really what I want to hear."

"Why not?"

"Beautiful? How about *hot*. I'll even take *cute* over *beautiful*."

"Okay, fine. Santi, you are *hot*!"

He smiled and ran his finger down her forehead, over the bridge of her nose, past her lips, and down her neck, stopping at her heart. He looked back up at her.

"What?" she asked.

"Nothing."

"Santi, what? I can tell you want to tell me something."

"No, I promised I wouldn't."

"Okay, well, now you *have* to tell me."

"No. Come on, Andrea. I don't want to."

"But I want you to. Please."

He nestled his face into her neck. She felt his heart pounding through his chest. He took a deep breath and whispered into her ear.

"I'm falling in love with you."

Silence fell. Time held still. Andrea felt her ache filling with Santiago's love. "Santi…I'm falling in love with you, too."

The words she had never said. The feeling she had never felt. She smiled at Santiago. He smiled back.

"You're pretty amazing, *llave*."

"Santi, confession time."

"Go ahead. I can't wait."

"I really don't like it when you call me *llave*."

"What? Why?"

"Because it's something you should say to your guy friends. 'What's up, *llave*?' Not something you should say to a girl lying naked in your bed."

"Obviously this is a *gringa* moment."

Santiago got out of bed. He grabbed the tattered book he had been reading the day Andrea met him and jumped back on the bed. He flipped through the pages, cleared his throat, and read out loud:

"In the suburbs of Havana friends are referred to as 'my earth' or 'my blood.' In Caracas, a friend is 'my bread' or 'my key': bread because of bakery, the fountain of good bread for the hunger pangs of the soul; and key...

- Key, because of key—Mario Benedetti tells me.

And he tells me that when he lived in Buenos Aires, during the time of the terror, he carried five keys on his key chain that were not his: five keys, of five houses, of five friends who saved his life."

His green eyes smiled at her. His finger gently touched her bare hip.

"Get it, *llave?*"

"Yeah. It's beautiful," she said, and then she fell silent for a moment, thinking. Then she asked,

"But what is the 'time of the terror'?"

"You're so cute, it's hard to be mad at you."

"Another *gringa* moment. I know."

"He's talking about the dictatorship in Argentina. Over thirty thousand people were killed."

"Why?"

"Because they wanted change. Benedetti is one of the most important writers in Latin America, but not even that could save him during the dictatorship. Only his *llave*s could."

"Did he write that book?"

"No, Eduardo Galeano did. It's called *The Book of Embraces*. It's a classic. You should read it."

"I will, but right now I should get home."

"No. Come on, stay a little longer."

"I wish I could, but my *tía* said I had to be home by seven. If I'm late she'll call Mané's house, and then I'll really be in trouble."

"All right. I'll take you home."

A short while later Andrea and Santiago stood at the edge of the marble steps leading up to Andrea's apartment. They kissed good night under the silver moonlight. She walked slowly up the white marble stairs, a woman conquered by love.

The elevator doors opened, and she was surprised to see William. The collar on his shirt was stretched out of shape, and his hands shook as he cleaned his glasses. As soon as he saw Andrea he frantically put the glasses on, and Andrea noticed that his brow was covered in sweat, his skin pale and ashen. Andrea hesitantly stepped into the elevator.

"Hi, William. Are you okay?"

"Good evening, Señorita Andrea."

He pushed the elevator button and stared straight ahead. The elevator was silent. Andrea felt an overwhelming nervousness coming from William.

"William, is everything okay?"

"I need you to come with me when I speak to your aunt."

"Why?"

"Just do as I say."

The words cut through Andrea's heart. *He must have seen me at Santiago's house!* Andrea panicked. If her aunt found out she had been at Santiago's house, she would be grounded her for months. She would never be allowed to see Santiago again. Tía Esperanza was obsessed with making sure Andrea and Valentina remained "good girls." She kept them on tight leashes when it came to boys. Going to Santiago's without permission, when his parents were not home, was absolutely against all of Tia Esperanza's rules.

Andrea needed to find out exactly what William knew. The elevator door opened and he stepped out, Andrea following behind.

"William, where are you coming from?"

Ignoring her, he opened the front door and walked down the hall. Andrea trailed him, her heart in her throat. Her mind was reeling. She was desperately trying to come up with a lie she could tell her *tía*. What if William had seen her in Santiago's bed? Surely she would be shipped back to the United States. Andrea's knees buckled at the thought. William knocked lightly on Esperanza's bedroom door.

"William, are you sure you want to do this?"

"I have to, Señorita."

Her *tía*'s carefree voice drifted through the door.

"Come in."

William opened the door and Andrea followed him into the room. With each step she felt her world crumbling around her.

Esperanza was painting a large canvas. She looked radiant, enveloped in the reds and purples around her. She turned around to greet her visitors. As soon as she saw William she froze because Roberto was not with him. William and Roberto had left together for the countryside that morning. Esperanza had pleaded with Roberto not to go to their farm; rumors were swirling that the countryside around their farm was giving shelter to the sons and daughters of the FARC. Roberto had ignored Esperanza. His blood was in that land, he said. His sweat had watered the mountainside. His tears had taken care of his workers for years. They would protect him.

"William, yes or no?"

"Yes, Señora."

The paintbrush fell out of Esperanza's hand. A single drop of red paint stained the lush white carpet. Tía Esperanza staggered to the bed. Andrea didn't understand what was happening. She did not know what William's yes had confirmed. William rushed toward Esperanza and helped her sit down.

"I'm so sorry, Señora. I did what I could, but—"

"William, what's going on?" Andrea interrupted. "What happened?"

"There were so many of them."

"Tía, what's he talking about? So many of who?"

"I haven't gone to the police yet. They told me I had to wait five hours before telling you, so I waited. I didn't know what to do."

"Who told you? Where is Roberto? Tía, where's Valentina?"

Esperanza snapped back into reality.

"Valentina. Where is Vale? She needs to get here now."

"Yes, Señora," William said. "I'll pick her up from her basketball game."

"Tía, what's going on?" Andrea pleaded.

"Roberto's been kidnapped," said Esperanza.

"What?"

"They've taken him to the jungle," said William.

"Who? Why?" asked Andrea.

"I don't know," William answered. "They were in military uniforms. They had guns. But they didn't say who they were."

"I have to call Miguel," Esperanza said.

"Miguel? Shouldn't you call the police?" Andrea asked, confused.

"Roberto always told me if I ever needed help with anything to call Miguel."

Andrea never understood why Miguel was always around. He seemed so out of place with the rest of Roberto and Esperanza's friends. Their friends were elegant, gracious, and gentle. Miguel was rough around the edges. He was loud. His words were too blunt, too harsh, too rough. He was a short man with wavy red hair. His double chin was almost as big as the potbelly that jiggled like Jell-O when he belted out the boleros he loved to sing. His voice was powerful and sultry, a complete mismatch to the gruff person who sang words of heartbreak and passionate love.

Miguel appeared at their house in what felt like seconds. He held Esperanza's hand as they whispered to each other in a corner. He spoke and Esperanza nodded her head in agreement. Andrea watched her aunt make a phone call, and minutes later the police invaded their apartment. Hours later everyone knew it was the FARC that had taken Roberto.

Andrea listened to William as he told the police officers about his last moments spent with Roberto. Roberto had been sitting in the back of the car as William drove up the dirt road that led to his farm in San Francisco. William jumped out of the car to unlock the front gate while Roberto looked out the window. He loved the smell of his farm; the sweet air, the green trees, and the open space always gave him a sense of peace. Roberto had traveled the world, but he never found a more beautiful or more peaceful place than the homestead nestled among the mountains of his farm. William got back into the car, and they drove to the front of the main house just as they had for years. Nothing seemed out of the ordinary. Roberto got out of the car and walked toward the front door. In the distance, a man's voice he did not recognize called out, "*Patrón!*" No one called him *Patrón* in San Francisco. Sensing something was wrong,

Roberto picked up his pace. Suddenly a loud gunshot went off behind him. Roberto froze. He slowly turned around. A group of ten men in army fatigues with large rifles hanging from their necks surrounded him.

"Come here," they ordered him.

Roberto approached the men.

"We've been waiting for you for a long time, Don Roberto."

"My name is not Roberto."

"Oh, no? Well, then we might as well kill you right now, because if you're not him we don't want you to go snitching on us."

All ten men pointed their guns at him.

"All right, all right. I am Roberto Valencia."

"Come with us."

"Where are we going?"

"Don't worry about it." They turned to the chauffeur. "You. What's your name?"

"William."

"William Chacón, if I'm not mistaken. You're going to stay in the house for five hours. Then drive directly to his house and tell his wife, Esperanza, that we have him. Tell her to wait for us to contact her. Don't even think about leaving a minute early because my men will be watching you, and they won't have any problem killing you."

The ten men surrounded Roberto. They began walking. William, with his heart in his throat, watched Roberto disappear into his beloved mountainside.

William's words hung heavy in everyone's heart. The police officers barraged him with questions. His heart broke with guilt after each answer. He felt he should have done more, but he was just one unarmed man against ten men armed to the teeth.

The night was long and dark. Ringing phones, police officers, and family friends filled the house. No one slept at all that night. Advice was offered as freely as water: *Do not go out alone. The family cannot negotiate with the kidnappers. A committee must be formed. Become friends with other families in the same situation; it will make you feel better. Talk to the media. Don't talk to the media. Get more bodyguards. Don't let fear control you. Keep living as before.*

Esperanza did not find any comfort in anyone's advice. The unanswered questions tortured her. How long would it take for the FARC to communicate the ransom? Where were they taking him? How long would he be gone? Was the rest of the family safe? Would they kill him?

Esperanza disappeared into her bedroom, hoping to find a moment of peace. Andrea and Valentina stayed close to each other all night. They did not say a word. They did not shed a tear. They just held hands, listened, and watched. Miguel called the girls over to him. His bloodshot eyes had large bags underneath, and the creases across his forehead were deep with worry.

"Girls, you are going to have to be strong for Esperanza. She is holding the weight of the world on her shoulders, and you two are going to have to prop her up. Do you understand what I'm saying to you?"

"Yes, sir."

"Good. Now go make sure she's okay."

Esperanza was lying in her bed, looking small and alone on the white sheets. Roberto's side of the bed seemed vast. His absence weighed heavily on her heart. Andrea kissed her *tía* on the forehead, then stepped back and watched Valentina do the same. Valentina hovered over her mother, holding back her tears. Andrea squeezed her hand, reminding her to be strong.

"Good night, tía," Andrea said gently to her aunt. "Let us know if you need anything."

Andrea pulled the curtains closed, creating a dark cocoon to keep them safe from the horrors of the outside world.

"Girls, will you please sleep with me tonight?" Esperanza asked.

"Of course, mami," Valentina answered.

Esperanza lifted her blanket, and Valentina and Andrea squeezed in beside her. They held one another tightly, hoping their combined strength would let them bear the weight of the frightful future that awaited them.

Andrea's nightmares startled her awake. Her *tía* was sound asleep next to her. Valentina was not. She sat up and saw light from the bathroom seeping under the door into the pitch-black bedroom. Andrea quietly got up and opened the door. Valentina was crouched on the floor, silently crying into a towel. Andrea pulled her cousin into her arms.

"*Prima*, I'm so scared."

"I know. Me, too."

"I kept dreaming that he had a chain around his neck and he was tied to a huge tree. He was screaming my name, but I couldn't find him because the jungle was too big."

"It's just a dream, Vale."

"But that's what the FARC does. They keep people in the jungle for years. For years, *prima*!"

"That's not what's going to happen to him."

"I never told him I loved him. He's the closest thing I've ever had to a dad, and I never told him I loved him."

"He knows you love him, Vale. Don't worry, he knows."

"But I want to tell him."

"And you will. He's going to come home, and you'll hug him and tell him you love him."

"But what if he never comes home?"

"He's going to come home, Vale."

"Are you sure?"

"I'm one hundred percent sure."

Valentina grabbed Andrea and held her tight. Andrea realized she was going to have to hold Valentina up. She was going to have to be strong for Valentina, so Valentina could be strong for Esperanza. Their ability to endure was inextricably intertwined: None of the three could survive without the others.

In the days following Roberto's kidnapping, from the outside, life appeared normal. Esperanza woke up at the same time every morning. The girls kept going to school. But small changes reminded everyone that life was far from normal. The girls no longer took the bus home; instead, William picked Andrea up the second she finished school and then rushed across town to pick up Valentina. Esperanza stopped painting. She spent her days debating hypothetical ransoms with her negotiating committee, trying to motivate lackadaisical police officers, and listening to the stories of mothers, daughters, sons, and fathers kidnapped and held in the farthest corners of the Colombian jungle. Esperanza felt the pain of the thousands of people who were tied to trees, who were being eaten alive by monstrous mosquitoes and dying a slow, torturous death of loneliness. Esperanza yearned for contact from Roberto, from his kidnappers, from the police. The silence was driving her mad. All she could do was sit by the phone and wait for it to ring. Ten days passed. The phone did not ring. Esperanza was frantic. Valentina was despondent. Andrea was angry.

Andrea came home from school on the tenth day of silence to an unexpected message. It was short and simple: *Your mother called. Call her right away.* Andrea picked up the phone and dialed the number to her old house, feeling as if she were reaching back in time to a past life that was no longer hers. Mariana answered right away. During her time in Colombia, Andrea had heard her mother's voice only a few times. She did not make the effort to speak with Mariana. When her mother called, Andrea hid in the corners of her new life. She wanted to forget everything she had been before she came to Colombia. Mariana was an unwelcome reminder of the stranger she had left behind. It was easier to simply forget the past than to try to understand the source of her darkness. But this was a phone call she could not ignore. She knew Roberto's kidnapping changed everything. Andrea heard the worry in her mother's voice as soon as she said hello.

"*Piojito*, how are you?"

"I'm fine. How's Gabi?"

"He's good. He misses you. How's your *tía*?"

"She's okay. I mean, as good as can be expected."

"Have you guys heard anything?"

"No. They haven't called yet."

"Andrea, I was thinking maybe it's time for you come to home."

"Why?"

"I'm worried about you. If something were to happen to you—"

"No. I'm not leaving my *tía* and Valentina. I won't leave them alone."

"But—"

"That's not what family does. We don't leave when shit gets hard!"

"They would understand. I'm just trying to protect you."

"Mom, I can't leave my *tía*—"

"Andrea, listen to me—" said a deep voice on the other end of the line.

"Gabi?"

"Yeah. You have to come home."

"You can't tell me what to do."

"I'm not telling you what to do. I'm just worried about you. We both are. Mom's not sleeping. I'm not sleeping. We miss you. Please come home."

"I can't. My *tía* needs me here. Valentina needs me. I have to be here for them. They've been here for me."

Silence.

"I'm not leaving, not now."

"If I convince Mom to let you stay, do you promise you'll come home when all this is over?

"I promise."

Mariana was silently proud that her daughter had the strength to carry the burden of the whole family on her tiny shoulders. Andrea was standing on her own two feet. Colombia's soil was a pool of blood, a grave of broken bones and spent gun cartridges, but her daughter was refusing to be knocked down.

Mariana got back on the phone.

"Okay, *piojito*. I want you to promise me you'll be careful. I would never forgive—"

"I promise, Mom. I'll be okay. Don't worry."

Andrea hung up. Her life was on the verge of unraveling. She needed to grab on to something that was grounded, secure, certain. She headed for the bathroom. Months earlier, Andrea had traded in her plastic razor for a proper razor blade. Now she pulled it out of its hiding place, tucked into a corner under the sink. She washed it under a cool stream of water. For months Santiago's kisses had dulled her ache, but now her mother's pleas for her to come home and the weight of her *tía*'s needs had awakened it with a vengeance. She pushed her yarn bracelets out of the way and focused on her smooth, soft skin. Her heart raced as the razor came closer to her wrist. Her mind screamed to hurry; her ache begged for relief. She gently slid the razor across her wrist. Her blood formed a beautiful red line as it escaped from her body. She held her breath. She waited for the stillness she desperately needed. It came for only a brief second, and then suddenly she was drowning in the darkness of her ache once again. She was panic-stricken. Her secret had never betrayed her in this way. Confused and desperate, she lifted up her skirt and hastily slashed her legs over and over. Blood poured down her thighs. She searched for her salvation in the pools of blood on the floor. Her hands shook as she waited for her peace.

A loud knock on the door snapped her back to reality.

"*Prima*, I need to use the bathroom."

"Can't you use mine?"

"No. I want to take a shower in my bathroom."

"I'm about to take a shower, Vale."

"Take a shower in your own bathroom."

"I never use that shower."

"Well, neither do I."

"I'm busy!"

"In *my* bathroom. You've been in there forever. Get out!"

"Just give me a second."

"It better not be dirty in there, *prima*."

Andrea's mind raced. Did Valentina know about her secret? How could she? She was meticulous about cleaning. Her scars were hidden underneath bracelets and long sleeves. She was so careful about her secret not even Santiago had seen the scars underneath her bracelets. She needed to get out of the apartment. She needed to escape from her family's watchful eyes. She was angry and frustrated. She needed Santiago. She needed to rest her head on his chest and hear his heartbeat. She hurriedly cleaned the bathroom and rushed out. She ran to Santiago's house, hoping his love would smother the fire that was threatening to consume her.

"Fuck the FARC, Santi," she said when she reached him. "Fuck all of them. How can they live with themselves knowing they are destroying people's lives? Do you know how many people my *tía* has talked to with kidnapped family members? Hundreds! Some people have been in the jungle for years! Years! Fuck them all! They all need to die and rot in and hell. All of them!"

"I'm not disagreeing with you. The FARC is horrible. I don't agree with what they do. All I'm saying is it's complicated."

"Complicated? What is complicated about kidnapping people and putting them in the jungle for years and years? What's complicated about killing people?"

"Why do you think they do it?"

"They're greedy bastards. They want to get rich off of people's pain. They don't want to work. They just want an easy road to success."

"Maybe now, but do you know why the FARC began in the first place?"

"I don't want a fucking history lesson right now!"

"It's important that you know why they exist."

"I know why they started their stupid war. They're communists. They wanted a revolution."

"Come on. I want to show you something."

Andrea and Santiago rode a bus south, past the twisty roads of La Candelaria and into the shifting shadows of Ciudad Bolivar. Dirt roads lined with half-built houses blasting music welcomed them into the poorest neighborhood of Bogotá. People came to Ciudad Bolivar not by choice, but because guns were put to their heads and they were told to leave the lands of their birth. Cocaine, oil, African palm, and gold were the reasons men with guns invaded their lands and forced them to walk down the long trail of tears to Ciudad Bolivar.

Santiago stopped at a two-story building surrounded by a large brick wall topped with piles of twisted barbwire.

"They really want to keep people out of here," Andrea said.

"No, they really want to keep people in. Come on."

They walked through a heavy metal gate. The courtyard was filled with pots of budding flowers in every color of the rainbow. The vivid flowers seemed out of place among the dull concrete and crumbling bricks. Inside, the building was spotless, but showed its age in its cracked ceilings and yellowing walls. A small woman with leathery, wrinkled skin sat behind a large desk.

"Hola, Santi. It's not Saturday. What are you doing here?"

"Hola, Doña Osana. I want my friend Andrea to meet everyone. Is Manuel here?"

"Yep. They just finished class. Go on up."

Santiago led Andrea up the stairs to the second floor, where they were greeted by another thick metal door. Santiago quickly typed in a code on a large lock and the door clicked open.

"Santi, what is this place?"

"It's a transitional home for kids who just got out of jail. A foster home for kids whose families can't keep them anymore. A place for street kids to sleep."

High-pitched screams surrounded them as the door clicked shut behind them.

"SANTI!!!!!!!"

A swarm of kids jumped all over Santiago. They wore blue cotton pants and light blue long-sleeved shirts. Some wore shoes, some had only socks on, and some were barefoot. The hard knocks of the streets were ingrained on all their faces, but they all had the innocence of children still ablaze in their eyes. The older kids were Andrea's age. They stood in a corner laughing as the younger kids pulled Santiago to the ground with their kisses. Santiago tickled the younger ones until tears rolled down their cheeks and they begged for him to stop. In all the commotion no one noticed Andrea. When the laughter finally subsided, a young girl with unevenly short-cropped hair stepped toward Andrea. She had dried snot around her nose and her two front teeth were missing. She extended her hand and pointed at Andrea.

"Santi, who's that?"

"That's Andrea. I wanted her to meet everyone."

"Hi. It's nice to meet you all," Andrea said.

"My name is Cindy," said the girl. "I'm ten. You have really pretty hair. Mine used to be long, too, but I had to cut it because I got lice here."

"The good thing," Andrea replied, "is that hair always grows back. Right?"

Cindy nodded in agreement and stepped back behind the rest of the kids. Everyone stared silently at Andrea.

"Santi, is that your girlfriend?" someone asked.

The room burst into laughter, whistling, and catcalling. Andrea could not help herself. She joined in the chorus of laughter.

"Yep. She's my girlfriend."

The whooping and hollering bounced off the walls. The rest of the day was spent laughing with the little ones, talking about the future with the older ones, and listening to all of their stories. Each tale etched itself inside Andrea's heart. She took the stories with her when she said good-bye and promised to come back.

"Santi, thank you for bringing me here. It…it was great."

"I'm glad you liked it. Even though at one point I was scared you were going to cry."

"I was about to."

"You shouldn't be scared of them."

"I wasn't. It's just…it's a long story."

"What?"

"It's complicated, Santi."

"Exactly. Just like Colombia is complicated. It's horrible that Roberto has been kidnapped, but you also have to try to understand why the FARC exists. I'm not talking about why they kidnap; there is no excuse for that. This country has been at war for thirty years, and we have to try to understand why, or else we'll never get out of the shithole we're in."

"To end the war, all we have to do is get rid of the FARC."

"Getting rid of the FARC doesn't solve Colombia's problems. Some of those kids in there don't have any other option but to join the FARC. Why? Because we have never dealt with the why the FARC began in the first place. Getting rid of the FARC does not take away the fact that those kids don't have any hope with how the system is set up right now. The system needs to change for them to have hope. Does kidnapping help change the system? No fucking way. But it's complicated. That's all I am trying to say."

"It's not so fucking complicated when your uncle has been missing for almost two weeks!"

Andrea was on an emotional roller coaster as the bus swerved in and out of cars and around potholes toward her home. She had grown up surrounded by hopelessness. She saw how it twisted and contorted young girls into rag dolls. Hopelessness slowly squeezed and stomped dreams to death, leaving empty shells that stole, fought, and killed without question. Only a few months earlier she, too, had been an empty shell, but by the grace of luck she had been brought back to life. Her empty shell had been filled with her grandmother's laughter, the cold air blowing over the Eastern Cordillera of the Andes, and the rollicking *R*'s of the singsong Spanish she had grown to love. Andrea felt heavy. She was confused. She kissed Santiago good-bye in a haze and prayed for refuge in the sanctuary of her bathroom.

During the time Roberto had been lost in the jungle, Andrea never knew what or who to expect at her house. Men on telephones seemed to be lurking in every corner, whispering their latest theories to other unknown men sitting behind desks in faraway places. The only quiet refuge was her bathroom. Now Andrea closed the door behind her and locked it. She pulled the razor blade out from its secret hiding place and pushed her bracelets out of the way. She needed to try one more time. She dug a corner of the razor blade into the meaty part of her wrist. As the blood oozed around the cold metal corner, Andrea waited for her ache to quiet, but it raged on. She dragged the blade along her wrist, but her ache only grew heavier, darker, more consuming. The trail of blood wrapped around her wrist. She stared at her blood as it ran down her arm. Her secret had failed her again. Time stopped as her ache wrapped its darkness around her heart and failure settled into her bones. Unsure what else to do, she placed her wrist under the stream of water. She watched her blood mix with water and the salt from her tears as it disappeared down the drain. She wanted to go with it and leave behind the pain that was raging inside her.

Andrea walked down the long hall into Esperanza's room, hoping to find a distraction from her internal hell. Esperanza was lying in her bed, staring at the television like a zombie. She seemed far worse than Andrea.

"*Tía*, you have to get out of bed."

"I'm too tired."

"Come on, *tía*. How about you take a shower, and we'll finish the ice cream in the freezer. "

"No, *mija*. I really don't want any."

"Please, *tía*. I really need some ice cream and I don't want to eat it alone. Please."

"*Ay*…fine. Let me take a quick shower."

Esperanza disappeared into the bathroom. As soon as she turned on the shower the telephone rang. Andrea answered it quickly. The connection was bad, but Andrea recognized Roberto's voice right away.

"*Hola, mija.*"

"Roberto! Where are you?"

"I don't know, but I'm all right."

"Let me get *tía*."

"No, I don't have a lot of time. I'm here with the *muchachos*, and they want me to make sure everything is okay with what they're asking for."

"Roberto, no one has contacted us."

"What do you mean, no one has contacted you?"

"No one has called. No one has written. We haven't heard anything from anyone."

"That can't be right."

"I know for a fact—"

"I have to go. Tell your *tía* I love her and I'm okay."

Roberto hung up the phone. He smiled at the toothless old man who watched his every move without ever looking at him. Roberto pulled a few crumpled bills from his filthy socks and discreetly handed them to the old man. Roberto had been astounded to find the bills in his pocket on his first night in captivity. As soon as he realized his captors' mistake, he knew the money would be the key to his salvation. The old man was the first door he unlocked with his crumpled bills.

Roberto sat down on the only other piece of furniture in the house, a rickety wooden stool. He was confused. His captors had been telling him they were in constant contact with Esperanza. They told him about detailed conversations they had had with her. They whispered to him at night how his freedom was only days away. Now his stomach dropped into the tortured depths of fear. The lies could mean only one thing. Every morning he was awakened by the butt of a gun and ordered to walk. He walked up mountains, through streams, in torrential downpours, and under the blaring sun. He walked and walked and walked. The young men with guns told him they were taking him to a safe house while they awaited the ransom, but Roberto now understood they were taking him south, deep into the jungle, where they would chain him to a tree and use him as their political pawn. This was a fate more terrible than death. It was a fate Roberto refused to accept. He promised himself as he sat in a forgotten corner in the country of his birth that he would rather die fighting for his freedom than live chained to the hell of the insufferable jungle.

An emaciated young man in army fatigues two sizes too big tapped his gun against the decrepit house. The sun was setting behind the mountains. Another night spent in the jungle. The thought sent shivers down Roberto's spine. The scrawny man led Roberto out of the small town and down the hill to a main road. They waited in silence. Roberto had stopped asking questions a few days after they had kidnapped him, having realized his captors were kinder to him when they talked about soccer, their families, or the homes they had all left behind.

Roberto looked up at the sky. Yellows mixed with purples and pinks created a canvas of exploding colors. He could not remember the last time he had contemplated the beauty of a sunset. A shooting pain ripped through his heart. He could not remember the last time he had told Esperanza she was beautiful. The first time he saw her he had been spellbound by her beauty. For months he told her every day how beautiful she was, but time slowly did its job, making him blind to her gorgeous eyes, her seductive lips, and her stunning hair. Roberto had been blind to her beauty for years now.

Roberto heard an engine in the distance. A small truck sped along the road toward the town. Looking at the sunset became too painful, so he focused his attention on the truck as it approached him and his emaciated captor. A tall man with a muscular build stepped out of the truck. Unlike all the other men, he did not have a rifle hanging from his neck. He stepped toward the young man, and they spoke quietly to each other. Roberto's eyes turned from the men to the truck. Roberto could not believe his eyes. The driver's door was open, and hanging in the ignition were the keys! Roberto's heart raced and his breath became shallow; he knew what he had to do. He looked at the men. They were engrossed in conversation. This was his chance. He ran to the car, jumped into the driver's seat, turned the key, and slammed his foot on the accelerator. The truck skidded down the road in reverse. He saw the muscular man pull out a gun from underneath his shirt, point it at him, and pull the trigger. A shot rang out, echoing across the mountainside. The windshield shattered. Roberto looked down, bracing himself for a river of blood, but there was none. He kept flying down the road in reverse. The road curved around the mountain and finally his captors were out of sight. He turned the car around and sped down the road. Roberto kept looking in the rearview mirror, waiting for the men to appear, but they never did. Instead, a few minutes later he came to a huge Mack truck parked across the entire width of the road. Roberto slammed on his brakes. He honked incessantly, but the truck did not move. Going back where he came from was out of the question. He needed to get around the truck. He stepped out of the stolen truck and ran to the edge of the road, peeking around the Mack truck.

"Hello? Is anyone here?"

Two men with guns stepped out of the brush. One said, "We will always find you."

Roberto dropped his head in resignation. One of the men talked into his walkie-talkie: "We got him. Alive."

"Good. I'll be there in five," came the crackling answer.

The man with the walkie-talkie put the gun to Roberto's temple and said, "If you try to do that again we'll kill you."

The following week was grueling for Roberto. As punishment for trying to escape, they made their walks through the jungle longer and cut down his already meager portions of food. The only time anyone spoke to him was to taunt him about his failed escape, or to tell him how much joy they would take in killing him the next time he tried to run away. Roberto was determined to get away, but he knew the only way his captors might let their guard down was if they thought he was broken. So he played their game. He pretended to be depressed, scared, and without hope, and sure enough, ten days later Roberto was given another opportunity to run.

"I've got good news for you, Roberto," said the man with a muscular build who'd shot at him days earlier.

"What?"

"You're not going to have to walk tonight."

"Why not?"

"We have horses for the next few days."

"I'm not the best rider."

"Well, I hope you're a fast learner, then."

On the outskirts of their makeshift camp stood five horses. They were scrawny, dirty, and on the verge of death. Roberto's horse was in the worst shape. Its hip bones looked as if they were about to tear through its skin. In its large black eyes Roberto could see it was tired of carrying men into and out of the depths of the jungle. Roberto stroked the horse's large head and whispered sweet nothings into its ears.

"Come on!" yelled one of his captors. "We have to ride through the night. Get on now."

"Is he a calm horse?" asked Roberto. "I don't really like horses."

"How the fuck should I know? They aren't ours. Let's go! Now!"

Roberto clumsily mounted his horse. The men kicked their boots against the horses' sides and trotted down the unmarked trail. They rode in complete silence, each keeping one eye on Roberto, the other on the thick bush, looking for lurking enemies. Night fell quickly under the canopy of trees. The skies opened and shed the tears of all the mothers whose sons' blood soaked the soil of Colombia.

Unable to bear the heartbroken cries of the thousands of mothers of the disappeared, the moon refused to shine. The stars were cloaked behind the thick black clouds. The night was so black eyes did not serve a purpose. All they saw was blackness. The raindrops were as big as *feijoas*. They splattered onto the ground, drowning out every sound. Roberto knew this was the moment to fight for his freedom or die trying. He had made the men believe he was afraid of horses, but Roberto knew horses like he knew women. He conquered them. He mastered them. So when the men let their guard down, hypnotized by the darkness and the constant beating of the rain, he grabbed hold of the reins on his feeble horse. Roberto's legs squeezed against the sides of his horse. It pushed forward, ahead of the pack. In the darkness, the men did not see him. In the rain, the men did not hear him. He squeezed the horse harder. It moved faster. Harder. Faster. Faster. Harder. Roberto listened through the splattering of the raindrops, trying to decipher how near or far the others were. Suddenly Roberto's horse veered to the left. Roberto knew that a horse always goes home, so he let it go wherever it wanted to go. He dropped the reins. He kicked the horse, hard, and it cantered through the mud, in the pouring rain, all night long, until it arrived at its home. Home was a small village with thatched-roof houses scattered about. Each house had a small plot of land in which grew yucca, plantains, and corn. Chickens pecked about freely. Roberto dismounted from his horse and removed the reins. He stroked its head and whispered into its ear, "Good girl. I promised you if you helped me get my freedom, I would give you yours. Go on, now."

Time was of the essence. He knew that by now his captors were looking for him. He tidied himself up as best as he could, but his overgrown beard, his sunken cheeks, and his filthy clothes were a dead giveaway that he had just escaped from the jungle. He knocked on the first door he saw. A woman with a child on her hip answered. She was short, round, and dark-skinned, with jet-black hair. As soon as she saw Roberto, she called out to her husband. Roberto heard the fear in her voice. Her husband came to her side instantly. He was a bit taller and a bit darker. His body was lean and muscular from working the land. He locked eyes with Roberto's, and then grabbed him by the arm and pulled him into his house.

"I don't want to know anything. Not even your name," the man told him.

"I need to get to a police station or a military outpost."

"The closest one is three hours away by boat."

"I have money. I'll pay you to take me there," Roberto pleaded.

"Your money won't buy my children another father if they find out," the man said.

"Let me buy your boat, then."

"They'll find you."

"Well, I can't stay here."

Silence. Roberto turned to leave.

"Wait," the man said. "The boat is in the back."

The muddy river snaked around the man's house. The boat was really a canoe with a small engine rigged to the back of it. It was tied to a tree trunk a few yards away. The back of the boat was filled with bananas. Roberto trembled as his freedom teased at the tips of his fingers.

"We'll hide you under the bananas, but no matter what happens, you cannot move," said the man.

Roberto scrunched into the back of the boat in the fetal position and the man piled the bananas on top of him. The three hours spent underneath the mountain of bananas was almost more difficult than the entirety of his kidnapping. With every stop Roberto felt his freedom slip further away from him, and with every start he felt the roar of freedom return. Finally the boat made its last stop. The man got out of the boat, freed Roberto from beneath the bananas, and helped him out.

"Thank you. Thank you so much."

Roberto reached into his sock and pulled out a roll of bills. He handed it to the man. The man waved it away, saying, "You might need it later."

"I have enough of it at home," Roberto replied.

"You might need it to get home. Just keep going straight, and you'll see the army barracks after about twenty minutes. Go."

Roberto turned around and ran as fast as he could until the cinder-block building appeared in the distance. Then he ran faster, his legs shaking. His heart felt like it was about to explode. When he finally arrived, he pounded on the door. A large man with a black mustache opened it, his gun pointed directly at Roberto's head.

"My name is Roberto Valencia. I was kidnapped. I just escaped."

"How did you get here?"

"A man on a boat just dropped me off."

"What's his name?"

"I don't know. But if you call Bogotá, if you call my wife, they'll tell you I was kidnapped."

"I'm not sure we can do that."

"Why not?" asked Roberto.

"It's dangerous to be seen with escapees."

"I'll pay you."

"You'll get out of here and forget about me," the officer said.

"No, I'll pay you right now. I have money."

"Let me see."

Roberto pulled out the stash of crumpled bills. The soldier's eyes lit up when he saw the money. He grabbed the bills and waved Roberto in. He sat behind his beat-up desk and made the call that set Roberto free.

"Hello, ma'am. Do you have a family member who's been kidnapped?"

Esperanza had refused to leave the house since missing Roberto's first phone call. She sat by the phone as if it were a newborn baby, in need of constant attention. When the phone rang, Esperanza picked it up immediately.

Her heart sank when she heard the officer's words. *He's dead,* she thought to herself.

"Yes, my husband," she replied.

"What's his name?"

"Roberto Valencia."

"He's escaped—"

"He's alive?"

"Yes, ma'am. He is standing right here next to me."

Esperanza screamed at the top of her lungs: "Roberto's alive! He's escaped! He's alive!"

Time twisted and turned and sped up and slowed down until Esperanza, Valentina, and Andrea stood at the airport awaiting Roberto's arrival, tightly holding one another's hands as a way to remind themselves that they were not imagining Roberto's return. They watched as the helicopter hovered over the tarmac. As soon as it touched the ground, Roberto leapt out and ran toward the women he had fought so hard to see again, who enveloped him in their arms, tears, and laughter. Soldiers with guns strapped around their necks, ready to fire at unseen enemies, surrounded the family. Blaring sirens, a caravan of speeding cars, and countless motorcycles followed the family home. Their apartment was full of soldiers with guns and strangers with cameras. The press was desperate to capture the image of the man who had miraculously escaped from the FARC and the jungle alive.

Roberto, Esperanza, Valentina, and Andrea sat in the kitchen holding hands. They could not let go of one another, afraid that if they did, they would slip through one another's fingers and fade into the jungle. Miguel sat across from the family with a huge smile on his face. Next to him was a man whose many shiny medals on his chest announced to the world his importance.

"It's good to have you back," Miguel said to Roberto.

"It's even better to be back, Miguel."

"Mr. Valencia, have you thought about what you're going to do?" asked the man with the medals.

"I'm going to enjoy my family, Mr....?"

"Captain Mora. I understand that is what you would like to do, but time is of the essence, and you have to decide where you will be living."

"Living? Here. In my house."

"If I may, Captain Mora," Miguel interrupted. "Roberto, you can't stay in Colombia. You escaped from the FARC. You've embarrassed them. This is only the beginning of the press. They're making you out to be a national hero because you screwed over the FARC. They won't let this slide. They'll come after you again. They might even come after your family."

"We can't guarantee your safety, Señor Valencia," said Captain Mora.

"Enough!" declared Roberto. "Girls, please go to your rooms."

Andrea and Valentina sat in silence in Valentina's room, waiting. Their future was being determined by a complete stranger's muffled voice.

In the kitchen, Roberto asked, "Miguel, do you really think I should leave?"

"Yes, I do. It's best for everyone."

"Would you leave?"

Silence.

"I don't know," Miguel finally replied.

Roberto turned to Esperanza.

"Mi amor?"

"No matter where we go, it won't be home."

Silence.

"She's right," said Roberto. "When the roof on your house has a hole, you don't pack up and leave. You fix the roof." Roberto then said the words that once again changed the course of Andrea's life: "But at the very least, you send the guests home."

His wife nodded in painful agreement.

The sound of Esperanza's heels echoed down the hall as she approached Valentina's bedroom. She opened the door. The wrinkles around her mouth had softened, and her eyes were abuzz with life again. She seemed lighter. She looked stunningly beautiful.

"Andreita," she said gently, "go and say your good-byes tonight. You're going back home tomorrow."

"What about you guys?"

"We're staying here."

Andrea's heart sank as Valentina grabbed her hand. Andrea's time in Colombia had come to an end.

chapter

TWELVE

Andrea mustered all of her strength to begin her journey's inevitable end. She knocked quietly on Santiago's door. He opened it, and Andrea stared into the green eyes she had fallen in love with the first time they met. Staring into their beauty now broke her heart. She leaned in and kissed him tenderly on the lips that fit hers so perfectly. She knew she would never find lips as wonderful as his. As she moved her mouth over his neck, her tongue led the way to his ears. She whispered gently, "I'm leaving for the United States tomorrow."

The air was sucked out of the room. They stood as close to each other as they could; this moment was the closest they would ever be to each other, because as each second ticked by, their paths moved farther away from each other. Santiago took Andrea's face in his hands and rested his forehead against hers. Andrea wrapped him into her arms. She took off his shirt and pulled off his pants so that he stood naked in front of her. She took in every inch of his beautifully imperfect body. With her hands, she gently explored his every curve. She wanted to burn his touch into her fingertips so that when she was alone she would be able to close her eyes and pretend the hands that touched her were his. She kissed Santiago for hours. Their tongues twisted and danced until his taste was inside her. It was sweet and earthy, with a twinge of a broken, mended, and once again broken heart. Santiago pushed himself inside her. She felt complete as he made love to her for the last time. She memorized his beautiful green eyes. She learned by heart how his tongue licked his lips with every gentle thrust. She stored away the memory of how his hands gripped her hips as she rocked back and forth on top of him. They grabbed each other's hands and led one another into pure ecstasy, then lay in naked silence until the sun rose.

"Santi, I have to go," Andrea said sadly.

"I want to give you something."

He grabbed the tattered book with the torn cover that he had been reading the first day they met. He flipped open the book and scribbled something inside.

"Don't read it until you're on the plane, okay?"

"I promise."

Andrea put her clothes on. They felt heavy and rough against her skin, the complete opposite of how Santiago's hands felt on her body. The air around them was thick with sadness. Santiago walked Andrea to the front door.

"Santi, it's better if we say good-bye here. My house will be crazy. We won't have any privacy."

"Okay."

The whites of Santiago's eyes were bloodshot. His eyes welled with tears, and he looked everywhere except at

Andrea. She fought back her own tears as Santiago's voice floated gently into her ear.

"I love you," he whispered.

"I love you, too."

They locked eyes for a brief second, and then Santiago disappeared behind his front door. Andrea stared at the wooden door where only seconds before Santiago had stood. She stayed motionless, hoping he would open the door and give her one last kiss, one last hug, one last moment. Andrea stood crying on his doorstep. All she had now were her memories of Santiago.

In the blink of an eye Andrea was back in the same SUV that had picked her up so many months earlier. William was behind the wheel, Roberto was in the passenger seat, Valentina sat to one side of her, and Tía Esperanza sat on the other. The car was quiet. Andrea silently said her goodbyes to the street corners that kept her secrets, to the mountains that pushed the cold into her bones, and to the sky that held her dreams. Andrea looked up at the clear blue sky and found comfort in its familiarity. No matter where she was, the sky would always be the same. No matter where she was, she would always share the sky with the friends, lovers, and family members who were no longer in her life. The sky would always be over Bogotá, just as Bogotá would always be inside her. Andrea reached over and squeezed her aunt's hand.

"*Tía*, I need to make one last stop."

"Andrea, we can't."

"I just need to make this one last stop. Please."

"Roberto?"

"Whatever you need, *mija*."

The car pulled up to the dilapidated house. Andrea did not know what she wanted to say, but she knew she needed to say something. She walked slowly toward the maroon door and rang the bell. The wasps in her stomach that had been asleep since her last visit started to awaken. There was silence behind the door. She rang the bell again. No one was home. She let out a sigh of mingled disappointment and relief. She pulled a pen and a piece of paper from her bag and quickly wrote a note to her father:

I'm going back home. I came to say good-bye, but you weren't here. Take care. Andrea

She slipped the note under the door, then turned around and walked back to the idling car. She felt the love of her family embrace her as they sat silently in the car, driving toward the airport. The wasps in her stomach were silent. Her rage was still.

The airport was a whirlwind of police officers, security checkpoints, passports, and the final good-bye. Andrea was going to the City of Angels, while her family was staying in the city of her birth.

A woman's voice crackled over the loudspeaker, announcing Andrea's flight. She hugged Roberto farewell, kissed Tía Esperanza good-bye, and grabbed Valentina's hands in eternal gratitude. Valentina had opened her heart to a stranger and taught her how to believe in herself again. She had shared her family with her. Now they each fought back the tears threatening to roll down their cheeks until, unable to take it anymore, Valentina wrapped her arms around her cousin. They sobbed on each other's shoulders until the crackling loudspeaker demanded that Andrea board the plane. She walked down the narrow Jetway and took one last look at the life she was leaving behind. Roberto stood tall in the glow of appreciation. Esperanza held his hand, grateful for a second chance. Andrea interlaced her arm in Roberto's, ready to finally have a father.

On the plane, Andrea hunkered down in her seat for the long ride back home. She pulled out the book Santiago had given her and ran her fingers over the ripped cover. How many times had Santiago's hands touched the exact place her fingers were now touching? She brought the book close to her face and inhaled his smell. For a brief moment she felt as if he were close to her. She opened the book. Her eyes focused on the words that were scribbled on the page:

Llave, it was a pleasure falling in love with you. Everything was beautiful. This is one of Galeano's jewels. A book full of inspiration. It is also very beautiful.

Santiago

Andrea traced the word *llave* with her finger. She was amazed how one word was able to bring her so much comfort, how one word could hold so much history. She opened the book and read:

In the suburbs of Havana, friends are referred to as "my earth" or "my blood." In Caracas, a friend is "my bread" or "my key": bread because of bakery, the fountain of good bread for the hunger pangs of the soul; and key...

- Key, because of key   Mario Benedetti tells me.

And he tells me that when he lived in Buenos Aires, during the time of the terror, he carried five keys on his key chain that were not his: five keys, of five houses, of five friends who saved his life.

She closed her eyes, exhausted. Change was exhausting. Fear was exhausting. Her ache was exhausting. Tucked away in her backpack was her razor blade. She had packed it for just this moment, hoping it would bring her comfort. Peace lay in the airplane's bathroom. She only needed to stand up, walk a few paces, and enter her sanctuary, but her feet were as heavy as steel. Her eyelids felt as if they were glued shut, and her wrists were pleading for rest. Her exhaustion pushed her toward sleep. Her dreams brought back to her the lessons learned, the tears shed, and the laughter shared inside Colombia's magical homes and on its maddening streets. She saw her hopes for her new life interwoven with her fears from her past.

A loud crash woke Andrea from her dreams. She looked out the window and saw the tarmac rushing past her. She looked up and saw the glistening lights of the City of Angels. She was home.

Andrea watched as everyone exited the plane. The weary travelers were eager to breathe in fresh air, to hug their families, to sleep in their own beds. Meanwhile, Andrea wanted to stay in the safety of her purgatory. The flight attendant smiled at her impatiently; even she was ready to go home. Andrea removed the razor blade from her backpack. Its cool steel edges were now filled with betrayal. It no longer held the possibility of peace. She opened her hand and let the razor blade disappear into the forgotten cracks of the overhead bin. She knew peace lay elsewhere.

Andrea walked down the empty Jetway. The murmured English around her prepared her for the world that awaited her. Standing alone at the end of the walkway was her mother. Andrea was surprised how time had changed Mariana. Her hair was as wild and as chaotic as ever, but her shoulders seemed broader and stronger than before. She was taller than Andrea remembered her. Mariana's eyes were not the beady, imposing eyes of her past; instead, they were eyes that were fearless, filled with unconditional love and dreams of a better future. Mariana's smile lit up her face, and Andrea saw her mother's beauty for the first time. She interlaced her hands in her mother's and pulled her close. They held each other in silence. Mariana's tears turned into sobs, and Andrea held her tighter. Mariana melted into her daughter's arms. Andrea gave her mother the love she had found in the arms of her family. She gave her mother the strength she had found in the bravery of her countrymen. She gave her mother the hope she had found in the *llaves* that saved her life.

Gabriel was the *llave* who gave her safety.

Esperanza was the *llave* who gave her freedom.

Valentina was the *llave* who gave her friendship.

Santiago was the *llave* who gave her love.

Mariana…her mother…was the *llave* who gave her everything.

Andrea whispered into her mother's ear, "Thank you, *llave*, thank you."

ACKNOWLEDGMENTS

I could not have embarked on this adventure without the love and support of many family and friends, all of whom I am blessed to have in my life.

Thank you:

To my partner in life, art, and love, Michael Skolnik. The years spent at your side have given me the courage to always try the impossible. Your unrelenting support and encouragement pulled me through the darkest moments of this journey. I love you.

To my mother, Liliana Legge, thank you for always answering my calls, no matter the time of day, to help me with the details I was imagining in coffee shops in New York but that unraveled in the streets of Buga, Bogotá, and Los Angeles. Your strength is my beacon of light.

To Tita, for all the stories you told me throughout the years. You made me want to know the ghosts of the past, the complexities of the present, and the joy of the future.

To Tía Luisa, for letting me into her home when I was lost, and for helping me find myself.

To Juliana Quintero, for giving me some of the best memories of my life, many of which live in these pages.

To Rick Mendoza, for loving me the way only a big brother can.

To Mato, my best friend, for taking two years of my work, a lifetime of suffering, life how I dreamed it, life how I wished I had lived it, and the truth and lies of the past, and translating them into the language in which they happened. I adore you.

To Gloria La Morte, my sister in art.

To Diane Stockwell and Lillian LaSalle, for believing in me from the very beginning.

To Farah Bala, Laine D'Souza, Gabriel Noble, Marjan Tehrani, Topaz Adizes, Noni Limar, Genna Terranova, Bradford Young, Tiphani Montgomery, Reshma Saujani, Max and Erika Skolnik, Martha and Simon Skolnik, Pamela and Charles Lapham, Brandy Selznick, Brandon, Ryan and Victoria Mendoza, Monica Martinez, Manuela Peralta, Camila Vasquez, Alejandro Vasquez, and Camilo Barrantes, whose love and support got me to the end.

To Smooch and Grounded, for letting me sit in your coffee shop for hours, days, weeks, and months on end.

And to the ones who didn't stay.